PRAISE FO.... ....UT NOVEL,
A WO.... ...WEEN US

*Longlisted for the Guardian Children's Fiction Prize
Shortlisted for the Branford Boase Award –
Highly Recommended by judges*

'An outstanding debut novel . . . Thoroughly researched and beautifully written . . . Syson's novel convinces with a light touch and a flair for vivid detail . . . [an] accomplished wartime romance.' *Guardian*

'*A World Between Us* by Lydia Syson transfers the love triangle to the Spanish civil war. The core love story, with all its near misses, coincidences and fleeting encounters, is given higher stakes by its setting. Equally absorbing is the relationship between Felix and the untrained Spanish nurse she takes under her wing, revealing the climate of suspicion and fear of "enemies within" that develops as the war grinds on. Syson brings history alive through careful detail.' *Observer*

'[A] fantastic historical fiction debut . . . featuring a wonderfully passionate and resourceful heroine. Recommended.' *Bookseller*

'Syson's writing is saturated with colour and detail and sets up the historical background without destroying the mood.' *Jewish Chronicle*

That
BURNING SUMMER

That
BURNING SUMMER
LYDIA SYSON

HOT
KEY
BOOKS

First published in Great Britain in 2013 by Hot Key Books
Northburgh House, 10 Northburgh Street, London EC1V 0AT

A CIP catalogue record for this book is available from the British Library.

ISBN: 978-1-4714-0053-7

1

This book is typeset in 10.5pt Berling LT Std

Printed and bound by Clays Ltd, St Ives Plc

Hot Key Books supports the Forest Stewardship Council (FSC),
the leading international forest certification organisation, and is
committed to printing only on Greenpeace-approved FSC-certified paper.

www.hotkeybooks.com

Hot Key Books is part of the Bonnier Publishing Group
www.bonnierpublishing.com

To Martin, who first took me to the Marsh,
and Adam, who flew me over it.

Issued by the Ministry of Information in co-operation with the War Office. and the Ministry of Home Security.

If the
INVADER
comes

WHAT TO DO — AND HOW TO DO IT

THE Germans threaten to invade Great Britain. If they do so they will be driven out by our Navy, our Army and our Air Force. Yet the ordinary men and women of the civilian population will also have their part to play. Hitler's invasions of Poland, Holland and Belgium were greatly helped by the fact that the civilian population was taken by surprise. They did not know what to do when the moment came. *You must not be taken by surprise.* This leaflet tells you what general line you should take. More detailed instructions will be given you when the danger comes nearer. Meanwhile, read these instructions carefully and be prepared to carry them out.

I

When Holland and Belgium were invaded, the civilian population fled from their homes. They crowded on the roads, in cars, in carts, on bicycles and on foot, and so helped the enemy by preventing their own armies from advancing against the invaders. You must not allow that to happen here. Your first rule, therefore, is :—

(1) IF THE GERMANS COME, BY PARACHUTE, AEROPLANE OR SHIP, YOU MUST REMAIN WHERE YOU ARE. THE ORDER IS "STAY PUT".

If the Commander in Chief decides that the place where you live must be evacuated, he will tell you when and how to leave. Until you receive such orders you must remain where you are. If you run away, you will be exposed to far greater danger because you will be machine-gunned from the air as were civilians in Holland and Belgium, and you will also block the roads by which our own armies will advance to turn the Germans out.

II

There is another method which the Germans adopt in their invasion. They make use of the civilian population in order to create confusion and panic. They spread false rumours and issue false instructions. In order to prevent this, you should obey the second rule, which is as follows :—

(2) DO NOT BELIEVE RUMOURS AND DO NOT SPREAD THEM. WHEN YOU RECEIVE AN ORDER, MAKE QUITE SURE THAT IT IS A TRUE ORDER AND NOT A FAKED ORDER. MOST OF YOU KNOW YOUR POLICEMEN AND YOUR A.R.P. WARDENS BY SIGHT, YOU CAN TRUST THEM. IF YOU KEEP YOUR HEADS, YOU CAN ALSO TELL WHETHER A MILITARY OFFICER IS REALLY BRITISH OR ONLY PRETENDING TO BE SO. IF IN DOUBT ASK THE POLICE-MAN OR THE A.R.P. WARDEN. USE YOUR COMMON SENSE.

I am a falcon. A peregrine, a traveller. Yet godlike. Alone in an azure abstraction. Air purer than danger. Like a heartbeat my engine throbs as I soar above a sea of cloud. Canvas and metal, these wings are my wings. A thought. A muscle. They lift, and tilt. We are one.

A break in the whiteness. The sea below me glints. The horizon shifts. I see my prey. My heartbeat quickens. I move in for the kill. Not yet. Not yet. When they see me it will be too late. Now.

RULE ONE: IF THE GERMANS COME, BY PARACHUTE, AEROPLANE OR SHIP, YOU MUST REMAIN WHERE YOU ARE. THE ORDER IS 'STAY PUT'.

1

'Just *do* something, can't you?' Peggy yelled at Ernest, starting to run herself. 'Now you're finally here.'

The last ewe braked and swerved again, yellow eyes hunting for an exit, away from the huddle of farmers standing on the platform near the ticket office. Her head dodged from side to side, neck wrinkling. Naked and deciding, her clipped body swung left then right on thick stick legs. Then she made a bolt for it.

'Quick!'

Ernest's face twisted in panic as he lunged for the sheep, arms flapping. Peggy was sure her brother's eyes were shut. But so were hers, almost, screwed up against the whipping coastal wind that flicked her tears away. It whirled the bleating up and around and away, and Peggy's head ached with the confusion of noise. She didn't feel much more use than Ernest.

Then another animal darted away from the flock, charging headlong towards the fence in that stupid sheep way. Peggy roared and swerved too, all instinct herself.

The looker's collie was quicker than either of them. Even before Ernest could pick himself up, the dog had rounded up both contrary creatures. The two sheep thundered up the ramp and into the wagon, broad arrows stark on their bare backs, tails and back legs filthy with fear.

There was a muted shuffle of hooves on wood as the animals made room for the last few tegs. A railwayman slid the door shut with a dull clang and the bleating inside became instantly more muffled and anxious. The animals kept on calling to each other, checking from wagon to wagon, eyes and wool pressed at the iron bars.

Then the whistle shrieked, and flags waved. Peggy and Ernest backed away from a warm cloud of black coal smoke and damp steam. The engine gathered its strength for the journey, and the train began to move. Nobody waved. They all just stood and watched it go, wordlessly. Before long, the rhythm of the track had drowned out the cries of the sheep. Just the wind was left, and a few wheeling gulls.

The figures on the platform slowly shook themselves into life again. Sheep droppings and straw littered the station and the smell of lanolin hung in the air. A few odd clumps of wool fluttered on the hurdles of the empty pens. Not much. The shearing gangs had got to work early this year. No point in the Enemy getting their wool.

The railwayman removed his cap with a sigh, wiped his gleaming brow and went to look for a yardbroom. A couple of farmers clapped each other on the back. They exchanged a swigging kind of mime and marched off in the direction of the pub.

The looker stared after the disappearing train. Peggy busied herself with an inspection of Ernest's knees. She must stop treating him as if he were six, instead of nearly twelve, but she couldn't bear to see the old man's face, so stricken.

'Not too bad,' she said to Ernest. 'And your specs are all in one piece, so that's good.'

'I know. I didn't say it was bad,' he snapped, backing away from her. 'I'm fine. I'm perfectly fine. And I *was* trying to help, you know.'

'Sorry. Shouldn't have shouted at you.' It was so hard not to sometimes. Habit, mostly. And the older he got the more aggravating his awkward aspects seemed to her. It wasn't surprising he was finding it difficult to settle. They all were, really. So very near, and yet so far from home. Even their mum didn't seem specially comfortable at the farmhouse. You'd never think she'd grown up there. Of the three of them, Peggy felt she was definitely making the best of things. But it was funny how staying was so very different from visiting.

'I'll tell Auntie Myra . . .'

'It's all right. You don't have to tell her anything. It won't make any difference anyway.'

A mild explosion made them both turn. The looker was blowing his nose.

'Bless you,' said Peggy.

The old man looked at them curiously, as if they'd just appeared from nowhere. He had the kind of eyes that didn't seem used to looking at anything or anybody quite so close to him.

'Hrramph.' He gave his nose a firm and final wipe.

'Do you know where the sheep are going?' asked Peggy. *Do you know if they're coming back?* She shuffled her feet, wondering how long she should wait for an answer.

'Happen it be West Country, they say. Or Midlands. Don't rightly know.'

'Somewhere they can't end up as German dinner,' offered Ernest.

Peggy rolled her eyes. 'It's not that, Ernest. Uncle Fred says it's all about the breed. Romney Marsh sheep are special. They need to preserve the purity of the breed.'

'Oh.' Ernest looked doubtful. 'Really?'

It didn't make much sense to Peggy either, now she came to think about it.

The looker's gaze shifted.

'Fred Nokes your uncle?' he said.

'Yes. My mum's big brother. We live with him now.'

'Over by Snargate?'

'That's right.'

It was Ernest's turn to shift from foot to foot as he felt the looker's eyes moving over him, up and down, up and down, and then away. The deep furrows between his eyebrows turned into ditches. So how does a hefty figure of a farmer like Fred Nokes end up with a puny runt of a nephew like Ernest? That was what he was thinking, Peggy could tell. And she knew Ernie knew too.

'The army took our house,' she added quietly. 'Last month.'

The looker slowly put away his handkerchief and with equal deliberation brought out a tin of tobacco from the bib of his dungarees. He rummaged for just the right strands, stuck a wad into his cheek, and his jaws began to move. Ruminating. Peggy and Ernest continued to stand there, not sure if the conversation was over, letting the sadness settle. And then

4

Ernest went and put the question Peggy had been forming in her head, but hadn't liked to ask.

'So what will you look for now, with the sheep gone?'

Did lookers look *for* sheep, or look after them, Peggy wondered. Both, probably. Their huts dotted the Marsh, miles from everywhere, little one-room brick houses surrounded by pens. Many were in ruins these days. Waking in the night in lambing season, when they often went to help their uncle with the orphans, Peggy had sometimes seen a light twinkling, way out across Walland Marsh. Looking was a lonely old life.

'The Enemy, I dare say.' The looker screwed up his eyes and scanned the huge sky.

'We've all got to look out for the Enemy now,' said Ernest, suddenly more talkative. 'Do our bit. *You must not be taken by surprise.* That's –'

'That what your uncle says, is it?' The looker made it sound like 'runckle'.

'Yes, I mean, no. I mean, it's in the leaflet. I expect you've read it.'

Oh, shut up about that wretched leaflet. Peggy came close to bursting the words out loud. *Just shut up.*

'I don't read.' Brown-coloured spit suddenly streamed from the corner of the old man's mouth. 'But yes, I do know what it say.'

An uncertain look crossed Ernest's face. Peggy watched a blush begin to creep up from under his collar to colour the tips of his ears.

'Come on, Ern. Get your bike. Auntie Myra said to come back as soon as the sheep were gone. Remember? You go

5

ahead. I've got to take something to the post office for Mum.'

'Oh yes. I'm coming. Bye then.'

The looker just nodded. As Ernest turned, he muttered something under his breath.

Abyssinia, Peggy repeated to herself. It was what Dad always said, and neither of them could quite break the habit. It was the last thing he said before he left, when Ernest was asleep but she had woken up and come downstairs when she heard the crying. *I'll be seeing ya.*

Then Ernest started up all over again.

'The leaflet says –'

'Ernest.' Peggy stopped. She turned to face her brother, put a hand on each shoulder, and fixed him with glaring eyes. 'Listen to me. And please, please, *please* remember what I tell you this time. I. Don't. Want. To hear. Another word. About. The. Bloody. Leaflet.' She stared a bit harder. He looked suitably shocked at her language. 'Got that?'

Ernest twisted away from her grip.

'But, Peggy, you can't just pretend –'

'Pretend what?' she demanded cruelly.

'You know. Pretend it's not happening. We've got to be ready.'

She inhaled noisily, ready to let out a deep and sarcastic sigh. Then she thought better of it. Instead she released her caught-up breath in a calm and orderly fashion, and counted to ten. It was no good getting angry with Ernest. He didn't start the war. None of this was his fault.

But she just wished he'd never got his hands on that leaflet. They were managing fine till then. Ever since Ernest had come in and found Auntie Myra and Uncle Fred and Cousin June leaning over the government's instructions together, the kitchen suddenly as silent as death, he had been obsessed. Absolutely fixated on the wretched rules. So Peggy repeated now what Uncle Fred had said then.

'Ernest, just remember. It says "*If* the invader comes." Not "*When* the invader comes."' Uncle Fred had tried to make a joke of it, of course. 'If,' he'd roared, with a burst of laughter. 'Bloody big if, if you ask me, pardon my French.' (And for once, Aunt Myra did.)

Ernest wasn't laughing.

Still unable to find words of her own, Peggy resorted to mimicking the annoying little phrase the soldiers used to call out at her when they caught sight of her serious face as she walked past the Camp on her way home from school, when Lydd was just a normal town, and you never had to think about the men going away to fight on actual battlefields. Before they requisitioned their house. Before they started using Dad's studio for target practice. 'Cheer up, love, it might never happen.'

Such a stupid thing to say.

2

A second earlier he would have sworn the skies were clear. Sworn on his mother's life. Henryk didn't get a glimpse of the pilot that hit him.

The instruction to scramble had come very late in the day, just before anticipation had turned to dismay. At 20,000 feet the squadron was told to look out for a formation of two hundred enemy fighters. They found them. Henryk survived that engagement, disconnected his radio and set off in pursuit of a single bandit heading for France. That one had got away.

Returning to base through a clear sky, anticipating the usual reprimand, Henryk heard an icy crash.

A jagged hole the size of his fist gaped in the canopy behind his head. Almost at once the cockpit filled with the sweet chemical tang of glycol. It came gushing from the coolant tank like a geyser, spraying Henryk in the face and chest, covering his goggles. His joystick went slack.

This engine's finished, he thought. *This plane is finished. I'm finished*. A chilling calm briefly froze all reaction. Did he care? He didn't know. Maybe not. But nobody wants to burn to death. He'd already pulled the pin of his harness in an automatic gesture. That freed him from his seat.

In a single movement he shoved back the hood, wiped his goggles, and tipped into noise.

He fell. Not straight down as he had always imagined. Headfirst, he rolled, forwards and forwards, turning and turning in an endless downward somersault, with no idea how to stop himself.

Whoomp. Whoomp. Whoomp. Whoomp.

One after another, there was a wrench on each leg – rip, rip – and his flying boots, pulled off by the force of his fall, flew past his ears. He didn't even feel his gauntlets go.

Rip cord. Find the rip cord. The other side, remember. Tucked up into himself, still hurtling and spinning, Henryk edged his hand across his chest and pulled. Nothing. The drogue chute had failed. Must have been shot through with the coolant tank. He felt the weight of the main parachute like an attacker on his back, pushing him round ever faster in his spin, clinging onto him, wrapping itself like a parasite round his shoulders, blinding him. And Henryk fought it off like an attacker. Kicking and struggling he forced his body to open. Fought to uncurl. The shriek of rushing air was agonising, a roar like he had never heard before.

Suddenly there came a jolt, then a second one, followed by an uncrumpling, and silence. Time slowed to a standstill. Henryk drooped painfully from his harness, unable to take in what had happened. The wind. It must have crept into a loose fold. It had unwrapped him. It had undone him. Now he would not die. And he could not work out how he felt about that.

His limp body hung in space like a discarded garment. Blue above and green below. Almost nothing there at all. Flat green, intersected with glinting lines of water. A few scattered buildings. Not much to worry about. No sign of his Hurricane at all. A lark passed him, singing furiously. Henryk wondered if there was any chance he could stay suspended, floating like a soap bubble.

Pop. He could just disappear, couldn't he?

No. He had to stop thinking that way. It was too dangerous. Henryk pressed his forehead against the webbing of his harness, digging it into his skin. Shame engulfed him with a physical force. For the thousandth time, his thoughts returned to the note he had found in his jacket when he reached Rumania. He had it with him still. Ten months on, it was filthy and wearing away at the folds. Gizela must have hidden it in his uniform when they came to say goodbye. Her spiky writing, hard and determined, had pressed with such force that the lined paper was holed at the full stop.

Below, he saw the roof of a church, like an ark, encircled by water.

Until we have our freedom again, your only purpose must be to fight for it.

He could see leaves on stunted trees. A pair of swans.

Was he released from Gizela's order? Perhaps nothing could release him now . . . perhaps he was tied more firmly still.

The ground hit him, and he doubled up.

3

Ernest didn't go straight home, despite Peggy's instructions. He couldn't resist a glimpse of the sea. It was early days for the passage birds, but he'd spotted a skua last July. Worth a try. He cycled down his favourite backpath to the shore, the quiet way, and abandoned his bike in the holly grove at the end.

The sea was just out of sight. Stones and sky filled up the space, like they always had. The sky was vivid blue and cloudless and criss-crossed by unravelling strands of white left by vanished planes. Ernest took a lungful of salty air. He stood and listened, facing France, concentrating. There. He could hear it again. A dark, low rumble, coming over the unseen water on the wind.

And then he remembered the first rule. *Stay put*.

It made no sense to Ernest. It sounded like a game of musical statues. But if you were in the wrong place when the invasion started, should you 'stay put' where you were, or get back to where you were meant to be? And did that mean the farmhouse, the yard, the outhouses, the fields . . .? He must find out if you were allowed to hide while you stayed put.

What if a German came marching in his direction right

now, heading straight for him, dripping wet from the sea? There was nowhere to hide on the shingle, and if he was in disguise, Ernest wasn't sure how he'd even know he was an invader. It would have to be a very high tide though. You could walk forever across the sand in water only up to your knees.

His footsteps on the shingle sounded like an army on the march. Ernest walked more quickly, and the stones tumbled more quickly too. His invisible companions were speeding up, drowning everything else out, almost as if they were following him. Stop. He was working himself up. He must put an end to these thoughts. Ernest's fingers began to creep into the pocket of his shorts, but he made himself remember the leaflet's words without looking this time. The Scholarship might have been a disaster, but he was determined to pass this test.

If you run away you will be exposed to far greater danger because you will be machine-gunned from the air.

When the headmaster read that line at school, Ernest actually had to sit down. His legs went loose and watery, and his neck burned. It must be a mistake. You couldn't just go machine-gunning ordinary people, running along an ordinary road. In the middle of ordinary life. But when he asked Uncle Fred, it turned out you could. It had happened already in Holland and Belgium. It really had. It was probably happening in France.

. . . you will also block the roads by which our own armies will advance to turn the Germans out. The thought of it. Stuck between armies on that triangle of land, so close to France.

Ernest wished Peggy would take everything more seriously. It was all very well making light of it, always trying to pretend everything was normal, but it quite clearly wasn't.

He made a quick swerve to avoid falling into a huge mound of seakale, white flowers bending in the wind, silvery-green leaves fleshy and firm. And that was as far as he got. Coming over the next rise of shingle, he was faced with a wall of coiled wire, barbed and springy, and twice his height. It stretched in both directions, as far as he could see. All the way to Dungeness. All the way to Rye. There were low concrete buildings dotted along the coast which hadn't been there before: blockhouses, greyer than the tawny shingle, with dark narrow window holes like half-closed eyes.

He began to sweat. He was in a wronger place than he'd thought. There must have been some checkpoint he'd missed. You were meant to have a pass to come here, he remembered. But they couldn't block every sheeptrack. Someone would see him now. They'd ask him for a pass and he didn't have one. He should have thought about that before. *That's just your trouble. You don't think*. That's what everyone always told him. But it wasn't true. He did think. All the time. He wished he could stop thinking sometimes.

Ernest turned and ran, back to his bike, slipping and sliding on stones that rolled away from him. He swung his leg over the crossbar, and headed back towards the Marsh, the wind roaring in his ears.

Between the road and his old house was a new fence, hung with signs in threatening capitals.

WARNING
COASTAL DISTRICTS OF ROMNEY MARSH, LYDD AND NEW ROMNEY

Under DEFENCE REGULATION NO 38A any stealing or scrounging from evacuated houses or damaged premises in these areas renders the offender liable to be charged with the crime of LOOTING
And subject, on conviction, to be sentenced to PENAL SERVITUDE OR DEATH

Penal servitude. That was hard labour, wasn't it? He wasn't sure if you could scrounge from your own house. They had left in such a hurry. But then again, Dad's binoculars probably weren't there any more, and the house was no longer theirs, and at least Ernest had rescued his own. He sped on.

Passing the church, Ernest looked up at the clock on its tower. The bells had been silent for more than a month. If you heard them now, it meant only one thing: the invasion. The corner of his gas-mask box dug into his back as he pedalled, reminding him that he hadn't practised putting it on yet that day.

Left at Hawthorn Corner, and the flatness stretched out for miles. But you'd think someone had thrown a junkyard down in these fields, from a great height. Here and there, old bedsteads pointed rusty springs at the sky. He saw an upside-down plough and a little further on, huge stakes driven into the earth, angled towards France.

When the road bent right to run alongside the sewer, Ernest

began to feel better. They'd have a job machine-gunning him from the air here, protected as he was by the line of low trees and bushes that followed the water. He slowed down a little. And anyway, he wasn't running away, but quite the opposite. But how would they know he was trying to stay put? Still, he'd skirt round Brookland, and stick to the quieter lanes, and then he'd be even less visible. On the footpath from Poplar Hall the trees met over your head.

Then he did hear a plane. Faintly at first, but getting louder with speed. It sounded odd. Different from usual. Lower maybe, and uneven, as though the engine was catching its breath. Could be one of ours coming home, hoped Ernest, but it was hard to tell without looking. A glance round and up at the sky over his shoulder. He wobbled, righted himself, lost his footing on the pedals and wobbled again. As the bike swerved into the long grass at the side of the lane, its front wheel hit a rock, and the world turned upside down.

The roaring grew louder. Ernest didn't have time to grope for his specs. From the sound of things, he ought to be getting to his feet and running for his life after all. But his legs were all tangled up in the bike and his shoe was stuck, and wasn't he meant to 'stay put'? So he crossed his fingers and tried to lie as still as he possibly could.

Blurred black smoke stained the clouds. Perhaps the plane was moving at a strange angle. Ernest squinted. The rhythm of the engine stuttered again, and his heart beat faster. But the danger was over almost before he'd begun to take it in. No machine guns rattled. No bombs fell. The plane simply headed in across the Marsh, unsteady and ever more blurry.

Feeling around for the glasses, his hand closed on stinging nettles. Ouch. He sucked the rising bumps, and squinted up again. If he squished his eyelids in a special way he could make things a bit clearer. For a short time.

He wished he could be like Victor. There's a flying pencil, he'd say, when all the others were still shielding their eyes from the sun. A Dornier, he'd repeat, scornful of their ignorance. Knew every silhouette, friend and foe, from miles and miles off even. All the numbers too, the ones that Ernest could never remember, and the engine sizes and all that kind of thing. Merlins and Vickers and all that. And the uniforms. Ernest wished he had a brother in the RAF too, someone who could tell him stuff like that. He corrected himself quickly and guiltily. Victor Velvick had *had* a brother. Not any more.

Then he noticed the sudden silence. Just a moment of stillness. Followed by a kind of tearing, rushing sound, as if somebody was ripping the clouds.

Something was falling out of the sky. Not just falling, but hurtling down, like a meteorite or something. Orange and black. That was all Ernest could make out. The plane was on fire. What else could it be? He struggled to extricate himself, and tried to work out where it would come down. Walland Marsh? Thereabouts.

Then nothing. Silence, briefly broken by the laughter of frogs.

Ernest finished untangling his legs from the bike frame, and got himself and the machine upright again. He spun the front wheel a few times to check it wasn't buckled. At last the glint of sun on glass caught his eye. His spectacles were balanced in the reeds at the edge of the drainage ditch.

4

The post office looked busy, which was annoying. Not much Peggy could do about that. She hugged the parcel to her chest to hide the address, and pushed open the door. The bell's brassy jangle sounded louder and harsher than usual in the silence of voices that descended.

There were six or seven women clustered around the counter. Peggy knew them all. They fell away when she came in, as if they'd agreed in advance. She was sure they must be staring, but she refused to look anywhere other than straight ahead. She swallowed – they probably noticed – and then she marched forward, up to Mrs Velvick, plonking her parcel face down on the counter. The postmistress paused with her right hand raised high, inky stamp waiting to fall. You'd think Sleeping Beauty had just stumbled upon the spindle, thought Peggy, eyes fixed on the locket that hung on Mrs Velvick's black-knitted bosom.

'Good afternoon, Mrs Velvick,' said Peggy, spreading her arms a little further apart on the counter, and leaning over the package. Heat rose through her body. Her neck prickled. 'It's a lovely day, isn't it?'

Mrs Velvick didn't speak. That locket. Had she always worn it? Peggy had a dim memory of the older Velvick boy.

He had only been a few years ahead of her at the Council School. If she stared hard enough, she could conjure up his freckled face. It must be him in there, surely. If you got your nail under the silver catch, opened that little oval door. All that was left of him now.

The post-mistress pulled the parcel towards her, and tilted it alarmingly, causing Peggy to start.

'I'll have to see how much it weighs,' said Mrs Velvick without expression, turning towards the scales.

So Peggy tried a different tactic. She spun round swiftly and smiled brightly at everyone. When she looked properly she realised that Jeannie's mother was there. That helped.

'Hello, Mrs Ashbee. How's Jeannie? Enjoying the new job?' Peggy got quickly into her stride, and swayed slightly from side to side as she spoke. 'Oh, goodness! Mrs Aldridge . . . I didn't see you there . . . have you had a postcard from Daphne yet? June said she'd heard the little ones were having a super time at Weston-super-Mare.' That was a lie, of course. She'd heard no news at all about the children who'd been evacuated as soon as the term finished. She laughed, tossing her hair like June and including everyone in her gaiety, so that all attention stayed fixed on her smile. 'Well, I suppose they would, wouldn't they? It being "super" and all that!'

God. If only she could shut up. They'd be wondering what had got into her. She shot a look back over her shoulder. Mrs Velvick was moistening stamps on her little round sponge. Her thin grey eyebrows were a good inch higher than usual, pushing tight lines of wrinkles into the skin of her forehead, exposing more than ever the dark hollows and red rims of her eyes.

'I almost wish I was still young enough to be evacuated myself,' Peggy went on, spinning round, waving her hands, keeping moving, keeping all eyes on herself and away from the parcel. 'Such an adventure! But of course Ernest and me have our warwork on the farm to do. Uncle Fred says he doesn't know what he'd do without us. Ninepence, did you say, Mrs Velvick? Goodness! Well, here you are.'

The coins clinked on the counter.

'Anything else . . . Miss Fisher?' Mrs Velvick narrowed her eyes.

The parcel was safely in the sack behind the counter. Nobody could possibly have read the words on the label. Though anyone would think Peggy was tipsy, the way she was carrying on. Tipsy! At sixteen, and half-past four on a Tuesday afternoon. As if.

'No, no. That's lovely, thank you very much,' Peggy chirped, turning back to the others again. 'Actually, I ought to be getting back now. But I'll say hello to my mother from you, shall I, Miss Winterbourne?'

'Oh yes, of course. Would you do that, dear?' Miss Winterbourne looked a little flustered, and put a hand up to pat her grey bun. Peggy could never remember which Miss Winterbourne was which when only one was there – the three elderly sisters looked exactly the same to her – but what did that matter? She had no intention of passing on any such message. Her hands now blissfully free, she waved merrily, taking care to look every woman in the shop firmly in the eye as she left.

'Cheerio, then!'

5

He could have been anywhere. Lying with twisted hips, white silk billowing half-heartedly around him, Henryk gazed up at a sky that told him nothing. It was the exact shade of blue he remembered from that first attack, late last summer, back in Poland. Once again, he was struck by the wrongness of its pure intensity.

The sky was not quite empty. Immediately above, a v-shaped flock of geese crossed his vision, honking a few times as it passed.

That twitching in his fingers had started up again, and in his right calf, and then just behind one eye. Limb by limb, Henryk began to test his body. Between his legs, he felt bruised and achy – the jerk of his harness had been like a kick in the crotch. As he shifted, feeling tenderly for damage, the movement released an even stronger ache in his armpits. His head ached too.

He was exhausted but he would have to wait for sleep to come. Sit it out. Three days on Benzedrine and his mind was like a runaway train. Wakey-wakey.

Henryk curled up in the grass and thistles like a baby, and rubbed the itchy skin on his jaw. He pulled the slithering material around him and over his head. Its softness against his face weakened him further. He could have wrapped himself up in it entirely, cocooning his body in its gentle shroud. The white silk absorbed the sun, its warmth and light quickly penetrating to his skin and hair. It did nothing to relieve the aching coldness grinding in his chest.

There had been no shrouds for his sisters. No graves either probably, though he wondered if he would ever know. Passing feet on pavements, perhaps. Eyes averted. Strangers and friends turning away. And nothing he could do, then or now. He might as well sleep forever himself. He might as well. He might as well.

A harsh burst of noise from the ditch at the edge of the pasture shocked him back into awareness. He sat up quickly and dizzily. The mocking noise came again, followed by a splash, and Henryk realised with a weak laugh of his own that his audience was just a frog.

But he wanted to keep it that way. Ignoring the pain in his ankle, Henryk knelt to pack up his parachute. He fumbled with the straps, hardly able to believe that nobody had seen him land. But the more he looked around, the more he could believe it. Again, he had the sense of being marooned in a landscape where nothing was as it seemed. A slight dip or rise might prove an impasse or a crossing place. Some things you could see coming for miles. Others sprang up in your face at the very last moment.

Like the dragonflies which flew over the ditchwater, electric-blue bodies constantly dipping and zigzagging, as if avoiding tracer. Changing course to keep out of the way. Dragonflies as big as birds, birds as small as butterflies; white butterflies like fluttering leaves of paper, notes scattering in the wind, escaped pages of books. All rising from nowhere to hit your gaze.

About fifty yards away, Henryk noticed a low line of trees, thicker than most. He reckoned he could make it that far. It would get him out of sight.

6

Mum arrived back at the farm as Ernest skidded round the gatepost. Their bicycles almost collided.

'Oh, Ernest, calm down, do,' she said, feet braced on the ground. She seemed quite shaken. 'What's the hurry?' And she forced out one of her stiff little laughs, the kind she only did when there was nothing to laugh at.

'A plane. I saw a plane. Another one. It must have come down over there somewhere. Didn't you see?'

He was waving his arms towards Appledore, though he wasn't entirely sure it was the right direction.

Alarm was infectious. Peggy came running out too, followed by Aunt Myra, and June with her sleeves rolled up, and the baby in her arms, both looking as immaculate as ever.

'What is it?'

'A plane. Ernest saw a plane.' Was there a hint of pride in Mum's voice?

'One of ours?' asked June.

'I don't know.'

'Never mind. It's not easy.' Mum hurried to head off Aunt Myra's tutting.

'Have you told your uncle? No, of course you haven't.'

'Give him a chance, Mum,' said June. 'How could he? They're practising tonight, aren't they?'

Aunt Myra wasn't listening. She wasn't much of a listener at the best of times, and Ernest wasn't always quick at getting his words out. His aunt usually had more than enough to say for both of them.

'Will you . . . no, maybe I'd better go,' said Mum. She looked grey and exhausted, pushing back the hair that had escaped her headscarf and setting her pedal again, ready.

'I'll go,' offered Peggy.

'No, I need to,' Ernest said quickly. 'I was the one who saw it.' He didn't see why Mum had to keep on working in the munitions factory when it made her so tired. Uncle Fred was always saying there was no need: it was far too much on top of all the farm work, and there'd be even more soon with all the men leaving, and wasn't that a reserved occupation anyway? Ernest was sure Dad wouldn't like it, if he knew, which maybe he didn't. But Mum never took any notice. Just talked about 'her bit', and came back later and later. 'At the Red Lion, are they?'

'That's right. You'll be quick?'

'Of course,' Ernest shouted over his shoulder, speeding off already, thrilled to be useful. 'And Mum – don't forget to put your bike away!'

It was hard to see how a German parachutist might invade London on a bicycle – surely they'd be bringing tanks with them? But best not to break the rules.

Ernest cycled to the pub so fast that he could barely get the words out as he charged into the side garden. Six or seven farmers and farmhands were standing round a blackboard in their shirtsleeves, chanting gutterally and incomprehensibly at Uncle Fred. They all looked sweaty – straight from the fields – and wore armbands with LDV in black letters. A pile of pitchforks and shotguns leaned against the fence. Gordon Ramsgate, who had once been in Peggy's class, was gripping an ancient muzzleloader. The Local Defence Volunteers were learning German.

'*Pistole Ablegen!*' they roared in unison. 'Put down your revolver! *Hände Hoch!* Hands up!'

'Not you, you chump!'

Ernest, still panting, had raised his own hands without thinking.

'Just a moment, lads.' Uncle Fred gave him an encouraging look. 'What's the problem, Ernest? Did Myra send you?'

'Yes. No. Mum did. There's another plane come down.'

'On our land?'

'Don't think so. Don't know. Maybe. But I definitely saw it fall. It was on fire. It was awful. You've got to find it.'

'Hang on a minute. Calm down. Just tell me nice and slow.'

'I think it's over that way.' Now he really wasn't sure where he should be pointing. 'Or over there.' Ernest felt himself getting hot and bothered. He wondered if the others were laughing at him, but he had his back to them and certainly wasn't going to turn round to find out.

'We don't want any false alarms, now,' said Fred, catching someone's eye.

'It isn't a false alarm. Honest. I saw it.' Ernest held on to some invisible handlebars, and swivelled them experimentally,

25

trying to work out where the sun had been when he came off his bike earlier. He turned and pointed again, this time in a slightly different direction. 'It was going that way, definitely. I saw the smoke. I really did.' And before they could ask, 'But I don't know if it was ours or not. I couldn't tell.'

'That's OK. You wouldn't be the first. Let's go then, quick march. See if it's recoverable.' Then Fred added, '*Umkehren weiter marschieren* . . . Umkayran vyetah marcheeayrun. What does that mean?'

A chorus of voices replied, 'Turn round and keep walking.' Which they then did.

I mustn't forget this either, thought Ernest, looking back at the blackboard. *Hände hoch, Hände hoch.* "Handy Hock, Handy Hock," he recited under his breath as he marched.

Most of the volunteers had biked over, but between them they did have two vehicles: Fred's Austin 7 van and a Hillman Minx belonging to Mr Gosbee, whose farm was furthest off. They crammed in, pitchforks and all, Ernest kneeling in the back, head stuck through to the front between his uncle and a neighbour, doing his best with the directions.

They seemed to go on driving for hours, round and round, circling the back lanes, but never spotting the least disturbance. In fact, there were even fewer flights overhead than usual. The men tried to press Ernest about the plane.

'Was it twin prop or single prop?'

'See bumps on the wings, did you, sticking out, like?'

'Any sign of a parachute?'

Ernest thought hard before he replied. He could feel them waiting.

'I couldn't see. No. I don't think so. I really didn't see.'

Uncle Fred sighed, and changed gear without speaking.

The sun got lower and lower in the sky, and Ernest felt more and more uncomfortable in every way. DO NOT RUSH ABOUT SPREADING VAGUE RUMOURS, he repeated to himself unhappily, one fist hammering dispiritedly at his feet, which were numb with pins-and-needles. He couldn't bear to meet the other passengers' eyes.

Conversation dried up.

Then came a hoot from behind. Mr Gosbee had pulled up. He was gesturing at the pasture to the right where a circle of young heifers stood, backs to the road, heads lowered, curious.

'Mmmm,' grunted Fred. 'Let's have a look over there then.'

The tenant herdsman who farmed this land had spotted the animals from the back of the Hillman. Now he began to lead the way, striding out over the grassland. Ernest hesitated, then folded back the bonnet of the Austin, unclipped the distributor and pulled up the rotor arm. Slipping them both into his pocket, he ran after the men.

'Gaa-r-nn!' The farmer began to shout and shoo away the cattle as he approached. They mooed at him and lolloped off, revealing what looked to Ernest something like a giant molehill, half-submerged in the field. You couldn't even call it a crater. It was more of an earthwork, the land torn up and thrown back, like when you dig a hole in sand and it just fills itself right in again. A scar on the field.

As he came closer, Ernest noticed jagged fragments of metal and wood scattered on the surface. Two thin wisps of smoke seeped skywards from the earth.

There was nothing much to say after that. Everyone quickly removed their caps and held them awkwardly in front of their chests. Ernest thought he heard someone mutter the word 'goner' and then Mr Gosbee led the gathering in a mumbled prayer.

This wasn't the first time the Marsh had swallowed an aircraft whole. Last time there had barely been a trace either. It was incredible. How could something so huge just disappear like that, and a person with it, too? Victor had gone with the search party when a plane came down at Brookland. He'd been hoping for a new souvenir, but came back disappointed. 'Good thing too,' he'd told everyone the next day at school. That there was nothing to be recovered, he meant. Someone had told him it was a Messerschmitt for sure, and Victor said the only good German was a dead German.

'Good lad,' said Fred quietly, as they got back into the van. Ernest couldn't see what was good about what he'd done. He hadn't exactly saved anyone's life.

RULE TWO: DO NOT BELIEVE RUMOURS AND DO NOT SPREAD THEM. WHEN YOU RECEIVE AN ORDER, MAKE QUITE SURE THAT IT IS A TRUE ORDER AND NOT A FAKED ORDER. USE YOUR COMMON SENSE.

7

Peggy woke in pitch-blackness. For a moment she couldn't think where she was. Then her fingers touched the cold iron bedstead, and her heart stopped racing. She must have been dreaming of their old house. It had confused her. But everything was fine. Nobody was crying, or shouting or arguing. It was just the fox cubs playing, their strangulated screams sounding for all the world like terrified children. That was a new thing. The foxes had always stayed on the hills till this year. But it didn't matter. Peggy was safe at the farmhouse, in the very bed that Mum had slept in as a child. She could just hear Ernest's light breathing across the room.

The bedsprings creaked as she rolled over but he didn't stir. She pulled the sheet over her shoulder, nestled her head back into the pillow and waited for sleep to drift back. Nothing happened. The very opposite, in fact. The noises of the night seemed to intensify and she felt more awake than ever.

Straining her ears, lying as still as she could, Peggy analysed each sound she heard in turn. Soft scuttling on the ceiling above. She used to think it was rats, but since Ernest had shown her the starling's entrance hole under the eaves, she hadn't minded the scrabbling footsteps. Much further off, like a distant summer storm gathering strength, a low boom rumbled across the Channel and right over the Marsh from France. Last month the guns had been much louder, especially in those horrid days when they were evacuating the British Expeditionary Force. Everyone from round here, anyone with any kind of boat at all had set off as soon as the call came. When they came back they said Dunkirk was just like Camber. Sand into sea. Big boats couldn't get close. They said they were picking up soldiers from the water, half-drowned, or worse. And there was Ernest, thinking all the while that one of them might even be Dad. But Mum had kept silent and looked away, as if there was even half a chance he could have got to France in that time, as if not saying wasn't just as bad as lying. It didn't give Peggy much choice.

Paris had fallen weeks ago, but that hadn't brought an end to the thunder from across the sea. What were the Germans doing there now, Peggy wondered. Mucking the place up completely? Her anger at the unfairness of everything began to well up again. She was quite desperate to go to Paris. She longed to sit at a café under a parasol, sipping black coffee at a table on the pavement, a Garbo hat adding beautifully to her mystery. From under its floppy brim, she'd safely stare at the ladies tripping past with their elegant shoes and little dogs in coats. *Who is this English rose?* Parisians would whisper as they went by. *She has such . . . such an unexpected beauty.*

Well, that was one way of putting it. Not that it would ever happen. There'd be nothing left of Paris by the time she finally made it there. Ruined forever before she'd even set eyes on the city.

A tide of guilt made her sit up in bed. Her mother had been so cross last time she'd begun a sentence with the usual 'What if I never . . .' She should think herself lucky, stop feeling so sorry for herself, think of other people, etc. etc . . . Grow up. It *was* childish. But at this rate she'd go straight from being a child to being an old lady, without a single one of the fun bits in between, and surely nobody deserved that. A Miss Winterbourne.

She was wide-awake now, and thoroughly on edge. Perhaps she should just go and check the henhouse door. After all, it was Ernest who'd closed it last. And if he *had* forgotten to push the latch right in, the consequences didn't bear thinking about. She threw back the sheet and flapped her nightie to tempt a cool breeze up her body. If there was a moon, she might be able to see if the door was swinging open from the landing window.

As she tiptoed across the wooden floor, Ernest moved and muttered something in his sleep. Then he spoke again, more clearly. He sounded indignant. 'I'm *not* a looter. I tell you I'm *not* a looter.'

Checking that no light could escape from behind her, Peggy unpoppered the heavy blackout curtain, and peered into the night. Pairs of searchlights streaked up into the sky from Rye, systematically sweeping the heavens. Little else was visible: the Marsh looked as empty as an ocean.

Except for one thing, Peggy noticed. Somewhere between here and there, a tiny orange glow appeared. She watched it carefully, moving unevenly up and down, coming and going. A distant looker's lantern, she decided: checking on lambs. But it was too late for lambs, and the lookers over that way were no longer needed, were they? Anyway, seeing in the dark was said to be one of their skills. And you could be fined for attracting bombers. She didn't think even a cigarette was allowed outside at night during blackout.

A hoarse bark reminded her of her task. She grabbed a pair of socks from her drawer and sat on the stairs to pull them on. Uncle Fred's snoring continued to whistle softly through the house. A last look, but the light was gone, so she poppered up the drapes. Then she felt her way down the stairs, through the kitchen and into the scullery to find her boots.

Stepping out of the back door, where farmyard smells took over from coal smells, her eyes and ears seemed to work better. Must be all those carrots I ate, Peggy thought, heading for the henhouse. Her boots flapped loudly against her bare legs. There was a dull thud of wood on wood, and a terrified squawking erupted into the stillness. Peggy began to run.

8

Too startled to work out where the bolt might be, Henryk leaned against the wooden door and cursed the birds. The shock of their sudden racket had set his legs shaking again, and jangled up his mind completely. He should have stayed away. He should never have risked this. All he'd wanted was a little food and shelter, while he worked out what to do. He didn't know how to calm Polish chickens, let alone English ones. When he tried to make soothing noises, all that came out was a strangled kind of whimper, that wouldn't quieten anything or anyone.

At the sound of running feet, Henryk looked up quickly. Thwack, thwack. Thwack, thwack. Closer and closer. And a cloud of white approaching, like a ghost coming out of the night. A ghost or an angel. He tried to move and the white-draped figure crashed right into him, hard head forcing a grunt from his chest. Henryk's arms instinctively enfolded the shocked body in front of him, and what English he had deserted him entirely.

With his face in this girl's hair, for a moment he could think of nothing but home. He began to sob, silently and uncontrollably, his whole body heaving.

'Ah, Gizela,' he groaned. 'Gizela, Gizela. *Przykro mi. Przepraszam.*'

Stiff furious arms fought their way out of his grip, boots kicked at his shins, and a voice hissed at him.

'Let me go or I'll scream.'

Henryk released her immediately. He was horrified at his own loss of control. This was no way to behave. How could he have done such a thing? Standing there in his filthy flying suit and soaking wet socks, rank with chicken muck and mud and marsh ooze, a burning pain wrenched at one ankle. But he knew what he had to do next. He pulled himself up as straight as he could manage and attempted to click his heels together. It was agony. He clenched his jaw and stepped forward. Taking the girl's pale hand, Henryk bowed low over it, and kissed it very neatly and precisely.

French, he thought. She must understand French.

'*Enchanté!*' he whispered.

She pulled her hand away, tucking it under the other arm as if it had been burned. He could just about see her face now. Her mouth had fallen open, and she was staring at him, completely bewildered. She was the same age as Gizela, more or less, he thought. No, probably a little younger, a little shorter. Less angular. But probably no less spiky, to judge from his bruised shins.

The fox barked again, far away now. With a few disapproving clucks and a rustle of feathers, the chickens settled back to roost.

What was this girl going to do now? She was staring at him. He felt her stare. Couldn't really see it, but he could feel it.

Henryk's thoughts sped away from him again, but he forced himself to concentrate. He tried to anchor himself in England.

The Island of Last Hope, they called it. *Good afternoon. How do you do?* How do you do. But it wasn't the afternoon. And then suddenly he remembered the right words. He whispered them slowly and carefully:

'Hello, old bean. Think I must get weaving. All teased out, I'm afraid.'

That was it. He'd heard his FO say exactly that, only three nights ago, after a particularly difficult operation.

Holding his breath, Henryk tried to sidle away from the girl. Just disappear. Just disappear. That was it. He needed another pill, really. He'd give anything for another pill. Waves of exhaustion kept swamping him. He shook his head, convinced now that if he just slipped quietly away into the night, she'd forget about him. She'd think she had been dreaming. Perhaps he actually would disappear. Best to stop breathing. People didn't breathe in dreams. If he breathed she was more likely to scream, or call for help. Lamps would be lit behind the blacked-out windows of the farmhouse. There would be more voices, and footsteps, and shouting perhaps. Alarm. He would have to explain and then they would take him in.

For a moment the idea seemed incredibly appealing: warmth, and dry clothes, and kindness. Henryk thought about a soft bed, sheets, blankets and a fire and he began to shiver, though it was far from cold. He teetered on the edge of temptation. Perhaps he should stop resisting. Perhaps he'd be able to manage, after all. Finish what he'd started. Do what he'd come to this island for. Nobody need know he'd tried to run away. He wasn't a deserter yet. Just another lost, bailed-out airman, trying to make his way back.

At the thought of returning to the airfield, his whole body began to shake and tremble again. He had to use every last bit of remaining energy to force his limbs into stillness. And as soon as he stopped thinking about keeping them still, the idea of climbing up into the cockpit of a Hurricane returned in full force, and the shaking started up again. If he let himself go now, if he gave himself up to warmth and kindness, he'd be lost. He couldn't do it. It simply wouldn't be worth it. Because then he would have to start all over again. And he didn't think he could do that. Not again.

'Toodlepip, then.'

9

'Stop!' Peggy hissed. 'Right away!'

The stranger was already vanishing into the darkness. She couldn't just let him go. How would that look? There were enough rumours flying round about her father as it was. If anyone found out she'd let an invading German disappear, just like that, without so much as a word, the Fishers' name would be worse than dirt.

'Don't turn round,' she added.

Silence. Had he stopped? He must have stopped. You can't run away without making some kind of noise.

Stay put, she silently mouthed, and, edging along the path by the henhouse, she began to cast about for a weapon. At last her fingers knocked against a long wooden handle, which she caught just before it fell. She sensed the chickens stir and resettle their feathers. It turned out to be a stiff broom, rather than the rake she'd hoped for, but better than nothing. Keep it up, high above the shoulder, all the weight above and ready to come crashing down, and then he won't hear the giveaway rustle of bristle rather than steel on stone.

'You can't escape,' she said firmly, wondering at the clarity of her thoughts. Her voice sounded thin in the night air, and feeble even to her ears. 'If that's what you're planning.'

Still no reply. The solitary invader must be lurking just around the corner of the chicken shed, perhaps as frozen by fear as she was. Waiting for reinforcements to arrive. Peggy's eyes were stiff with staring into darkness and both her thoughts and her breathing sounded unbelievably loud. In fact, everything seemed rather unbelievable. Still just as terrified, she started to feel like a heroine in one of May's thrillers. It didn't seem possible that she could be in the story herself, actually taking part. Clutching her nightdress to stop it flapping, she took a quiet step forward and listened again.

Suddenly the stillness was broken by a quiet gasping sound. *Be quick, calm and exact*, she told herself firmly, suddenly grateful for Ernest's endless recitations. *The ordinary man and woman must be on the watch.*

It was no good running off to get help. The stranger could be miles away by the time she got anyone out of bed and into the farmyard, and nobody any the wiser as to where he'd gone. Or, worse still, the farm could be surrounded even now. *Try to check your facts.* That light she had seen earlier . . . was it just his cigarette?

There's nothing harder to walk in quietly than gumboots. With ridiculous, exaggeratedly high steps to avoid the sideways slap of rubber against her calves, Peggy began to creep around the henhouse. Her chest felt tight and bursting. Fingers on the edge of the wood, she leaned forward, breathing in the smell of creosote. Another smell hit her nostrils too. She'd caught a whiff of it earlier as she struggled to escape from the stranger's arms. A peculiar sweet and chemical smell she didn't recognise.

40

Oh God. He must be closer than she'd realised.

She wanted to scream now, loudly, and the tightness rose in her throat, but she was too paralysed to make a sound. Shifting just a fraction, she felt her nightie snag on the splintery wood at her back. The clouds had cleared and the starlight was much brighter. She took another step forward and made herself look, then leapt back in fright.

A huge pair of eyes glinted up from a crumpled heap on the ground. Then she realised that they weren't eyes at all, but goggles, pushed to the back of the man's head, over his leather headgear, so that as he buried his face in his knees, they stared glassily up at her. He was curled up like a child playing hide-and-seek, as if by making himself as small as possible, and not looking back at her, he might become invisible. Even disappear.

Impossible in that light-coloured flying suit, of course. He couldn't have stood out more. Peggy squatted down beside him, pulling her nightie over her knees. He curled himself up tighter still, tucking his head in more firmly. She could see the tension in his outstretched neck. Taut tendons and the beginning of dark cropped hair. Nothing on his feet except sodden filthy socks, unravelling in places where jagged holes revealed dirty bare skin.

REMEMBER, THAT IF PARACHUTISTS COME DOWN NEAR YOUR HOME, THEY WILL NOT BE FEELING AT ALL BRAVE, she recalled. Something about this man made Peggy feel he was very much on his own.

'Hello,' she said quietly.

No response.

41

'Are you hurt?' she tried.

The body in front of her began to shake. Squeezed up too tightly to balance, it suddenly rolled helplessly onto its side.

He was crying. Awful. Impossible to be frightened at all now. Peggy felt sick instead, sick with embarrassment and awkwardness. What man wants a girl to see them cry? She stretched out a tentative hand to within a few inches of his shoulder, and then pulled it back.

'You can't stay here all night, you know.'

What could he understand? She had no idea.

'And I'm really sorry about this, but I'm going to have to turn you in. We've all got to do our bit, you see.' She sighed, and wondered what her dad would say if he heard her now. 'But would you mind taking those goggles off your head? I really, really don't like them.'

Very slowly, a hand emerged from the folded limbs and slid off the goggles, and the body slowly began to uncurl.

'Please.'

Just one word. But it was English. That was a good sign. When he had spoken before, the words had sounded to Peggy like something learned by rote for a play, or for homework. He hardly seemed to understand what he said.

'Please,' he said again. 'I cannot go back.'

'To Germany? Don't be silly. Of course you can't. They won't let you.'

'Germany?' He finally looked at her, frowning, eyes flickering, and then looked away quickly, as if she were a light that hurt his eyes. '*Nie, nie.* No. To the airbase. The RAF. To fly.'

Peggy stared at him.

'RAF? The Royal Air Force?'

He nodded, and began to scrabble at his flying suit. Peggy got ready to run. What was he doing? He pulled it off his shoulder, and stabbed a finger at his upper arm.

'Poland,' he said, very slowly and carefully, as if addressing a small child. She didn't want to lean forward, to get too close. 'Poland,' he said again, in a voice of despair, and for a moment she thought he wanted to rip something from his sleeve – a badge she supposed.

Poland? And then Peggy remembered what June had told her when she came back from a dance at Folkestone a few weeks ago. How all the girls there had been simply mad for the Poles. Those crazy Poles. Charming, brave, utterly dashing, they laughed at danger, and spoke of nothing but revenge. Folkestone girls couldn't get enough of them, June said. They were all throwing themselves at the new arrivals. Quite shameless. So he was Polish. But June must have got it all wrong . . .

'You don't want to fly?' Peggy asked. 'I thought . . .'

And the shaking began again.

'Oh.' Peggy felt utterly helpless. 'But I can't . . . you can't . . .'

She stood up, and looked down at the wretched creature at her feet. His toes were grinding into the chicken-scratched bare earth.

'You'll have to . . .' But she couldn't finish the sentence. It felt too cruel. Overwhelmed with misery, Peggy thought about her father. She hadn't been kind to him when he said goodbye. It had been too difficult just then, with her mother in pieces. It made Peggy want to be kind now, very much indeed. She let out a deep sigh.

'Well, I suppose I could find you somewhere to hide, just for tonight. Till we think what to do.'

The pilot lurched to his feet. Peggy's confidence faltered when she saw how he towered over her. She hoped he wasn't going to start all that heel-clicking and hand-kissing again. But there was no need to worry. He couldn't even force his face back into a smile.

'Thank you. My name is Henryk. How do you do?'

10

'I'm Peggy.' The girl's voice was clear and calm, and her hands hung awkwardly by her side. He resisted the urge to take them in his own, to cover them with grateful kisses. Peggy.

They both looked down at his feet. Henryk's ankle was twice the size it had been.

'Boots,' she said. 'You need boots. And dry clothes. And a stick. Wait there.'

She flapped down the path.

It's not too late to run, thought Henryk, propping himself up against the chicken shed. Listening. She might not come back alone. He did have one other option if that happened, but it was a very last resort.

He waited, feeling the weight of his weapon inside his jacket.

When the flapping approached again, he saw the girl's outline had changed. She had a bundle in her arms. Her hands were full of boots and she was using her chin to keep the clothes from falling.

'I can?' he offered politely, reaching towards her.

'You're lucky. My mum put the trunk with Dad's stuff in one of the outhouses, so it wouldn't be in Aunt Myra's way. I've got some of his work clothes for you – I just had to grab what was on top – but no stick, I'm afraid. I'll see what I can do tomorrow if you still need one.'

He wondered if she expected him to get changed there and then. He carefully placed the pile of clothes on the floor, and made to pick up the first garment.

'Oh not now. Not here.' Setting a pair of heavy leather boots down on the ground in front of him, she began to gather up the clothes again, wrapping them into a more secure bundle. 'You're bound to get wetter before you get dryer, I'm afraid. But you'd better put these boots on first, or we'll never get anywhere. Do you think they'll fit?'

Her torrent of words slowed down at her final question. Henryk grabbed its meaning with relief. He nodded.

'I try.'

A little big, but too small would have been worse. He couldn't tie up the left one at all, so he tucked the laces inside out of the way, and tried to stand up without wincing.

'*Dziękuję*. I thank you very much.'

Her mouth stretched into something like a smile, and she nodded.

'This way. Don't worry about the dogs. They won't mind you if you're with me. You were lucky before, weren't you?'

'Lucky?' he said, checking. He thought about it. 'Yes, lucky.'

One step and it was obvious he wouldn't make it far without her help. She ducked round to his other side, and offered her arm. He couldn't refuse. Cool and downy, it felt, and slender and strong, but not actually strong enough to take his weight. Very business-like, she realised the problem after just a few steps, and simply took his own arm and put it across her shoulder, so that she was supporting him with all her body.

Again he could smell her hair. It made him want to gulp down great lungfuls of its scent. The only girls he'd met in England up till now moved in clouds of perfume and hairspray, and laughed too loudly, and looked at each other all the time. His fingertips brushed accidentally against the trimming on Peggy's nightdress sleeve and met with skin. He quickly withdrew his hand, and made sure there was a layer of cloth between them before he gripped her arm again, with the strength he needed to make it useful.

They moved painfully through the dark countryside. Henryk could sense the movement but not the direction of her thoughts beside him. She seemed sure of the way, despite the darkness. The stars were very bright. They edged round a potato field, stumbling on the ridges, and she got him over a stile and then a low, unfenced footbridge. A tricky manoeuvre, as his squadron leader would say.

'Thank you,' Henryk said. It was all he could say right now.

'It's all right,' she said politely.

Henryk kept wanting to say something more. He wasn't sure if she realised the enormity of what she was doing. He wasn't just AWOL now. He really was a deserter. He should tell her. Explain somehow. This would put her in danger. Didn't she realise?

'You are very kind,' he said, and she laughed, quite loudly, so he looked around nervously.

'Don't worry. Nobody can hear us here.'

He nodded. He wished he knew how far they still had to go. Or what to say. You are my only hope. Peggy, he said to himself, over and over again. Peggy.

47

Then he realised she was asking him a question.

'Sorry?'

'I just wondered what happened. You know, how you. . .'

She must be able to feel him trembling, remembering. But when he tried to bring back the details, the awful rushing and thudding started up again, and he felt he might black out. He may have stuttered a few words. In this state, he could hardly tell what was in his head and what came out of his mouth.

'Hit.'

'You were hit, yes. You're not burned, are you? Look, don't you think a hospital would –'

'No. No. Please. No hospital.'

'And what about your plane . . . oh, I see . . . and you must have a parachute, somewhere?'

The sudden roar of planes overhead saved Henryk from answering. He pulled her down with him, flattening her against the hard path. When they stood up again, she brushed herself down and seemed to shake off her nerves as easily as the clinging goosegrass. But the further they went, the more often she looked behind her. All the while, the distant searchlights raked the sky.

Finally they came to the last ditch. A low building stood beyond it. Henryk was ready to turn and flee. What if she had led him into a trap? All that turning back . . . were they being followed? Perhaps she had secretly alerted someone when she went to get the boots and the clothes.

Then he recognised the church he had seen from the sky. A church the shape of an ark, and surrounded by water too, as though the flood had only just receded and it was time for the world to begin afresh. A building all alone, with flat fields all around it. Through the reeds, Henryk saw the light catching the water surface and realised the sky was no longer as dark as it had been. Dawn was on its way. The night noises were changing their pitch and tempo. New birdcalls were beginning. Peggy stopped. She looked around as she spoke, glancing here and there, but not at him.

'The vicar used to come from Brookfield once a month, but not any more. Not since the war started. Not enough people, you see. It's not worth it. So you'll be quite safe here. I'm sure you will. I thought we could get as far as the Looker's Hut – that's no good for anything now, not with the sheep gone – but it's just that bit further, and I'm awfully sorry, I really am, but if I don't leave you now, I'll never get back before they wake up at the farmhouse.'

She saw his face and slowed herself down.

'Can you get across the water by yourself, do you think?'

Henryk nodded again.

'Jolly good. You'll find the key in the door. I'll come back with food as soon as I can.'

She stayed long enough to help him into the water. A shock at first, its coldness soon soothed his ankle. He took a tentative step with his good foot, which squelched into mud, and felt glad of the boots, and when he looked back to say goodbye, and thank you, a thousand more times, the ghostly white figure was already retreating across the field. He had yet to think about hunger – the pills they gave him to stay awake helped with that too. But seeing her go made him feel a different kind of emptiness.

At its deepest, the water came up to his thigh. He had to cross very slowly, holding the bundle of clothes high in front of him to keep it dry. By the time he reached a shallower part of the bank opposite, a muddy place all pitted with hoofmarks, the sky was lighter still. At his back, a faint glow of pink was beginning to appear.

The church was too small to have more than one entrance: a plain wooden door in a plain brick porch. Its iron key felt weighty in his grip, its handle elaborate. He had to put the clothes down to turn it with both hands. There was a porch, and then another door inside, half-open. He moved the clothes, looked back in the direction Peggy had taken, and scanned the lightening sky one last time. Withdrawing the key, he carefully shut the door behind him, and locked himself inside.

He listened, stiffening, ready for a fresh surprise as he pushed open the inner door.

Stillness. And boxes. The church was full of wooden boxes, like animal pens, with benches inside each, and wooden doors too. He felt his way into the first one, jumping at the metallic clunk of the latch as it fell back into place. Soaking wet as he was, he laid himself down on the floor. Tiles gave way to wood, barely less hard. He didn't deserve a bed. And he hadn't the energy to change his clothes anyway, or make himself more comfortable. He kicked off his soaking boots. A trickle of water emerged, and traced the gradient of the floor. The smell of dust and cobwebs reassured him that the girl – Peggy, he whispered again – had not lied.

Like a clockwork toy winding down, his mind began to slow at last. He forced his jaw to stop its grinding. Before Henryk fell asleep, a ray of sunlight crept in. The only decoration in this plain, plain church was a series of wooden oval plaques, stuck high in the rafters. In the roof above Henryk, one golden inscription was suddenly illuminated, long enough to read the words:

We wait for thy loving kindness, O God, in the midst of thy temple.

11

Aunt Myra counted out the tasks on her fingers, and Ernest felt his panic rising. He was bound to forget something. He stared at her moving lips. Uncooked sausages. And then he thought how like sausages her fingers were too. But the fat kind, not the thin ones, like her lips. Sausages, or pale blood puddings.

' . . . and when you've fed the chickens, fetch in the washing from the line, and put the nappies in June's room and don't forget to check on the baby while you're in the orchard. And you might get a bowl of cherries for our tea since you're there.'

'All right.' *Chickens. Washing. Nappies. Baby. Plums. No, cherries. Chickens. Washing . . . Yes, I can do all that. But I need the basket*, thought Ernest. Where's the basket? He put down the pig slop bucket and went to look. It wasn't in the outhouse. Maybe Aunt Myra had left it by the line when she hung up the washing. Best check first.

Past the vegetable patch and the chicken run and he could hear the baby had woken up. The big black pram was twanging on its springs, and trembling with angry crying. Ernest ran over and peered in. He began to rock the pram.

'Hello there. You're meant to be asleep, you know.'

The baby stopped with a hiccup. She stared at him, tears pooling in her eyes, lower lip quivering. She seemed to be holding her breath.

'Give me a minute,' Ernest said.

He turned to pick up the basket and the baby let out a new howl.

'Oh, baby . . . Claudette . . .'

Like everyone else in the family, Ernest couldn't get his head round the baby's name. His cousin June had named her daughter after Claudette Colbert. It felt like the next best thing to being a Hollywood star herself, which was June's real dream. Claudette's dad was in uniform and well away by the time she was born, so he hadn't had much say in the matter, though Ernest sometimes wondered what he thought.

Ernest went back to rocking the handle of the pram, and tried to stretch across the grass to reach the basket with his other hand. Then he had the idea of moving Claudette. So he pulled the pram behind him, dragging it over to the washing line. The baby's head jolted from side to side as it lurched over the tussocks. Strangely, she seemed to like these violent movements. Didn't she? Laughter or tears? The harder he looked, the less sure he felt. Claudette's little face lit up a bit more every time she saw his.

Ernest decided the best thing would be to put the washing basket on the front bit of the pram – the apron, June called it, for some reason. But when he poppered it up, it blocked the baby's sight, and she didn't like that. A few games of peepo later, Claudette calmed down and Ernest could get on with his tasks.

It was a white wash. Nappies, nappies, nappies, some tea towels and a tablecloth and some of his own vests and Peggy's plain knickers and June's rather fancier ones and – about three times the size – his Aunt Myra's knickers. Ernest unpegged these with his eyes shut.

Basket piled high, baby calmer – as long as he kept peeking round the washing – Ernest started to wheel the pram back to the farmhouse. Then he remembered the cherries. Drat. He'd forgotten to bring out a bowl for them. Well, he couldn't leave the baby now. She'd scream the place down.

Under the dappled shade of the tree, inspiration struck. He explained his idea to Claudette.

'Look. We can make a nest in the washing for the cherries, can't we? Simple! We don't need that silly old bowl, do we?'

Popping one cherry into his mouth, he began to fill his nest with fruit. When he found a perfect pair of cherries, he hung them over his left ear. The baby reached out for them as they dangled, and she laughed.

'Do you want some earrings too? Here you are then. Two for me and two for you.'

Soon Ernest had a great pile of cherries sitting on the nappies. Back past the henhouse. The white leghorns all came rushing up to the fence at his approach. They were jolly noisy today. What was the matter with them? Through the vegetable patch. The beans were coming along. He'd be able to hide in their wigwam soon. Except he was a bit big for that now. At the back door, Ernest realised he'd have to turn the pram round to get it up the step.

Ernest walked backwards through the door, grinning at the baby.

He heard voices in the kitchen. An argument was brewing. Aunt Myra sounded outraged. Then Ernest heard June pleading.

'Mum, you mustn't. You can't ask her that. You can't possibly. What if it's not true?'

'Not true? Only too likely, I'd say. It's just what I'd suspected myself.'

'He went very suddenly, I suppose,' said June.

'It's no wonder she's not let on. Oh, the shame of it!'

'I can think of worse. Much worse,' said June.

'Don't imagine they can't too. In fact, I did hear . . .'

'Stop, Mum. You mustn't. Just don't say anything, please. You can see she's already upset. And what about Peggy and Ernest?'

'Hmmph.'

Ernest stepped backwards, straight into the slop bucket he'd put down earlier. He skidded, and fell, making a grab for the pram handle to right himself, which knocked the washing off. The cherries went flying; the baby started crying. Ernest's head crashed hard against the scullery door-frame. When he opened his eyes again, the scrunched-up face of Aunt Myra was right against his own. Her screeching made his ears hum. He could drown in her fury.

12

Peggy heard the crash from the hall. It was followed quickly by the baby's rising scream, and Myra's above that. Safe to waltz into the kitchen then, as if she'd only just happened to arrive, instead of listening as she had, for five minutes or more behind the door.

'You stupid, stupid boy!' Aunt Myra was shouting into Ernest's baffled face. Claudette's howls stepped up to an ear-fluttering pitch.

Clever boy, thought Peggy. Perfect timing, for a change. Good to have that subject closed.

'Oh, Ernest! What have you done?' Peggy said. She knew it was a kind of betrayal, to align herself with her aunt like that.

Ernest looked as dazed as she'd ever seen him.

'No common sense at all,' Myra kept repeating. 'If I've said it once, I've said it a thousand times. Not one drop.'

'I know, Mum, but don't keep saying it. It was just an accident,' soothed June.

'It's always just an accident.'

'He was only trying to help.' June scooped up the baby, popping the cherries from her ears into her own mouth. She rocked her against her shoulder with one arm while trying to separate potato peelings from the rest of the cherries with the other.

'Don't worry, I'll do that,' said Peggy, quickly stepping in before Claudette's head could swing back. 'Let me get a colander, and then I can give them a rinse.'

The kitchen hadn't been empty since she'd finally woken up, long after breakfast, and with an awful start – you never knew what time it was with the room so dark. June was hammering on the bedroom door, telling her she'd milked Marge already, and hadn't she heard the racket the cow had been making, and that she might have got away with it this time, but that was the last lie-in Peggy was getting this side of Victory. Peggy briefly wondered if she'd dreamed the whole thing. The mud on her nightdress hem told her otherwise. Anyway, nobody could make Henryk up. He was too extraordinary.

Ernest staggered to his feet, and managed to squish more cherries into the nappies in the process. Dark purple stains.

'I'm so sorry, Aunt Myra. I just didn't see the bucket there. I'll clear it all up, I promise. I'm ever so sorry. I didn't mean it. Look, I'll take my shoes off right away. And I'll make some tea, shall I?' he offered. 'Yes, tea . . . Why don't I do that?'

Peggy nodded at him, and gave him a little shove in the direction of the Rayburn. Best get him away and busy as quickly as possible.

'See! There are plenty of cherries here worth saving!' she said.

Peggy was trying to ignore the tight, dragging sensation in the pit of her stomach. It was like carrying around a boulder, this mistake she had made: huge and indigestible, it weighed her down. She put the colander on the table and set her face into an encouraging smile.

'You sit down, Auntie – you must be exhausted. I'll clear all this lot up and I can easily put the dirty things in the tub to soak again.'

'Boiling water for cherry stains. Stretch out the cloth and pour it through. Hasn't your mother taught you anything? Goodness me. Well, you'll learn when you have to. June can show you this time, and you'll know for yourself the next.'

Peggy's jaw clenched. She had to keep her mouth shut. June turned from the draining board, and gave her a huge wink. A perfectly painted black line flicked up at the end of long heavy lashes, making Peggy wonder if she wouldn't be better off learning June's mascara trick, instead of top tips for stain removal. Except, with her luck, make-up would probably be yet another thing she'd have to 'do without', thanks to this wretched war. And just as she was finally getting old enough.

Myra was still talking.

'Could be worse. Could be blood.'

On hands and knees back in the scullery, Peggy stared at the flagstones. The sun flooding from the open door lit the whole awful mess with brutal clarity. Whatever had she been thinking? People don't just go round hiding people. It was absurd. Specially with Ernest always trailing after her, with his binoculars and his questions and his rules. Noticing things. What about food? What about the law?

Her skin seemed to contract. For the first time she began to fear for herself. Maybe she was a traitor already. After all, she'd encouraged someone not to do his duty. That was a kind of treachery. Peggy didn't know how old you had to be to go to prison, or if being a girl made any difference. But they hanged traitors. She was sure of that.

June's voice sang out from the kitchen, sounding blissfully normal: 'I'll have a cuppa while you're on the job, Ernest.' Peggy knew exactly what she'd say next. 'I'm parched.'

'Would you like tea too, Peggy?' called Ernest.

'Yes please!' she called back, unfreezing, glad nobody had been watching her.

It was simple enough, Peggy told herself, scooping some carrot peelings back into the bucket. As soon as she could escape, she'd go back to the church and tell the poor pilot right away. Not much time had passed yet, after all. It wasn't too late. He'd be back at the aerodrome soon enough, putting all this behind him, and nobody need ever know what had happened in a silly panic in the middle of the night.

Nose wrinkling, she finished clearing up the slops. There had to be something here worth rescuing for Henryk, though even the chickens and the pigs were getting rather a rotten deal now, what with everyone having to be so careful about what they threw away.

A slice of burned toast balanced where it had fallen on the row of gumboots. Her own were still slightly wet. She hoped nobody had noticed, and shoved the toast into the pocket of her cardigan. Feeding the pilot before she sent him away was the very least she could do.

13

As soon as his eyes closed Henryk was flying again. Nothing could keep him out of the sky in his dreams. Before the war, he often found himself laughing in his sleep as he flew. It was an endlessly exhilarating miracle, and for the first six months of flying solo he never stopped dreaming about it. Why put an end to the most perfect liberty devised by mankind, even for a night? It was a glory like no other. He barely felt alive except when he was in the air.

Not any more. Now when he slept Henryk always returned to the same flight. This was the tenth, or twentieth time or thirtieth time he had re-lived it. It was always the third day of the war. The moment when rage had whipped away doubt.

No looking back at the mechanic, sweating on the ground. The man's encouraging shout was lost in the engine's rising roar and the thud of turning propellers, and the final lurch into freedom. In the air at last, and not a breath of crosswind, Henryk turned the nose of his plane skyward, climbing almost vertically in formation with the others. Witold, Kazimierz, Jan, Tadeusz, and Wacław. Slow and steady. It felt too slow at first. But height was the thing, and he had to be patient.

The fields below slowly shrank.

It felt so good to be on the move again. Three days, hidden with their P.11s, watching wave after wave of enemy aircraft pass overhead from the shelter of the trees. More pilots than planes on their side: time after time the squadron commander had stepped in to stop furious attempts to take off without orders.

'We can't afford to lose more aircraft.'

And now, finally, they were fighting back, and the British would soon send more planes, and the French were coming any moment too. It was just a case of holding on, till help arrived. Not long. Then Hitler would see what he was up against. He'd see what the Poles were made of.

Henryk barely noticed the chill as the rush of wind cooled his sweat-coated face. He knew the machine guns were checked and loaded. He trusted his aircraft completely, just as he trusted the groundstaff. His focus was all on the sky.

Which had never looked so blue. Another perfect day. It felt so wrong. This was the kind of late summer Sunday afternoon you needed to hold on to, so that its magnificence could last you through the winter. He should be taking his sisters to Kryspinów for their last swim of the season today. That's what they always did this weekend. Before the water turned too cold to bear. While the leaves were still green on the poplars. No. Stop. Don't think about this. Gizela's pleading eyes. Klara and Anna pulling him out of the door, laughing, bubbling over with excitement, towels stuffed in bags and spilling out as they spun round. Stop. His mother calling down from the top of the stairs, making sure Ana had her float.

Stop. Keep searching the sky. There's no time for thinking.

Where were these wretched planes then? How much longer could they take to arrive? Four minutes? Three minutes? Two? Henryk's eyes ached with the strain of looking. Up, ahead, left, right. Perhaps there had been a mistake. Over and again he scanned the blueness. Kazimierz adjusted his course, just a little to the left, and turned in the cockpit. His mouth opened and shut as he signalled, and then Henryk saw them too.

From below, the enemy aircraft looked like a dark cloud, a swarm of locusts bigger than any he had sighted yet.

Henryk continued to climb, pulling on the stick with increasing urgency. He was desperate to get closer, closer and higher. Now, through the propellers' blur, he could count the planes. Six flights of heavy Junkers, low-winged bombers. Another two flights below. A fat batch of Heinkels. And, with a sickening jolt inside, Henryk registered four more flights behind these, huge and grey. Here and there, like dragonfly next to these well-filled locusts, single Dorniers flitted.

Henryk's head roared. It was so hard to be patient. But you had to wait. You just had to wait. Till the last possible moment. It was all about keeping your nerve.

At last the Me 110s themselves appeared, noses up, as though the Polish fighters were not even worth their attention. Glittering in the brilliant sunshine, they radiated superiority in tight formation.

'Come on!' Henryk shouted into the noise. 'Come down and get us. You can see we're here. Why don't you come and fight?'

You would think they'd heard the taunting. All at once the Messerschmitts suddenly dived straight for the Poles. Henryk just saw teeth, sharp and white, fangs painted on the snout of the plane whose gunner was aiming right at him, guns stuttering. Teeth clenched, jaw rigid, Henryk returned fire, felt the recoil jerk of his own plane, and turned instantly on his wing.

The German plane flashed by, and turned too, but it was below him now. He had the advantage at last. Behind and above. And it was not for nothing the Polish planes were known as bees, angry ones at that, returning again and again to the kill.

Henryk looped back and back, and fired his machine guns until they failed to respond. Then he kept on hammering the button with his thumb, almost unable to believe this fight was over for him. But his ammunition was finished. All gone, so soon. The important thing now was keeping his plane intact for the next attack.

Heading back for the airfield, he caught a flash and another burst of fire at the edge of his vision. Oh Jesus! Number 3 was in flames. Witold. Like a comet, the machine plunged to the earth, a fiery, smokey tail streaming behind it. Escape looked impossible. Surely he was already too low and falling too fast to bail out? Henryk's heart smashed against his ribs, and then he saw white. A slow, soft blossoming of silk against the dark stripes of newly ploughed earth.

His relief came too soon. A streak of tracer followed. Then another. A second Messerschmitt had swooped in. Far away as he was, Henryk could see Witold's flailing limbs. They jerked repeatedly, then hung limp.

Henryk's sleep was disturbed by the jerking of his own body. His thrashing arms thudded against planks, and when he tried to sit up, the crash of skull on wood left his head ringing. He was trapped, boxed in on three sides. Only when he heard the depth of the stillness all around him did he roll over and out from under the seat of the wooden pew, and see where he was.

His first thought was the window. A church. A village? That girl?

He pulled himself up, registering pain in his ankle, the stiff, clinging dampness of his many layers of clothes, the dull ache in his heart. The box-like pews made the place feel like a courtroom. Even without witnesses, without a prosecutor, he felt himself on trial. The windows were criss-crossed with lead, the small glass squares thick and distorting. Henryk half-expected to look out and find himself fenced in by hostile peasants, ready to lead him to a prison cell. He had abandoned his post. It didn't get much worse than this. He deserved to be punished.

Henryk looked through the cobwebbed panes and saw nobody. Nobody, and nothing.

Almost nothing, at least. He was briefly dazzled by the glittering blue of the water through which he had waded in the night. It snaked through lush grassland, forming something like a moat to this isolated church. No gravestones that he could see. Very few trees and fewer houses, save a couple of red-toned roofs dotted about in the distance, none very close. A great deal of sky, and the sun high in it too. He had slept too long.

He raised a hand to rub at his bent neck. It was chafed and raw from turning his head, over and over again, constantly looking for the enemy. The bundle of fresh clothes still lay tumbled in a heap on the parquet floor where he had dropped it. The girl. Peggy. Was she coming back? And if she did, what would he say to her?

Little clouds of dust rose in the air and invaded his nostrils as Henryk inspected the pile of clothing. He shook out baggy corduroy trousers flecked with pale crumbling paint, a fisherman's jersey, and a canvas smock. It was stiff in places and also encrusted with some chalky substance. Thick, knitted socks. All apparently packed away in a hurry, unwashed, unironed. Not that he cared. But it made him curious about the man these clothes belonged to.

Before peeling off his uniform, Henryk removed a stone from his inside pocket. He kissed it once, and placed it carefully on the white painted bench in front of him. Then he sat down and withdrew his revolver. Nearly everyone in his squadron had carried a handgun during the Battle for France. Who wanted to come down defenceless behind enemy lines? So many planes destroyed on the ground, but this, at least, he had rescued.

Elbows on knees, head down, he weighed the gun in his hand, remembering. The solidity of the weapon no longer eased his nerves. Neither friend nor enemy, neither cold nor warm, it simply existed. Neutral, passive, a cog in a machine, it was a rank-and-file instrument, awaiting orders, which it would simply obey. You had to admire it, really.

Henryk turned it round, and closed one eye so he could look down into the darkness of the barrel. Not much to see. A faint smell of metal and grease. It was awkward holding it like that, wrist twisted. And he felt so stiff. His armpits still ached from the parachute harness. His ankle gently throbbed. He felt as hollow as the barrel down which he peered.

Well, he could just see, couldn't he? Find out what it felt like? See if he could? The roof of the mouth. That was meant to be the way. A straight path to the brain. It should be easy enough. A simple solution. His lips parted and his jaw loosened, his tongue retreating to the back of his throat. It made him gag. There's no flesh to speak of in that soft dark archway. It's too hard to take more hardness, hard like the mouth of a gun itself. It will bruise and splinter.

Henryk heard a noise, and realised he was making it himself. A soft, choking kind of sound, wet and dry at once, like breathing stuttering to a halt in the last hours of a long illness.

The safety catch. He couldn't do this with the safety catch on.

The truth was he couldn't do it at all.

14

Peggy drew herself sharply against the wall by the window so she could not be seen. Heart thudding, eyes shut. A white figure appeared in her mind just as clearly as she had glimpsed it moments before. She could trace the line of his back as he bent before the altar, a little distorted by the window glass, but clear enough. Not prostrate or even kneeling, but simply pulling on a pair of dry trousers.

When her breathing had become slower, she was tempted to look again. But she found she couldn't. The idea of being seen looking was too excruciating. She felt hot with shame even for thinking of it.

Peggy had made a wide circle round the church before approaching it this time, over the bridge. Why hadn't she led him round to the causeway in the night? No time. This way was better. You could just about see the building from the farmhouse. Coming from the far side was definitely safer. Creeping round towards the porch, she knocked gently on the door. A waiting stillness came from within and the handle of the string bag she was carrying cut into her hand, as if to chastise her for stealing the food it contained.

'It's me. Peggy,' she called softly. Heaven knows why. Out here on the Marsh you could shout and scream and the sound would vanish into the skies and nobody'd know you'd ever spoken. *You're trying to make this into a big adventure*, she told herself. How long would it take for him to pull on his clothes, and how would he look then? She called a second time, more loudly.

'Open the door. Henryk. I've brought you breakfast.'

The lock turned, and the door swung away from her.

'Sorry it's so late,' she said as she slipped inside, where she found herself immediately squeezed against Henryk. He had been waiting this side of the inner door so he could shut the outer one behind her. They tried to manoeuvre round each other. A familiar, comforting smell of lanolin, sweat and clay filled the tiny space. It was the smell of her father, rising from his old jersey, warmed by a new body. Unbalanced, Peggy sat down suddenly, on the bench behind the door. She took a breath to calm herself, and looked up to see Henryk's face. Dark with beard-growth, it had a hunted appearance already and his eyes were blood-shot.

'You are cold,' stated Henryk. 'You . . . brrrrrr . . .' He mimed shivering.

She hadn't noticed, but he was right. The air in the church felt icy after the fields' overbearing sunshine. There were goose pimples on her arms and legs, and her cotton frock felt all at once too thin and too short. A little girl's dress. A little girl who was trying to be a grown-up.

'Look what I've brought you.' She held up the bag brightly, and he backed into the church. 'You must be starving.'

'No, no, no. Not *starving. I* am not starving,' he said quickly, and Peggy wondered at his insistent precision. Then he made

68

himself clear. 'In Poland they are starving. I am . . . *peckish*.' A
shadow of a smile crossed his face, and he nodded, relieved.
He seemed proud to have got the word right. Peggy smiled
too, a nervous, uncertain smile.

'Well, it's not much. It's been a bit tricky, in fact. But I
intercepted some eggs, and managed to boil them in the kettle
without anyone seeing.'

She looked around, and wondered where to unload her
modest haul. Her mind kept fluttering. She'd tell him her
decision in a minute. He had to go: there was no doubt about
it. But first, food. Send him away fed, and then he could face
the music on a full stomach. Even a condemned man gets a
last meal, doesn't he?

The wooden board over the font would have made a good
table, but she couldn't possibly put it there. Instead, Peggy headed
for the box pew with the open door. Henryk's bulky flying suit
lay flopped in a heap in the corner, like a crumpled corpse.

'Oh,' she said, startled. 'I thought for a moment . . .' And
she shook her head and changed the subject. She knew she
was talking too fast, and too much, but she didn't seem to be
able to slow down. Everything was racing inside, her thoughts
faster even than her words. Just as busily, she began to lay out
and rearrange her finds on the paint-chipped bench. 'Very
stale bread, I'm afraid. My aunt was saving it for a pudding.
I'll tell her I gave it to the pigs by mistake. And look . . . I even
remembered salt!' Peggy held up a twist of paper. Her father
always liked salt on his eggs.

Looking at it all laid out like that, and then at Henryk, it
didn't seem very much, after all that effort. And him so tall.

Thinner in these clothes, which rather hung off him, the trouser cuffs too high. He must need so much food. No. She couldn't do this again. He wasn't her responsibility. She stole another glance at his face.

Henryk was considering what she had brought, hand on chin. She could hear the rasp of his fingers moving thoughtfully against his stubble. Then he leaned forward without warning and snatched something from the bench, so quickly that Peggy heard herself cry out. Not food though. He hadn't taken anything she had brought. She felt herself stiffen, like an animal preparing to run. She had been too easily fooled. He wasn't who he said he was. Who was he, though, and what was he going to do?

Just as he had seen her shiver a little earlier, he noticed instantly the sudden fear in her face. It was as if he could hear her thoughts. *Peggy Fisher, what have you got yourself into? And who are you going to call for help out here?* But it was all right. That's what he was trying to tell her. Henryk put a reassuring hand on her arm, and then slowly uncurled the other fist to show her.

A stone. A small grey pebble.

Henryk stared at it with a strange expression. Loving and anguished. It was infinitely precious to him, this uneven bit of rock. Peggy could see that without asking. Not like a diamond or a pearl or anything like that though. More like a songbird's egg, waiting to hatch. Henryk stroked it tenderly, bent to kiss it, and stowed the stone safely away in the pocket of his borrowed trousers.

15

The stone brought everything back. He had never seen a grown man crying before the day he left Poland. Not open tears. Not gulping and sobbing without control. Now he was pressed against hundreds of weeping men, many in uniforms like his own. The rumble of low-geared engines rose and fell in an insistent undercurrent, and petrol fumes flooded his senses. Henryk didn't know exactly when the Rumanians had shut the border but by this time hundreds of vehicles of all kinds had congregated behind it: thunderous military trucks, a few private cars – those that hadn't been abandoned on the roadside already, for want of petrol – but mostly horses and carts, wagons and wheelbarrows, all inching along, stopping and starting, jostling for space. A relentless river of people, tens and thousands trudging at the same pace as the traffic, shadows swinging across their faces. The crossing was now open again, but movement was so slow.

Henryk could only see about five of the other pilots in his unit. They had lost Wacław long ago, not surprisingly. How could he have hoped to keep up when he insisted on dragging along that bit of broken propeller? Jan was still just ahead though, and Kazimierz right beside him, keeping up a steady mumbling prayer, repeating it over and over, till it lost all sense and Henryk wanted to thump him.

I nie wódź nas na pokuszenie, ale nas zbaw ode złego. Bo Twoje jest królestwo, potęga i chwała na wieki wieków . . .

When the front bumper of a smart shiny Fiat nudged at the back of his legs, Henryk could hardly make himself look up. Stumbling, he glanced round, one hand shielding his eyes from the headlight's glare. A woman in a fur coat stretched forward in the front passenger seat and began rapping at the windscreen, trying to wave him out of the way. She even leaned over and started bashing at the horn herself. Henryk peered at the peaked cap and impassive face of her driver and guessed he was a chauffeur. No doubt as anxious to escape capture as his employers, but trained not to show it. Everyone was on the move now. The Soviets had begun to march into Poland from the East that very morning.

He ignored the car and its owner. There was nowhere it could go anyway. The road ahead was crammed, bottle-necking at the frontier post before the bridge. And he had his own orders: evacuation orders. Somewhere over the Dniester, new planes were waiting, sent to Rumania by the British. The fight would soon resume. That was the plan.

Everyone shuffled forward.

A startling bang resounded a little way ahead, causing a sudden opening up of the crowd. Silence, and then the shuffling started up again, more half-hearted than ever. But it stopped just as quickly and the whispering began. The news didn't take long to reach Henryk. Unable to bear the shame of retreat, a cavalry officer had shot himself in the head, right there, in the road, in front of everyone. Nobody was certain what to do. Once more, everything came to a juddering halt.

Henryk took a deep breath and pushed his way through the ring of onlookers, who stood like iron filings circling a magnet. Everyone else seemed paralysed by the fact that the dead man was an officer, and away from his unit. Henryk responded without really thinking. When you're the oldest in the family, and the only boy, you get used to taking charge.

'Will someone help me? Please?' Henryk's voice sounded strained and strange, even to himself. He bent down, hoping it would encourage another volunteer.

He wanted to get hold of the feet, but the dead man's head was closer. Henryk bent down with a grunt, and hoisted him up, one arm under each shoulder. The officer's unshaven jaw sagged, and blood spewed from the corner of his mouth. It came from the wound at the back of his head too, soaking into Henryk's sleeve. Edging sideways, out of the current of people and traffic, he twisted away from the man's blank eyes and matted moustache. Henryk's boots mashed against something that was both soft and rigid: he had accidentally crushed the officer's brocaded hat. This man must have fought in the wars of 1920 too. Unlike Henryk's father, he'd survived the events that settled the eastern borders of Poland, and secured her independence.

They left the body by the side of the road. At the last moment, the young cadet who had volunteered to take his feet reached into his pocket and pulled out a grimy handkerchief. He passed it once across his own forehead, brushing his eyes too, and then carefully spread it out over the man's face, covering his eyes.

'That's better,' he said, and coughed, and then he disappeared back into the shuffling.

It took another hour to reach the red-and-white barrier. Henryk wondered what could be causing such a blockage. Eventually, he realised. Nobody could bear to leave. Men were clinging to the barrier, barely able to let go. As each Pole crossed into Rumania, another took his place at the frontier. They caressed the wooden post longingly, trailing their fingers like parting lovers. Some kissed the eagle on it, or pressed dry lips to the ground beneath, where others scrabbled for handfuls of earth. Henryk recognised a pilot he hadn't seen since their training at Dęblin. Eyes shut, he was moaning softly as he embraced the guard's sentry box.

Henryk had been stuck on the edge of the crowd since moving the body. That made it easier to step aside for a moment without the people behind falling over him. As he watched, an immensely tall and skinny bomber pilot hoisted a friend onto his shoulders, who reached up into the lowest branches of the last tree in Poland and began to snap off twigs. He passed down leaves too, which were handed out one by one, with a solemnity more suited to communion wafers. Men received them with yet more tears. Their gratitude was almost pathetic.

Those won't last, thought Henryk. He remembered little Anna's disappointment last autumn. A vivid scarlet leaf she had collected one Sunday afternoon in the Park Krakowski had crumbled to brittle fragments in her coat pocket even before they reached home. *But I wanted to show it to Daddy. And then I was going to keep it forever,* she had told him. Forever and ever. *I'll find you another one, an even better one. You'll see.* He had brushed the tiny pieces from her hand as he spoke. *Really?* Trusting eyes. *Yes, really. We'll go and look now.*

When he was younger, Henryk always wished his stepfather could have been more dashing. More like his real father, he supposed. A cavalry officer. Then there was a time when he wanted nothing other than a pilot for a father. Now he was glad his widowed mother had married a music professor who was getting on in years, and that they had both enjoyed a second chance at family life. Too old to fight, too insignificant to care about. At least he'd always be there to look after Matka and the girls.

There was a faint kerfuffle ahead, and Henryk panicked briefly. Perhaps they were shutting the border again. Quick.

A stone. He needed to find a stone. He could keep a stone forever.

He dropped to his knees and fumbled with his fingertips, digging his nails into the soil to scoop out a pebble. Just as he managed to scrape one out, a boot landed heavily on his hand. He gave its owners' legs a determined sideways shove with his shoulders, and closed his fingers round his prize. He must find somewhere really safe to keep it.

Henryk unbuttoned his tunic, felt for the inside pocket, and slid the stone carefully down to the bottom corner of it. Immediately after buttoning himself up, he had another thought. He opened his jacket again, shook it a few times, and stuck his hand back into the pocket to make sure there were no hidden holes in the lining that might catch him unawares. Nothing to worry about. Except for a piece of paper. What could that be? He had no memory of putting anything in there.

He'd have to look later. He needed time, and light to see. Right now the whole world seemed too dark, and he wondered if the light would ever return.

The weeping grew louder, and the wind began to pick up too. Soon the first heavy drops of a late summer thunderstorm began to fall.

16

Peggy wondered if she could simply slip away. Now, while Henryk was in this dreamy state. She risked another glance at him. His eyes had gone blank, and though he continued to stare, it was as if he were looking through her and seeing something else entirely. The muscles of his face twitched slightly. He might have been rehearsing speech.

She began to practise herself, the words she might use to tell Uncle Fred she had led the pilot here deliberately, intending to lock him in before going for help – surely no less believable than what had happened.

Give him the facts. That was the order. GO QUICKLY TO THE NEAREST AUTHORITY AND GIVE HIM THE FACTS. But Peggy was less certain than ever what the facts actually were. Henryk hadn't asked for food, or transport, or maps, or where he was, or where his comrades were, or where the British soldiers might be. He hadn't asked for anything at all, barely seemed to know what he wanted.

Without making it too obvious, she glanced down at the uniform discarded on the floor. Next to the flying-suit was a jacket. RAF blue. It looked authentic enough to her, though she hardly thought herself a very good judge of these things.

Maybe she should tidy it away for him, and get a better look at the same time. Peggy felt almost wifely as she picked up the jacket, shook it out by the shoulders, and began to fold it up. There. There it was. An embroidered badge, at the top of the sleeve. That's what he was trying to show her in the night, when it was far too dark to see properly. POLAND, it said. He really was one of those crazy Poles. But crazy in a different way altogether, with not an ounce of the exotic slate-blue glamour June had described.

'Poland,' she said.

When she spoke his eyes flickered, back to the here and now. He wore that expression you see on people when they are tuning a wireless, trying to get a clear signal. Then he nodded at her.

'Yes. Cracow, I am from.'

'Oh.' She had so many questions, but she was worried she'd be drawn in, and it would just make everything harder later. 'Look. I have to go now. I'll be in such trouble if I don't hurry. So much to do. On a farm. You know.' She wasn't sure he did.

Something about him made her think he wasn't the country type. What was that place he had just mentioned? Crack-something. She would look it up when she got a chance.

Then another thing occurred to her.

'You never told me.' She swept her hands round like a ballet dancer, miming the cause of her anxiety, and the hem of her dress dropped back. 'Where is your parachute?'

'I hide it,' said Henryk. 'It is safe. Nobody find it.'

'Oh good. Because . . .' No, this was hopeless. The more she thought about it . . . 'Look,' she said, drawing herself up. She found her voice becoming louder and slower and distinctly firmer, rather like Aunt Myra's when she talked to Ernest. 'Look. Maybe all this isn't such a good idea after all.'

He didn't take the hint. She would have to spell it out.

'It's not too late. You can come back with me, right now. We can go to the Red Lion – that's the pub – and we'll phone the airfield, and then they'll just come and get you and everything will be all right.' She could hardly bear to look at him. 'I'll pretend I found you here instead . . . Oh, in fact, I've got a good idea! Yes, yes! I know! You hit your head. You forgot everything. And now you've remembered. It often happens, I'm sure. I've read about it in lots of stories.'

Peggy beamed at him, confident that she had found the perfect solution.

Except clearly it wasn't. As soon as she'd spoken she saw the fear returning, crawling along his bones and under his skin and into his eyes. It crept along her spine too, and she knew right away that he couldn't forget anything. That was why he was here, and not drinking in some mess with his mates, or playing cards or backgammon, or whatever fighter pilots did when they weren't flying.

Henryk shook his head. His mouth opened. He was about to start pleading with her. She didn't want that. She'd had enough of pleading. It didn't work. Look at her mother, pleading with her father. Not to take the peace pledge. Not to make a fuss. Pleading about the leaflets. Pleading about the letters and the newspapers and the meetings. Pleading with him to change his mind – he was too old to be called up yet anyway, he could just keep his head down, keep quiet, accept the way things were, it wasn't necessary. He didn't have to take a stand, make a scene.

'Don't. Please don't.' She found herself looking over her shoulder, as if they were being watched already. 'You'll be safe here. Until your ankle is better, and then . . . well, then we'll see.'

17

It must be a warning. Side by side, they hung motionless on the fence, noses pointed to the sky. Despair or defiance. Ernest stared at the wire twisting through the moles' necks, just under their whiskery chins. He couldn't see how hanging them there would stop the others tunnelling. Twelve, thirteen, fourteen of them, he counted, unable to take his eyes off the gibbet. Their paws were like little baby hands, with perfect pink fingers, and if you looked closely, you could see the dirt from their digging still clinging to the crevices. Soft bedraggled black fur. In the stomach of one creature, maggots were beginning to squirm.

Ernest backed away, bile rising. There was no getting away from his own guilt.

Uneasily, he went back to his search, methodically working through the hedgerow to find the perfect twigs. Hazel and willow worked best for the traps. They had to be just the right length and thickness. Pencil-size for the mumble pin, but you needed a long bit of willow for the mole stick. And that evening – unless there was an air raid – he and Fred would sit in the kitchen, whittling away in after-supper silence, comfortably absorbed. He didn't mind that bit.

Peggy would probably be able to help him find an excuse

not to go with Uncle Fred to check the traps later. She was good at thinking things up. Ernest couldn't possibly tell him the truth about how he felt, though Dad would understand, of course. *He* didn't think it was silly or squeamish. A dead animal, in your bare hands, that you've killed yourself . . .? Ernest shuddered, imagining the feel of a stiff, cold body, hard under velvet. Seeing the gibbet made it harder to forget the purpose of the whittling.

'That's the one,' he said aloud, feeling for his penknife. 'Perfect.'

He crouched down to cut the switch at its base, leaning against the trunk of the willow for balance. For some time Ernest moved along the bank, occasionally swatting at mosquitoes, enjoying the methodical task of stripping the leaves. At last he had a good pile, and he was feeling creaky and hunched, so he stood up and stretched.

A loud plop made him turn, but there was nothing to see except for the circles on the water surface below getting bigger and bigger. Like an ever-expanding target, Ernest thought, crouching down in the reeds at the edge of the ditch, where the water was green with duckweed. After a few minutes' observation, Ernest spotted the frog surfacing. One of the new kind, he was sure: the ones that made such a racket.

It was quite silent now that he was looking. Just its warty old head was above water, staring right at him, you'd think, with those big eyes stuck on top. A real beauty. Big and fat and spotty and such a bright green. Ernest waited for a while to see if it would do that funny thing. If you were patient, they puffed out their cheeks like pale grey balloons, one on each side, qwarking away. Like a question. Or they'd burst out into loud laughter. Bre-ke-ke-ke-ke-ke-ke-keh. Gut Sewer was full of these new frogs.

They had escaped from Percy the Poet's garden. That's what his aunt had told him a few weeks previously, with a sharp sniff. *Foreign frogs*, she said, peering with great suspicion into a jar of spawn he'd just brought home. *Those aren't ours.* She pursed her lips. Hungarian, if you please. At any road that's what she'd heard. Or was it Rumanian? The point was that they were aliens. Invaders.

Peggy had come over to have a look, and she shook her head too.

'Can't you see, Ernest? That's not proper frogspawn. Just look at it.'

He'd wiped his specs and looked more closely. And of course she was right. He'd wondered how he'd struck lucky so late in the year. There weren't many eggs. And they were much lighter than usual, a sort of biscuity colour, with far less of that jelly stuff all over them.

'It should never have been allowed,' Aunt Myra had said, with another sniff.

Ernest stood up and moved along the bank to the next cluster of willows, repeating the rules to himself. 'THE ORDINARY MAN AND WOMAN MUST BE ON THE WATCH,' he said. *Read these instructions carefully.*

83

18

Peggy felt the heat of the sun on her hair, and a rivulet of sweat sliding down the skin of her back. She would take a different direction this time, she decided. You had to put people off the scent.

While she walked, Peggy worried. About the next meal. And the one after that. And of course the one after that too. She thought about the farmhouse larder. Its shelves usually began to fill this time of year. Aunt Myra had been pickling onions only last week. She'd amassed a small stockpile of sugar before it went on the ration, but she couldn't go bottling fruit or making jam with her usual abandon. Nor could she stop complaining about the fact. June teased her about it, and got away with it. 'Don't you know there's a war on, Mum?'

Across the fields Peggy noticed a heron, poised over a dyke, still as a post. It watched the water below with a focus she envied. Fishing patiently. There was a thought. What about fish? That wasn't rationed. Perhaps she could catch fish. But what would she find in these waters but eels, and how could she possibly cook fish, or stop it going smelly in this heat?

A splash of bright red moving beyond the willows interrupted the ebb and flow of her optimism.

'Ernest?' called Peggy. 'Is that you down there?'

No answer.

'Ern?'

Her stomach cramped.

'Hello there. Just coming.' It *was* Ernest's voice. The reeds parted and he came scrambling up the bank, reaching out a hand so she could haul him over the last bit.

'Thanks,' he said. And then he knelt down and started fiddling with his laces, although she could see they were perfectly tight already.

'Looking for frogs?' asked Peggy casually. She wanted very badly to talk about something normal and meaningless. 'Did you find any? It's getting a bit late, even for the new ones, isn't it?'

'No, I was just getting stuff for Uncle Fred's traps, actually.'

She watched as he began to polish his spectacles furiously. So he was worrying about that again. She swallowed her impatience and made an effort to be constructive.

'Do you want me to ask if I can go instead of you? I honestly don't mind.'

'Maybe. I don't know . . .'

'Or is it the rabbiting you're bothered about? Poor you. He does mean well. *He* doesn't think you're spoiled, or "over-sensitive". He thinks you've been deprived, you know, never having had a rook rifle of your own. Mum said he wanted to give you one when you turned eleven.'

'Really?' Ernest's voice sounded dull.

'Dad didn't like the idea at all. You can imagine.' She hadn't really meant to mention their father. Ernest didn't look at her though. You'd think he hadn't heard a word she'd said, in fact.

'Hey, I've got an idea for you,' Peggy went on. 'Say you'll go shooting with him, and go along with it all, but then just keep talking all the time you're out. Really keep at it, you know. Don't stop, ever.' Looking at her brother, she saw what a tall order this would be for him, if not for her. 'Just be as loud as you possibly can, and stomp around, you know, like this, as you walk . . . then all the rabbits will run away and with a bit of luck you won't be able to get anything, and neither will Fred.'

'I can't do that.'

'Or . . . I suppose . . . I suppose I could volunteer for that too, couldn't I?' Why didn't *she* learn to shoot rabbits with Uncle Fred instead of her brother? That would kill two birds with one stone, so to speak. 'If you do my washing-up for me, that is. Fair's fair.'

What was he looking at? Peggy suddenly became aware of the empty string bag hanging in her hand. She should have hidden it in her knickers, or something. She began to scrunch it up, trying to get it out of sight in the palm of her hand before he noticed.

'What is it, Ernest? What's the matter?'

It wasn't the bag. Something in his head. A few moments later he broke the stillness.

'It's LMF,' he said.

'What? Ellameff?' It sounded like a foreign word. A place, perhaps?

'L.M.F.,' he repeated quietly, each letter distinct this time.

'I don't know what you're talking about.' Peggy was beginning to get exasperated. It generally took less time than she hoped.

'Lack of Moral Fibre. That's what they call it in the RAF now. Victor Velvick told me. He knows about these things. His brother must have told him.'

'What?' Peggy said again.

'When you're in a funk. You know.' He kicked at the ground. 'Too scared to fly. They don't want waverers. Dangerous. It's infectious, you see. It can turn a whole crew bad, Victor says.'

'But nobody's asking you to fly,' said Peggy uncertainly.

There was another long silence, and then Ernest spoke. He was almost inaudible.

'But it's just the same, isn't it? I haven't got the moral fibre to go trapping with Uncle Fred. Or rabbit-hunting. I'm too scared. I'm no good at that kind of thing. A coward. They used to shoot cowards, you know.'

She looked at him sharply.

'In the Great War,' he added.

'Yes, but not now,' she said. 'Traitors maybe . . . Deserters even. But not cowards.'

She found it hard to think that word in her head, let alone say it out loud. Deserter. Deserter. Deserter. There was something so harsh about it. It seemed to have so little to do with Henryk. It conjured up an image of a man running and running, across miles of empty sand, guns firing at his back. Until he fell.

Ernest and Peggy stared each other out for a few moments, daring the other to push the subject further. Then she shook her head. What could he possibly know? She had taken such care. Unless he had heard something about Dad . . .

'So where are your sticks?' she asked. 'You know. For the traps. I'll help you carry them home, if you like.'

He looked around, genuinely baffled to find his hands empty. 'Oh, bother. I must have put them somewhere.'

He turned to lower himself back down the bank.

19

Peggy was still talking nineteen-to-the-dozen, as Aunt Myra would say, when they burst into the kitchen just after one. The table was laid, but nobody was there. A man's voice was booming out from the parlour, steadily rising in excitement. It sounded like a racing commentary, and near the end of the race, too.

All three frowning, fingers on lips, Aunt Myra and June and their mum turned from the wireless in unison as they came in. Then Ernest realised his mistake. The announcer wasn't getting excited about horses.

'There's one coming down in flames – there. Somebody's hit a German . . . and he's coming down – there's a long streak – he's coming down completely out of control – a long streak of smoke – ah, the man's baled out by parachute – the pilot's baled out by parachute – he's a Junkers 87 and he's going slap into the sea and there he goes – sma-a-ash . . .'

'Dover,' whispered Mum. 'Attacking a convoy. It happened yesterday evening.'

You could hear bursts of shooting somewhere in the background, not far off – the ack-ack guns on the coast, Ernest supposed – and further away, the occasional explosion of a bomb. As last night's battle progressed, the five of them bunched closer and closer to the wireless.

'*The sky is absolutely patterned now with bursts of anti-aircraft fire and the sea is covered with smoke where the bombs have hit . . . Ooh boy, I've never seen anything so good as this – the RAF fighters have really got these boys taped.*'

Aunt Myra thumped her fist in her hand with relish.

'Give it to 'em, boys! That's the way! Oh yes, we'll show 'em.'

Ernest glanced at Peggy, who was leaning against an armchair, looking pale and dazed. Their mother switched off the wireless set, and the glowing dial darkened abruptly. For a second afterwards she rested her hand on its polished wooden top, as if feeling it for warmth and life. Aunt Myra was still talking enthusiastically about the battle report, and saying they mustn't miss the evening news on any account.

'Every night I pray to God to strike Hitler down,' she said, with satisfaction, looking around as if anyone who didn't do the same was letting the side down.

Ernest thought about the possibility of a well-aimed thunderbolt, and shook his head.

'I think He'd have done it by now if that was His plan.'

'That's quite enough of your clever remarks.' Aunt Myra swept from the room, the others following in a cowed line. As they passed the pram in the hallway, June quickly bent and snatched up Claudette, even though she was fast asleep. The baby began to whimper.

In the kitchen, Mum was all bustle again.

'Peggy, slice us a few tomatoes, would you, dear? Not too thick, mind. In that bowl, on the draining board.'

'Yes, Mum.'

'By the way, Myra, did you hear about Mrs Velvick? She was nearly done by one of Cooper's Snoopers last week.'

'No?!' said Aunt Myra, delighted. 'What happened?'

Mrs Teacup-Whisperer. Ernest wondered if his mother was trying to get on the right side of her sister-in-law. Buttering her up with a tidbit of gossip. Where was Uncle Fred? He'd put a stop to this. Muck-spreading, he called it.

'He sent his daughter in to do the dirty work, it seems.'

'Like a decoy? Well, I never.'

Miss Leaky-Mouth.

'I suppose so, yes. Begging for some extra sugar for her mother-in-law's birthday cake apparently. Awfully convincing, I heard she was too.'

'And?'

Their aunt plonked the bread-board down on the table, where it set up a slow circular rattle, like a drum roll. The rattle of doom, thought Ernest.

'Oh, not a hope. Mrs Velvick wasn't having any of it.'

'Really?'

'Not even when the girl offered her fourpence a pound. Well, you know how it is these days . . . she'd have been up before the magistrates like a shot if she'd let her have the sugar.'

'An example to us all!' Aunt Myra glowed with self-righteousness.

'Oh yes.'

'And quite right too. I heard what happened to Mr Morris in Winchelsea. No more than *he* deserved. But I can't see Mrs Velvick doing anyone a favour, least of all a stranger.'

Strangers, thought Ernest. That's what the posters meant. It was strangers you had to be careful of.

'Well, she's had a hard life, specially this year. To lose a son like that . . .'

'We all have our crosses to bear. How did she know the girl was from the Ministry, anyway?'

'Food Control Office. Apparently there was a man in a mac waiting outside. She recognised him. Nearly fell off her perch. But this isn't from the horse's mouth, you know.' Mum hung up her apron. 'It's just what Mrs Ashbee told me. Hurry up, Peggy.'

Ernest sat down at the table, and remembered not to tip his chair. June had taken no part in this conversation and was gazing out of the window across the farmyard, as though she'd just noticed something frightfully interesting. But when Ernest stood up to look too there was nothing to see at all. June was thinking about the wireless broadcast, he guessed, and other ships being bombed somewhere else. Troop ships. She was holding Claudette so fiercely against her that the baby began to struggle and moan.

'If the Nazis come here, I'll kill her myself before I let them take Claudie away from me,' June said, and sat down, very suddenly. 'I'd kill myself, too, if I had to.'

Suppose they didn't hear the church bells? thought Ernest. Suppose there was no time for anything like that? Suppose they killed you first, before anybody could even get to the felty ropes to pull out a warning? Suppose they were already hiding in the church tower itself, ready to strangle you with those very ropes?

'Oh bother,' muttered Peggy into the shocked room. Unable to get a purchase, the knife kept slipping right off the smooth hard skin of these freshly picked tomatoes. Now it had slipped through her own skin. She sucked her finger, wincing.

'Slice, don't chop, dear,' Mum reminded her.

'That needs sharpening,' said her aunt, whisking the knife from her hand with a flash of silver. 'Used to go through flesh like butter, it did. Pass me the stone.'

A mean low rectangle of margarine glistened in the dish. Ernest stared at it while he listened to the blade scraping across the whetstone, a rhythmic broken sawing sound that went on and on and on.

RULE THREE: KEEP WATCH. IF YOU SEE ANYTHING SUSPICIOUS, NOTE IT CAREFULLY AND GO AT ONCE TO THE NEAREST POLICE OFFICER OR STATION, OR TO THE NEAREST MILITARY OFFICER. DO NOT RUSH ABOUT SPREADING VAGUE RUMOURS. GO QUICKLY TO THE NEAREST AUTHORITY AND GIVE HIM THE FACTS.

20

June looked up from the mangle with a disbelieving smile.

'You'd rather grub around in the earth than do the laundry?'

More than anything, June hated weeding. It was the effect on her nails that she minded most. She inspected them now with a grimace.

'Oh, any day!' said Peggy. 'I HATE ironing. I loathe folding clothes. And I'm always pinching my fingers in that horrible thing . . . I'll love you forever if you'll swap.'

'And you won't change your mind the minute I've finished with this lot?'

'Of course not. That would be rotten. I want a permanent swap.'

'Go on then. You're welcome to it. But take this with you for the potatoes while you're going.' She swapped the full bucket of soapy grey water for an empty one. Its handle clanged mournfully. The pitch of the dripping became higher and more insistent: a half-wrung out pillowcase was still caught in the rollers. 'And wait till the sun's lower before you do any watering, won't you?'

'I know, I know.' Everyone thought she and Ernest knew nothing about *any*thing. Anything useful, anyway. Coddled. That was what Aunt Myra always said to Fred as soon as Mum

was out of earshot. Time they grew up. Their father thinks
. . . When I was that girl's age . . . Or worse, when June was
that girl's age, she'd been earning a living . . . etc . . . etc . . .
As for travelling all that way to the Grammar, what on earth
was the point of that when she could be paying her way like
everyone else?

Well, moving here had put a stop to school pretty quickly.
They all knew they had to earn their keep on the farm.

'And do wear gloves. Specially with that cut of yours.'

'I will,' Peggy called back, knowing she wouldn't, that it was
already too late. The mangle's squeak faded.

She'd worked it out during dinner. If she took over the
vegetable plot, it would become a hundred times easier to 'lift'
the odd thing here and there for Henryk. Nobody had time
to count carrots. They'd never notice if a few went missing.
Or more than a few. Besides, it was perfectly true. She'd far
rather be out here on her own where she could keep an eye
on things, than messing up the washing or breaking crockery
under Aunt Myra's gaze.

At the gate Peggy hesitated. There was a figure behind the
beanpoles, already at work, digging. Not easy with the ground
so dry. Little gasps of effort were escaping with every blow.

'Mum?' Peggy called, shading her eyes to be sure. 'Mum!
What are you doing? *I'm* in charge of the veg now. You've got
enough to do already.'

Her mother twisted, one foot raised on her spade. She didn't
answer immediately. Panting slightly, she waited for Peggy to
reach her, and then looked around before she spoke.

'I'm hiding this. I don't think we've got long now.'

There was no need to ask what she meant by that. As if in confirmation, a faint burst of anti-aircraft fire sounded from the direction of the ranges on Denge Marsh. Peggy frowned. An old wooden crate gaped ready to receive its treasure. Her mother had already wrapped it up, swathing it carefully in a couple of pillowcases, soft and worn, but Peggy had a good idea what it was.

The first pot Dad had ever given her. His wooing pot, he always called it, and for years the way he said that was guaranteed to make Mum blush and giggle, and the children wish they weren't there. More recently though, she kept silent when he referred to those days, and looked at the floor as if it had all been a mistake.

An old story, often told when Peggy was younger. He had stopped at a café in Rye, at the end of a weekend of walking and sketching on the High Weald with a trio of Art School friends. The pub hadn't opened yet, so they were making do with tea. As soon as Mum appeared to take their order, he was smitten.

Chemistry, he'd say, his arms swooping round her waist as he swept in from behind, all hands, and she pretended to push him away so she could get the supper on in peace. *It's an unavoidable reaction. Like the transformation of copper in a kiln from verdigris to lustrous red. You reduced me, Lizzie. You took my oxygen away and changed me forever. You make me iridescent.*

Slower-burning chemistry in Mum's case. She always took longer to react. It had taken three more visits to get her to talk to him. Seven more cups of tea. And then on the tenth he'd brought her this.

It was his final exam piece. A tall blue and green jar, wood ash glazes, the colours of the Marsh. Substantial. A satisfying lid, kept in place by a raised rim. Its handle was in the shape of a swan. Peggy loved the way he had planed the sides, with just a suggestion of geometry, that made you want to clasp it and run your finger down the seven vertical meeting points.

It was for their marriage fund, the first sovereign already inside when he gave it to her, and it had remained their savings pot ever since. There was never an engagement ring, which hadn't impressed Aunt Myra, but wasn't this better than a ring?

A ring would have been easier to hide, thought Peggy. Or sell, if need be.

'I've got to keep it safe, if . . . when . . . it happens.'

'The invasion?' *Just say it.*

Peggy began to slide the pillowcases away from the pot, and her mother nodded her permission. They both wanted to see it again.

'Yes. The invasion.'

'Oh.'

'You're old enough. You need to know. And I was going to tell you where I'd hidden it, of course, just . . .'

'. . . in case?'

The shimmering noises of the Marsh crept into their silence. The day could not have been more perfect. That Yorkshire man on the radio – the one with the calming voice Aunt Myra loved to listen to – he'd been quite right. There had never been a more lovely summer than this one. Loveliness like a beautifully painted silk curtain, which might rip at any moment.

Peggy made herself think how it might come, this invasion. Would it be by day, or by night? Tanks rolling relentlessly towards the farm. Explosions. Resistance. (June, with her baby. Myra, with her knife.) Occupation. And under all that destruction, a pot, waiting for its maker to return.

Impossible. How could any of that happen here? The sky was too blue.

'But we haven't begun the harvest yet,' she protested, as if the Nazis were just waiting for them to stook the corn neatly.

'Well, there may still be time. I don't know. I'm afraid there's not much in there now.' Mum shook the pot gently, and Peggy caught the clink of coins. 'But we don't want to be caught on the hop. Like I said, just in case.'

Peggy touched the curving swan's neck, and tried to push down the fluttering creature rising in her chest. There were lots of 'in cases' to consider. She thought about them all, and decided her mother was right.

'I'll help you,' she said. 'But let's move some raspberry canes on top. For protection. And it'll be too obvious otherwise. Look – there are lots of new shoots we can take. They're spreading into the rhubarb already.' She began to prise a fork under a stray plant, teasing at the soil, determined not to snap its long eager root.

'It's not just me,' Mum said, getting back to her digging. 'Everyone is hiding things.'

'Are they?'

'Myra and June have sewed £5 each into their stays.'

Peggy stared at her.

'Five whole pounds?'

'Yes. Notes. She hasn't told Fred though. It would make him angry. You know how he is. He won't believe it's possible.'

'Yes.' That was what Peggy liked about Uncle Fred.

'But you just can't tell, can you? And also, I heard . . .'

Her voice dropped to a whisper, and she looked around.

Then Peggy remembered. 'Stop it. You've got to stop it. You shouldn't listen to rumour, and you shouldn't repeat it. You know that.'

'It's true, though. I'm sure it's true. Myra heard it too. And if it's true, it's not rumour, is it?'

Peggy wasn't sure.

'Anyway, telling you doesn't count. You're my daughter. And you're not a child any more.'

'What did you hear?' said Peggy. Was it better to know, or not? Better perhaps to be a child. 'Where did you hear it?'

Once more, her mother looked around.

'At the post office, Mrs Velvick was saying . . . The banks . . . I heard they are going to burn the money when the Germans come. The notes, of course. They have to. They can't leave all our money for the Nazis and Fifth Columnists.'

Peggy shushed her. Did they burn the money in Czechoslovakia and Poland, and Denmark and Holland and Norway and Belgium and France? She didn't imagine the people there had time enough to sew money into stays before it was too late.

'You won't tell Ernest?'

A ridiculous request. As if Peggy's sleep wasn't disturbed enough already by his nightmares.

'But you're old enough to know.' Mum laid down her spade,

and tried to look Peggy in the face. She had shot up this spring and they were eye to eye now. Peggy considered the earth, and the hole, and the crate, and the pot, but avoided her mother's gaze. It was sensible enough to take precautions. She could see that. But somehow it felt as if they were preparing to bury Dad.

'You're old enough,' Mum said again.

Peggy really wished she wouldn't keep saying that.

21

Henryk only left the church when he needed to pee. He could desert his post, but nothing could make him pee inside a church. The first time he simply crouched, supporting himself with one hand on the ancient sun-warmed bricks by the mounting-block that was built into the end wall.

When he heard a dogfight start up over towards the coast he found he couldn't watch. He didn't even want to listen. Before he knew it, he had run back inside to squat on the floor of his adopted pew with his hands over his ears. He rocked, back and forth, back and forth, humming tunelessly to himself to drown out the sound of the fighters. The panic eventually subsided, and finally he felt he could breathe again.

After that he made a determined effort to be more practical. What if someone saw, from a distance, that the key wasn't in the lock? Wouldn't that make things look suspicious? Unlocking the door was terrifying, but Henryk decided it had to be done.

Next he gathered all the hassocks from around the church and pushed them together to make a mattress. He lay on it experimentally, and then replaced each one, exactly where he'd found it. He spread out his damp clothes, and decided they'd dry eventually, and then he would hide them again. And he found a cupboard near the door of the church, and pulled out some musty-smelling robes, and spread these out to air too, for bedding.

Near the stone font – empty under the wooden lid – there was an instrument. Not a piano, he realised when he saw the paddle-like foot pedals, slightly encrusted in animal dung in the corners. Too small. A harmonium? He lifted the lid, stroked the keys, and then, finally, pressed one slowly down. It didn't make a sound. He pumped the pedal a few times, and felt the pressure build, like bellows. Then he tried another key, a little faster. This time a single note burst out, uncontrollably loud. It was still dying away seconds after he'd slammed shut the lid and backed guiltily away.

For the rest of the day he read, half an eye always on the window. Without conviction or pleasure, he worked his way through the Psalms. The huge bible he found open at the lectern was bound in leather, and coming apart at the spine. Slowly and methodically, he worked at matching up the English words in front of him with the Polish words lodged deep in his memory. 'Yea, though I walk through shadow'd vales, yet will I fear no ill.'

When he reached Psalm 91 he hesitated. 'For he shall give his angels charge over thee, to keep thee in all thy ways.'

Angels, Henryk thought. One of the first new English words he'd learned. Angels were part of the instructions that came crackling into your headphones just before an attack. Bandits over Folkestone at angels fourteen, you'd hear, and that would be it.

Now he realised the real meaning of the word. It wasn't just a measurement. A thousand feet. He thought back to the white-clad apparition that had rescued him in the night. 'Peggy,' he said out loud. '*Mój Aniołku . . .*' That made sense. He heard the connection between the words for the first time. Angel or spirit? She was certainly haunting him. He wasn't sure how he would manage another night on his own here if she didn't come back. He glanced out of the window for the hundredth time, and watched the wind roll over the grass.

What could she possibly think of him? A coward, someone to feel sorry for, someone to pity. And she'd be right. What else was there to think?

'So sorry. Such a bother.' That's what Henryk must say to her when she came. If she came. It was a phrase he couldn't forget. Not since a fair-haired English officer had staggered into a still-turning propeller as he dismounted from the cockpit after too many sorties in succession. The pilot lay bleeding on a stretcher, waiting for the ambulance, saying the same thing, over and over again: 'So sorry. Such a bother. So sorry. Such a bother. So sorry. Such a bother.' Until he could no longer speak.

But a case like his own. That was quite a different matter. Aside from his ankle, there was nothing really wrong with him, Henryk persuaded himself. Nothing a little more time wouldn't sort out. Peggy would understand that. If he could just stay here a little while longer, just long enough to get his strength back, then . . .

Strength? Who was he fooling? It wasn't his strength he needed. Nerve. That was what had deserted him. Like water into sand, it had seeped away while he wasn't looking, and left him drained.

22

Several hours later, Peggy's face was streaked with dirt, the compost heap was piled high with weeds, and you would never know that she and her mother had done anything more dramatic than increase the size of their raspberry plots. She also had a substantial harvest of carrots, runner beans, a few more tomatoes, and a mountain of late gooseberries in the trug.

She set aside the vegetables she would take to the church later, picking out the best, straight and true. Anyone would think she was getting ready for the village flower show, she thought. Absurd, really, to take such care. But she could almost *feel* him waiting for her. And for some reason she wanted things to be perfect.

Peggy sat back on her heels, wiped the sweat from her hairline with the back of her wrist, and gave herself a few more moments to conjure up Henryk, and the pleasure she would see in his face when he saw what she had brought him. Maybe he'd kiss her hand again.

She smiled and held out her hand as if he were in front of her now. Her nails were bitten short, and for the first time she saw how stumpy and childish her fingers were, with dirt not just where you'd expect it but right under the soft bits

June was always trying to get her to push back nicely too. The knife-cut was also edged with black, and stinging now. She'd give her hands a good scrub before she left. She hoped she could stay a little longer next time so she could find out more about Henryk. He'd be longing for company, you'd think. She must find a way.

Peggy decided to hide the food in the old stable where they had started keeping the bikes. That way she'd have an excuse if anyone spotted her. Just checking Ernest had put his away properly. Like the leaflet said. You know. Hide your food and your maps and your bicycles.

Of course Ernest had covered all the bikes with fertiliser sacks now, not so much as a spoke or a pedal showing anywhere. You'd think they'd been tucked up terribly carefully for the night.

She flicked up a sack to put over the vegetables, and as she did so, another one began to slither off Mum's bike. At first she thought the piece of paper tucked into its brake cable was part of Ernest's precious salvage collection. *Speed old Hitler to his grave with all the paper you can save!* She was about to add it to the huge boxful by the door of the shed when something made her hesitate. The paper was yellow and lined – she'd never seen anything like it in the house. But it wasn't flimsy enough to be a receipt. And it was odd how it was folded over and over, until it was hard and firm and solid.

She began to unfold it.

ELIZABETH FISHER, she saw. Written in neat and even capitals.

It was for her mother then. So why not take it in and give it to her? Or just put it straight back, so that she'd find it for herself when she went off on her late shift a little later? Because. Just because, thought Peggy.

She listened. Nobody was coming. She quickly hid the vegetables she'd 'borrowed', then looked outside, listened again, and finished opening up the note.

It was all in capitals. A bit like a telegram. But there was no signature. Nothing at all to show who'd written it. The words made her feel cold and sick.

YOUR HUSBAND DOESN'T CARE IF THE GERMANS COME AND RAPE YOU. YOU DESERVE TO BE PUNISHED.

Peggy felt contaminated. She scrumpled up the paper in her fist, digging her nails into her palm. Then she marched straight to the privy and locked the door behind her, leaning against it and breathing heavily, while she waited for her knees to steady. She wouldn't read it again. What good would that do? Instead Peggy stood over the lav and tore it into a hundred tiny pieces, which floated down like confetti into the earthy darkness below. And then sat down on the wooden seat, and used the lavatory for its usual purpose, just to be sure.

23

Ernest sucked his pencil and wondered what to write next. He had asked Dad about the food, the uniform, and the weather so far, and was running out of ideas.

'For heaven's sake, boy, get that out of your mouth – you'll be poisoned!' said Aunt Myra, poking his shoulder.

'No, I won't.' Ernest slid his elbow over the letter, before she leaned over any further. This was none of her business. 'It's not actually lead, you know. It's graphite, and that's a form of carbon.'

He was about to explain that this was why pencil marks burned off under a glaze during the firing, but June had her finger on her lips and was quietly shaking her head at him.

'Come on, Mum, you'll be late for St John's. Aren't you learning mouth-to-mouth today?'

June bustled his aunt into her summer coat and hat and out of the kitchen. Ernest shuddered, and went back to sucking his pencil.

It was hard to keep writing without getting anything back. That was war for you, Peggy always said when he complained about the silence. And the less anyone at home knew, the less chance there was of giving something or someone away by mistake. Careless talk and all that.

'I know!' he suddenly said out loud, standing up and knocking his chair back into June, who was hovering right behind him.

'Whoopsadaisy! What do you know?'

'I'm going to go and check on the Hungarian tadpoles – the ones that didn't die, I mean. The ones in the sewer.' He didn't mind telling June. 'Dad will be interested to hear how they're getting along, don't you think?'

'I'm sure he will. Good idea. You run along. Oh – I nearly forgot to tell you – my dad said could you go and check the first lot of mole traps without him? There's an LDV exercise on – a roadblock or something, on the Appledore road – oops – I shouldn't have told you that! – but he won't have time today.'

'OK,' said Ernest, without meeting June's eye. He ran upstairs to put the half-written letter under his pillow for safekeeping. He didn't see how Uncle Fred would be able to tell if he'd done the job or not. He could always just say they were empty.

June was waiting with a trowel for him.

'Thanks,' he said, forcing a smile. Then he couldn't help asking, 'June, why do you think Uncle Fred hangs all the corpses up? I don't think the other moles can see them.'

'Oh, bless you, that's not your Uncle Fred. That's what the molecatcher does, to show he's been doing his job, you know. But he volunteered for the navy last month. Leaving us with yet *another* thing to do. Speaking of which, it's time I got on, no rest for the wicked and all that . . . I don't know . . .'

June started doing her put-upon act for Claudette, blowing out her cheeks and shaking her head and sighing loudly, and the kitchen rang with the baby's laughter.

Ernest headed back to the place where he'd heard the frog

a few days earlier. The new ones seemed to love this weather. They were much easier to find than the old kind this late in the year – always out sunbathing, just like the Greatstone holiday campers, before the army took over.

He let himself down to the water's edge with the help of a willow trunk, and moved slowly along the reeds, looking for a likely patch. The tadpoles seemed to prefer the shallower water. He used his trowel-hand to support himself against the bank, and rehearsed his lie to Uncle Fred. He'd have to pretend he'd reset the traps too, of course. That might be more of a problem.

'Damn!' he said aloud, driving the trowel into the bankside in frustration. A clump of loose earth tumbled down, and dissolved into the water below. Unusually loose earth, Ernest realised, looking more closely. He raised the trowel to his shoulder, and plunged it in like a dagger. A glimpse of white made him draw breath. It didn't take much more digging to reveal that there was a substantial amount of light-coloured material concealed beneath the soil.

Ernest felt sick. A body? A dead body? His knees went watery, and he almost stepped back into the dyke. He wanted to get away, immediately, before he saw anything worse. Breathing ever faster, he forced himself to stay. *Keep your head*, he told himself. *If you see anything suspicious, note it carefully.* He hadn't seen enough to note yet. He'd have to look properly. Could he do it without touching whatever it was with his fingers? Ernest used the trowel to brush away more soil, and almost laughed out loud when he realised it was much too squidgy underneath to be a body. The material was too soft and white to be a discarded feedsack either . . . unless it was a sheet flown loose from a washing line in one of those whipping east winds, which had flapped into the dyke, and buried itself here?

Or could it actually be a parachute?

He scrambled back the way he'd come, and stood panting and sweaty on the track, looking about him anxiously. Nothing had changed. The Marsh was still and calm. No paratroopers were descending from the heavens. No church bells ringing that he could hear. There was not the least hint of an invasion. But he couldn't take any chances. He'd seen something suspicious, and now he had to go at once and report it to the nearest military officer. The Appledore road. That would be quickest. He'd go and find Fred and tell him right away, and then it would be out of his hands, and he'd have done his duty.

What about June, or Peggy? No, not a word to them. No rushing about. No rumours. Straight to the point. He'd sneak in, get his bike, and sneak off again before they could ask where he was going.

At the roadblock, Uncle Fred was nowhere to be seen. There was a proper army man there, in a car, who would surely count as 'the nearest military officer', but he was shouting so furiously at Mr Gosbee, the LDV guard, that Ernest didn't dare interrupt.

'What the bloody hell do you mean?' The officer's red-veined face emerged from the front window of a shiny black Wolseley. 'I don't have to show you anything! Let us through immediately!'

'I'm afraid you do, sir,' said Mr Gosbee firmly. 'You both do.' He tipped his cap at the ATS driver, who was pretty and blonde, and then tried to turn the movement into a salute. 'Everybody has to show their papers. Sir.'

'Oh, for heaven's sake, man – don't you know who I am?'

'Yes, sir, Colonel, sir, I do, sir. Of course I do.' Mr Gosbee shuffled his feet, glanced at his LDV armband as if it had let him down, and then looked for reassurance at his gangly companion, Gordon Ramsgate. 'But you see, sir, I have my orders, sir, and . . . no, no, Gordon, I don't think that will be necessary, Gordon, put it down . . . I'm sorry, sir, but really would you mind . . .'

To Ernest's relief, Gordon lowered his ancient gun. Why did it have to be him there, the oldest of the Ramsgate boys? He was the last person Ernest wanted to have to tell about the parachute. Gordon was barely older than Peggy! Meanwhile, the Colonel's driver whispered something to her agitated passenger. Still huffing and puffing, he finally reached inside his jacket.

'Do you realise this is the fourth time we've been through this charade in the past hour?' said the Colonel, passing across the necessary documents.

The vehicle was waved on at last, and Ernest stepped forward, hoping his voice wouldn't let him down.

'Looking for Section Commander Nokes, are you?' asked Gordon, with a grin.

Ernest's confidence in his mission was faltering fast, but he nodded.

'I'm afraid you've just missed him,' said Mr Gosbee, more kindly.

'Oh dear. Where is he? Will he be long?'

Gordon placed a meaningful finger against his nose, and looked down at Ernest.

'Well, that would be telling, wouldn't it?'

'He was only asking, Gordon,' said Mr Gosbee. 'The Section Commander is on a special operation, just now, son, but we can't tell you where.'

They don't know themselves, thought Ernest.

'Can we help?' added Gordon.

Ernest supposed they could, in theory. They were now the nearest military officers, weren't they? Right. He was ready for this. Quick, calm and exact, he had to be.

'I've got something to report. I think I've found a parachute.'

'Very funny. And I've got Adolf Hitler living in my lav.'

There was a roar of laughter, and the men looked at each other.

'Suppose you found it hanging on the washing line, did you?' said the older man, beginning to hum.

'Quick, look over there!' shouted Gordon, putting up his gun again, and Ernest's head obediently whipped round. 'Oh, sorry, it's just a crow. I thought I saw a nun.'

Ernest's neck began to burn. There was no point in staying.

24

When the pills had worn off completely, Henryk's hunger returned with a vengeance. His jitters were getting worse too, and he felt almost as guilty about losing the plane as he did about losing his nerve. There could be no hope of repair – it must be category 3 – nothing worth recovering. Just another mess to track down in a field or a wood and pick over for souvenirs.

He sat on the floor of the pew and sighed. There were never enough planes.

They thought they'd soon be in the air again all those months ago. But despite what they'd been told, there were no aircraft at all waiting for the Polish Air Force in Rumania. A kind of welcome, perhaps, not always kind, and sympathetic looks from villagers. And then internment.

At least in the camp, the guards were happy enough to look the other way, for very little reward. Quite a few of the other cadets had been sneaking out each evening ever since they arrived, and they weren't looking for empty beds to spend the night in either. It didn't seem much harder for a courier to sneak into the camp.

Henryk and Kazimierz sat hunched on wooden pallets in the barn that was their barracks. Aching from another day working in the fields, they rolled cigarettes that got thinner each time. Though he liked to have something to do with his hands, Henryk had never cared much for smoking, so he handed his tobacco ration over to Kazik, who'd given up on his prayers after the fall of Warsaw. Now he just ranted.

'What are they going to do with us?'

'I don't know.'

'We can't just stay here.'

'I know.'

'We have to go on. We've got to keep going.'

'I know.'

'We can't just stay here.'

'I know.'

'But what are they going to do with us?'

'Shut up and listen, Kazik.'

They both cocked their ears. Henryk was right. The knocking came again. One two, one two. A stick beating on the rough wooden wall, hard enough to flutter the candle flame with each blow. And a voice, in Polish at last. Through a knothole, they received their orders. Learned where they'd find a change of clothes. Who to meet. When they might see their officers again.

Henryk barely remembered now quite how they got from there to Bucharest. Rivers. Forests. Generosity from peasants with bare feet, he remembered. Incomprehensible Rumanian army officers with white silk gloves who searched the pilots or let them pass at whim. A lot of walking. A few days into their journey they joined up with a man from another squadron called Piotr, which meant they could walk together, three abreast, taking the middle spot in turn so one of them could always sleep on the move.

How the policemen in Rumania loved to wield their silver sabres. Any opportunity, they'd take. Slash, flash, and a slice of flesh gone. It was mostly show though. Usually you could get away with it . . . it was just a case of handing over enough *lei* or a half-decent pair of boots and suggesting a drink to the health of King Carol. The next thing you knew you were sitting down to supper with the policeman's grandmother. But not always.

Stick with the women on the trains, that was the trick. The courier had tipped them off to it. They'd hop on at a bend or crossing and scatter themselves through the carriages, each pilot looking for a single lady, travelling on her own. The patrols didn't seem to question lovers.

Bucharest was altogether more frightening. The Gestapo officers were very much in evidence, patrolling the streets, making everyone scuffle, and the courier had warned that they couldn't be bribed. Evacuation was being managed from a small but grand apartment in the old part of the city. Henryk's name was ticked off a list extracted from one of the huge piles of paper covering the lid of a grand piano. Other files were spread across the dining-table and a double bed. Papers, more cash, and more instructions.

Kazik, some way ahead of Henryk in the queue, was sent to Constanza. Henryk had to make his way to Balchik, another Black Sea port. The idea was to get to France. The Polish government had re-formed in Paris, they were told. If they were lucky, they might meet again in France. Before they said goodbye, they crouched over a gutter running through a darkened alley and dropped their silver eagles through the grating. All that was left of their uniforms, but the pilots couldn't be caught with their Air Force badges now. Listening to the feeble tinkle as the metal bounced against the side of the drainpipe, to be swallowed up by the muck and sewage of Bucharest, Henryk felt he'd lost part of himself.

25

In the end Peggy managed to slip away again after supper, muttering something about a walk. By that time Fred was hard at work again, trap-making, with Ernest strangely grey and silent by his side. Aunt Myra had made a trap of her own for June, who sat on a stool at her mother's feet, hands held stiffly up in front of her face, a foot or so apart, wound about with grey wool. It kinked away from a sleeveless pullover her mother was unravelling to make up into socks, for the forces. Peggy's mum was already knitting, lips tight.

'I'll keep the scraps for your squares!' promised June, as Peggy exited, calling out thanks. She flicked her cardigan from a peg in the hall and pulled it on.

'Is she moping over someone?' Myra asked, loud enough for Peggy to hear from the back doorstep.

'Oh, you know our Peggy,' said June. 'She's like her dad, isn't she? Can't get enough of sunsets.'

Our Peggy, she absorbed gratefully. She shut the door firmly before she could hear the response, and ran.

'Hand of God' her father always used to say, whenever he saw a sky like this, and he was only half-joking: from a mass of dark swollen cloud, outlined in gold, radiant beams reached down to earth to touch the distant trees. Like a revelation. But glorious as this evening's sunset was, Peggy felt too poisoned by the note she'd found to be uplifted.

Rape. She wasn't sure exactly what that meant. Something worse than nasty, that was certain. And part and parcel of invasion, to judge by the dark comments she'd heard from time to time these past few months. It seemed to be reserved for women, though she wasn't quite sure of that. And girls perhaps?

When grown-ups used the word 'rape', they mouthed it, or lowered their voices at least, and quickly looked at her to see if she had noticed. Peggy had got quite good now at pretending not to listen, she thought. That pleased her. It was the only way to find anything out. That was how she had learned of the suicides in Hastings. An old couple, who'd lost three sons in the Great War. They took poison, Myra had whispered, disapprovingly, while Peggy pretended she couldn't hear over the clatter of pans in the sink.

Sometimes you had to give up on rules. Like telling the truth and shaming the devil. Not reading other people's letters. Believing grown-ups.

She should have kept that yellow paper. Evidence. There might have been some sort of clue she'd missed, a hint at its author. But all Peggy had wanted to do was get rid of it, as quickly as possible, and make sure there was no danger at all of her mother seeing it, ever.

The 'hand of God' dissolved and the sun began to sink. Lucky it had been so dry for so long. Not just for the harvest, of course. All through winter, and most of spring too, you could only reach the church by the causeway. And before that was built, people used to go by boat, Uncle Fred said. There hadn't been a service there for nearly a year. Peggy decided that if anyone ever saw her going, she'd say she was praying. For the war to end. Or for God to strike down Hitler. Nobody could argue with that.

Anticipation fluttered high in her chest. The thought of seeing Henryk again made her feel nervous, but there was a kind of pleasure in her fear. She mustn't talk too fast, this time. She must give him a chance. They had to decide the next step together. Peggy wanted to call out as she approached the porch, to make sure she wouldn't catch him unawares. Actually, she realised, she just wanted to say his name out loud, to hear how it sounded in her voice, and to know she could trust that voice not to squeak or crack.

The key was in the door, on the outside.

The church was empty.

Peggy stood in the aisle and looked around carefully. She peered into the white-painted pews, one after another, slowly and quietly at first and then much faster. She reached the last pew.

Nothing.

He had covered his tracks well. A disturbance of dust was the only sign anyone had been here for weeks. A few fingermarks on the lid of the harmonium. She traced these with her own finger. Some mud was smeared on the bricks near the font, and a little more in the lettering of the single memorial stone in the middle of the floor, caught in the curving J of *John Beale of this Parish*. A sense of air that had been stirred and settled.

Nothing you'd really notice if you didn't already know.

So that was that.

Bother, she thought bitterly, and looked at the bag of vegetables she'd carefully gathered, twisting and untwisting at her wrist. She'd swiped a jar of plum jam too, for pudding, and a little more bread, and filled a lemonade bottle with fresh water too. She'd even found clean socks. So much for that. Bother. Then she said it out loud, again, and just for good measure, and because there was nobody to hear, she shouted, loud as could be:

'BUGGER. BUGGER. BUGGER.'

She'd never dared say that in front of anyone other than Ernest. Once.

Then she sat down on a bench, with her back to the pulpit, and hugged her knees. She tested her teeth on her salt-tasting knees and screwed up her eyes and tried to persuade herself how much better it was that Henryk had gone. She hoped he'd had the sense to turn himself in.

It must have been hard. ('Accept the inevitable,' her mother had said. 'I won't,' her father replied. 'I can't. I don't believe it is inevitable. It shouldn't be. It's not right. Don't you see why?' 'No. I don't.') Couldn't he have waited, though? Couldn't he have said thank you, and goodbye . . . at the very least . . .? She would have written it in dust, she decided, as she stood up to inspect the black-painted edging.

But there was no sign. Waterlogged with regret, she sat down again in the pew they had shared just that morning, and blinked hard. She examined a woodlouse, desiccated and dangling in a corner cobweb. She counted the pegs in the rafters. She read the oval painted signs on the pale grey beams ahead that she'd never taken much notice of before, and found herself more mystified than enlightened.

Keep thy foot when thou goest to the house of God . . . She looked at her own feet. One sandshoe was beginning to come apart at the edge where the rubber met canvas. Keep thy foot? How could you not keep your foot? . . . *and be more ready to hear than to give the sacrifice of fools.* That was more like it. Not that she had sacrificed much yet – though she had certainly been prepared to – but she was definitely a fool.

Barely had she made herself ready to hear than a scrabbling noise started up. It came from almost directly beneath her. She jumped to her feet, scattering a few runner beans, and quickly leapt up onto the bench, cowering in the corner just under the lectern. The scratchy rustling sounded like claws and came from the base of the triple-decker pulpit that rose in steps from the box pew behind her. Henryk's head emerged first, twisting round to glance at her. Then he thrust his arms out, leaning on his elbows, and dragged himself forward, turning halfway through so he was on his back.

'I see you from the window. You come. I hide myself.' His face, more shadowed still with beard-growth, was serious and steady.

'You . . .' Peggy felt an idiot standing up there. 'Why? Why hide yourself from *me*? Don't you trust me?'

'I am wanting to know if I can disappear.'

Peggy didn't answer right away. Holding her dress against her thighs, she manouevred herself down to sitting, knees primly together, and refused to look at him.

'In case it is necessary,' he added.

Henryk pulled himself up and sat beside her, the food between them.

'You mean if it isn't me, next time? If someone else comes?'

'*Tak*. Yes.'

'But nobody ever comes here. That's why I brought you.'

'I hope not. But maybe it is changing . . . He frowned as he searched for the phrase. '"Better safe than sorry". Yes?'

'Yes, I suppose so. Better safe than sorry.'

She picked up a runner bean, checked it for dust, and snapped it in two. She offered one half to Henryk, and crunched the other herself, too loudly.

'Thank you,' he said. They chewed in unison. Uncooked, the beans tasted sweeter and sourer than usual, both at once. Different. Just as everything felt a bit different when she was near him. As though his very presence awarded her senses an extra power. On the skin of her arms she could feel the heat his body exuded. She seemed to hear and smell in a new dimension too. Sensations she'd never even noticed before became all-absorbing.

Peggy wasn't hungry, but there was something awkward in watching another person eat alone, and she had brought a huge pile of beans.

She looked sideways at Henryk, and wondered. She decided to be patient. He was planning to stay. Clearly. So there was some time, after all.

'That house. Over there . . .'

'It's empty. Don't worry. Mrs Frampton used to live there, but she's a widow and she went to live with her sister in Dorset. Didn't like the guns. You're safe.'

He nodded.

'You really are.'

'Thank you. Thank you again.' He half-bowed, and made as if to move towards her. Like a puppet whose master has tweaked the right string, Peggy almost put out her hand. The invisible pull was so strong. Her skin tingled where his hair might brush it if he bent his head to kiss it. First her fingers, and then the back of her hand. She could almost feel his touch now, slowly, softly sliding off, while she watched.

Except he didn't, and she didn't, and instead they both just sat there, feeling the space between them.

'Your English . . .' Peggy stopped. She didn't want to sound rude.

'It is very bad?'

'No, no . . . I meant the opposite. The first time . . . the night you came . . . I thought perhaps you couldn't, I mean, you didn't know . . . well, I just thought . . . and now I can see. It's really very good.'

Bother. She hadn't wanted to remind him of that night. Terror must surely have driven everything away.

But Henryk swallowed and then said, 'In the RAF they didn't like it. When we talked in Polish.' He smiled at her consternation. 'When we were flying, you know. It is difficult to remember. And sometimes . . . well, it is easy to get . . .'

He waved his arms, and looked from side to side, acting out alarm.

'Excitable, that's what they said we were. So we had to learn quickly. Mistakes are dangerous.'

She nibbled at her beans, to make them go more slowly, so there would be more for Henryk. He thought hard, and then

126

seemed to be quoting something he had learned by heart:

'"Reporting of enemy. DON'T get excited, and DON'T shout. Speak slowly and into the microphone."'

He swallowed again, though she knew he had finished his mouthful. He was remembering things he didn't want to remember. When you watched the dogfights up above, the machines themselves seemed the living things. It was so hard to think there could be actual people alive inside them, shouting and maybe screaming too, their screams drowned out by the sound of their engines. Cursing each other perhaps. How did you remember to speak slowly into a microphone with an ME 109 on your tail, coming out of nowhere? Or a whole formation bearing down on the country, and only you to stop it?

Peggy passed Henryk a carrot, hoping to distract him. His teeth took the top off with a resounding crunch.

'Too loud, for church,' said Henryk, with his mouth full, and raised an apologetic hand to cover it. She let herself smile then, and looked at him directly, happy to change the subject.

'There aren't many things you're meant to eat in church, are there, really?'

Henryk mimed taking the sacrament, and looked at her with questioning eyebrows.

'Oh, well, yes, I suppose there is that. I was thinking of proper food. There are scones, sometimes, I suppose, when there's a fundraising tea. Or rock cakes. They always go down well. And even I can make rock cakes.' She was beginning to gabble again, she knew. 'Everything's for fundraising now. Lydd was trying to buy a Spitfire when we left, but there was a long way to go. They cost so much.'

She regretted letting that out immediately. She'd have done anything to stop that twisted look returning to his face.

'I'm sorry. I didn't mean . . . Was yours a Spitfire, then?'

He shook his head.

'No. A Hurricane. Beautiful.'

'Oh, but it wasn't your fault, I'm sure. I mean, it can't have been, can it? You must have done everything you could, surely.'

'But I lost it. And they will find it. They will look for me.'

'I don't think they will find it,' said Peggy quietly. 'It's gone now.'

'Gone?'

'My brother saw where it fell. It must have been your plane. It went right into the Marsh. Buried itself. They'll never get it out. And nobody saw you bail out. You're safe. Really you are.'

26

As soon as she'd gone, Henryk felt Peggy's absence. They had begun to speak of his journey from Poland: his answers to her questions seemed to transfix her. It surprised Henryk how easy it suddenly became to talk about those buried months.

Arriving at last in Balchik, the pilots found themselves in a steep place with an end-of-season feel. Pale stone houses curving round the shore and sprawling on rocky slopes rising behind. The music of gypsy violins seeped out of courtyards and snaked from pavement cafés. It made Henryk melancholy as he waited for news, and watched the ships pass.

He eked out his day's allowance, tried to resist the sting of alcohol on an empty stomach, and wondered if he should let himself be tempted by the Bulgarian girls who crowded round the pilots' endless games of bridge. Finally the call came. Down to the quayside, where a Greek-flagged merchant ship with a huge and shallow hold was waiting for them.

Leaving land felt significant, and hopeful, until Henryk clambered down into the ship's hold and breathed in the stink of it. He was too much of a city boy to know if the last occupants had been sheep or goats, but the smell sent him reeling.

'*Psia kość*,' he swore, pitching into a stocky fellow coming down the steps behind him.

'Dog's bone?' the other laughed, pushing him upright again. 'Pig's shit, more like.'

Henryk quickly got to know Mirek better. They could hardly help it. By this time eight hundred airmen were squeezed into the *St Nicolas*, the last hundred or more soaking wet after having had to swim to the boat. A night passed, and a day, and another night fell. When they felt there was no air left to breathe down below, Henryk and Mirek pushed their way onto deck, and leaned over the railings.

'Why are we slowing down?' asked Mirek.

The sailors were signalling and shouting. There was land on each side now, narrowing all the time. Mountains with stringed clusters of lights that glimmered again in the water. Henryk had always loved maps. He worked out where they must be.

'We're going through the Straits of Bosphorus. No clashing rocks for us, at least,' he laughed, light-headed.

Mirek stared at him blankly.

'Jason and the argonauts, you know? Oh, never mind. They were going the other way, anyway.' Henryk turned away, and the brief surge of excitement he'd felt was crushed. If everything had been different, how glorious, how romantic this moment would be. Sailing towards Constantinople. He'd always wanted to see the world. Learning to fly was part of that urge.

Henryk had turned eight just a few weeks after Orliński flew back in triumph from Tokyo, the hero of all Poland. He'd begged his mother to take him to the local *aeroklub* for his birthday. And after that, he was hooked.

'So what country's that?' Mirek persisted, waving to the right.

'That must be Turkey. We're at the crossroads of the world. Europe that way, Asia over there. Pretty impressive, huh?'

Mirek rolled his eyes. 'There's only one thing that can impress me now. Getting into the cockpit of a plane and fighting back for Poland.'

They'd all thought that, then. Never imagined for a second there would come a time when the opposite might happen. Never dreamed of that moment when, in the middle of combat, you find yourself alone, isolated. Hidden in a cloud perhaps. Lower, higher, less visible than the rest. The brief possibility of escape held in front of you, just a temporary exit, a chance to get away from the fray. Stuck on that boat, desperate to be in the air again, neither Mirek nor Henryk could know what determination you would need to return to a scrap when, like a gift from heaven, you have unexpectedly been offered a way out, with nobody there to see you take it.

RULE FOUR: DO NOT GIVE ANY GERMAN ANYTHING. DO NOT TELL HIM ANYTHING. HIDE YOUR FOOD AND YOUR BICYCLES. HIDE YOUR MAPS.

27

The next day was Ernest's birthday. He'd been a two-o'clock-in-the-morning baby. That meant most years he just woke up, and it had happened: he was a year older. This time they were all awake and together at twenty-five to two, down in the cellar with eiderdowns and torches. And an enamel jug of tea, as if they were haymaking. A pack of cards sat untouched.

'Hitler must have known it was your special day, eh, Ernest?' joked Uncle Fred, with serious eyes. 'He wanted to make us light the candles on time, for once. Not so long now.'

Perhaps he could get Uncle Fred on his own tomorrow, and explain quietly. They could go together, and he'd show him, and maybe it would turn out not to have been a parachute at all. Maybe there'd be some other explanation, quite obvious to everyone else, that Ernest just hadn't managed to think of.

'The last thing we need down here is candles, Fred.'

Aunt Myra sniffed at the smells in the cellar and fretted. Paraffin, and cardboard, and last year's potatoes. They heard flight after flight of enemy bombers coming over the farm. Whump, whump, whump, whump, they went, hour after hour, relentless and threatening and unmistakable, but you didn't exactly want the noise to stop. You wanted it to keep going, so you knew the planes had got past you.

Ernest buried his face in his pillow and wondered if anybody would notice the farm in darkness, from above. What might show from up there? Could a wisp of rising smoke give them away? The gleam of iron on the pigsty roof? And what if the planes themselves were flying on and away, but silently dropping parachutists as they passed? Arms up, he'd heard they landed, a grenade in each hand. Even when they were dressed as nuns? You kept hearing about nuns. Hairy arms. Hairy hands. That's what you had to look out for. Nuns with hairy hands and Fifth Columnists. Who would surely know better than to hide a parachute in the side of a dyke.

Nobody wanted to turn the torch off, though they knew they were wasting batteries. It sat in the middle of their circle, like a feeble campfire, yellow beams lighting the underside of the hall floorboards, catching the cobwebs. Nobody even pretended to sleep, except for Claudette, who lay so still and calm that Ernest wondered if she was actually breathing. Just as his anxiety built up enough to make him want to poke her into life, her eyelashes briefly flickered, and he breathed again himself. Every ten minutes or so, Ernest crept his hand into his mother's, and pulled her arm towards him so that he could squint at her wristwatch. Sometimes she stroked his hair.

Impossible to settle when you're waiting for something.

A few minutes before two, Peggy began to shiver and look clammy. Ernest was surprised. He'd never seen her scared like that before. Real terror. He wasn't sure what to do about it. Then a peculiar noise erupted from the depths of her throat,

136

as if a crow were stuck in there. Half-rising, Peggy threw up through her fingers. Ernest sat up, transfixed, immobilised. But Mum was quick enough. The cellar had plenty of old pans and buckets stacked in one corner, waiting for the next tinkers' visit. She grabbed a huge saucepan and shoved it under Peggy's overflowing hands, and held her while she heaved and swayed.

June looked away, one hand over her own mouth.

Peggy stared wildly for a moment, dewdrops of sweat suddenly scattering her forehead, and then she rushed up the cellar steps and disappeared.

'Oh, where on earth has she gone?' Mum grabbed the sick-filled pan and ran after her. Ernest accidentally caught a whiff as it passed and worried how white Peggy's nightie was under the path of those planes. They'd be able to see it, ever so clearly, as she crossed the yard to the lav. Wouldn't they? From up there?

The others huddled and listened, except Aunt Myra, who had insisted on putting a preserving pan over her head.

'It just feels safer like this,' she said, with a spectral rattle. 'Have you all got your gas masks?'

Eventually they came back down, Mum supporting Peggy, whose legs weren't doing a very good job on their own.

'What did you see?' Ernest asked, wondering if he didn't need the lavatory himself.

Peggy shook her head, and gulped.

'Runny tummy,' Mum explained. 'Seems she ate some raw beans while she was doing the weeding.'

'Not feeding her enough, Myra?' Fred nudged his wife, and his shoulders shook a little.

'Well, I'm sure she won't be tempted again,' said June.

'I'm surprised you didn't know better.' The words echoed inside the preserving pan, surprising nobody. The voice of doom, thought Ernest. 'Good as poison, raw runner beans.'

Peggy's eyes went round and starey and she seemed about to rush straight back up the steps, but another wave of planes could be heard, and everybody froze again.

'I expect you'll feel yourself again soon,' he said kindly, when the bombers had gone. She had sat down, but was holding herself all tight and stiff, as if she might break. Or make another dash for it, at any moment. He hoped her illness wasn't going to wreck his birthday. It would be so unfair. He had high hopes for the day ahead. Mum must have heard his thoughts, because she gave him a huge, tired smile and said:

'Goodness, look at the time! You're twelve already. We almost missed it. Happy birthday, love!'

Their ragged chorus filled the cellar and Ernest basked briefly. He felt silent questions passing above him, and hoped a little bit more, and harder. Then Mum nodded, and stood up again, as much as you could down there.

'May as well. I'll get them, Fred.'

'You know where . . .'

'Yes, yes . . .'

'Be quick.'

'Of course I will. Won't take a moment.'

Mum hovered at the top of the steps, the door open just a crack. Yet again, they all listened. Ernest was torn between guilt at putting her in danger and wanting to find out if he'd guessed right.

June was doing quite a good show of looking excited on his behalf, but you could tell her heart wasn't in it. Her eyes were all smoky round the edges. Ernest hadn't realised before that she slept with her curlers in. Above them, they heard Mum's feet coming along the hall, not exactly running, but almost, and Claudette began to stir. The door opened and shut. Peggy opened her eyes, and reached for the sick-pan and Ernest tried to block his ears.

While the cleaning up was going on, Ernest turned his back on the parcels and inspected the floor of the cellar. He found a detached pan handle, and started to scratch away with it quietly, a new possibility constructing itself in his mind. What if they had to hide there when the invasion started? Supposing they were stuck for weeks on end? If there was a gas attack, say, or if the bombing got so bad they couldn't leave the farm at all. They could eat the potatoes, raw, he supposed, if raw potatoes didn't make you sick too. Or they could dig their way out, but it would take forever.

'Happy birthday again, love! This is from me.' Mum held out her present.

'And Dad?'

Peggy looked away, and Mum seemed to hesitate. Uncle Fred started coughing.

'Yes, yes, of course, and Dad . . .'

It was probably a book – too heavy and square to be a game or a model kit, and it was solid, not a box, and made no noise. She had wrapped it in an old *Beano*. He held it closer to the torch. Jimmy and his Magic Patch were flying through some mountains on the front, red bottom in the air.

'Thanks, Mum. Can I open it now?'

'Course you can. Didn't brave the bombs for you just to look at it, did I?'

Ernest began to unpick the first strip of tape. Nobody spoke. He made a pact with himself. If he could get every scrap off without tearing a single bit of paper, Dad would come before his birthday was over. You just had to be very patient, very gentle. It was perfectly possible. A bit more difficult with so little light down here, and it would be good if his nails were less bitten. Strang the Terrible came away intact, and then Big Eggo, in a splash of yellow. Mum had chosen all his favourites. He turned the parcel over, and started to tackle the other side. He realised he was breathing rather loudly, and then that everyone else was too. All watching him.

'Oh give it here, Ernest. I'll help.' June had lost her patience. She half-snatched it from him, and he held on. The sound of ripping paper silenced everyone.

28

He really minded. June didn't notice, but Peggy did, and so did Mum, who gasped, and touched Ernest's arm, because she'd seen the glint of a tear too.

But Ernest just shook them all off. He tore at the rest of the paper with careless speed. Then he ripped it up, deliberately, scrumpling each piece and dropping it.

'*Arthur Mee's Blackout Book*,' he read out loud, opening it close by the torch, with Peggy reading over his shoulder. Mum had remembered to put Dad's name, but it was quite obviously her writing. Anyway, Dad had never given a book in his life without putting a little picture by his name. They all knew that.

'That looks super, doesn't it? We'll have lots of fun with that, won't we?'

Everyone had become so good at pretending. Peggy forced brightness into her own voice and thought about Henryk, all alone in the middle of the Marsh, retching and retching and worse too, if she was anything to go by, cowering in a dyke, perhaps – he could hardly stay in the church – his stomach cramping uncontrollably, just like hers was now. Wretched, and far too visible.

Ernest had found a page of jokes. That's the spirit.

'What is the difference between a glutton and a hungry

man?' He tilted the book to the light to read out the answer. *'One eats too long, the other longs to eat.'*

Laughter.

Ernest looked up, pleased, and ran his finger under the next one.

'Which travels faster, heat or cold?'

'Oh, I think I know this one,' said Mum. 'Is it heat, because you can "catch" cold?'

'That's right. How did you know?'

The grown-ups looked at each other.

'Here's another good one. What is longer when it is cut?'

He gave them half a minute.

'A ditch.'

A cold and hungry man in a ditch.

Fred rapped on the preserving pan.

'Come on, Myra. It's our turn. Just come out for a moment, won't you? Ernest's big day, remember?'

She grumbled of course, and blinked at the light, then played her part.

'Yes, and we're going to make a man of you now you're twelve, aren't we, Fred? Where is it then, Lizzie? We haven't got all day.'

'Right here.'

Mum had brought down a bundle of towels: in case Peggy was sick again, she'd supposed. In fact, they'd been hiding Fred and Myra's present. Without them, its shape was a dead giveaway, even in its brown paper wrapping. Peggy watched recognition form on Ernest's face and willed him to pretend some more. It worked.

'Wow! Uncle Fred! I can't believe this!'

Fred beamed.

'We thought you were old enough now, didn't we, Myra?'

'Oh yes.'

Ernest felt the weight of it, then ripped off the paper.

'It's a Webley and Scott. Mark II,' said Uncle Fred. 'Thought I'd never lay my hands on anything light enough for you to handle. Can't get a weapon for love or money these days. I was ready to give up, I tell you. But I asked around, quietly, and in the end – in the nick of time really – I found a chap in Udimore who was prepared to let this go. Bit naughty really. Should have been handed in.'

'You've done it up beautifully, Fred,' said Mum. 'Looks good as new, doesn't it, Ernest? Lovely.'

'It was his son's.'

Ernest's voice broke into the expectant silence.

'It's fantastic. Thank you so much. I can't wait to use it.'

In the torchlight, the rifle seemed to glow in Ernest's hands. Fred had polished the wooden butt beautifully, and the barrel shone too.

'I'll take you out soon as I can. Shame we're so busy right now, and with so little help. Give it here, lad, and I'll show you how to load it.'

Fred unlocked it with a snap, pointed out where the pellets would go, and cracked the gun back on itself and straight again before passing it back to Ernest. Peggy wanted to tell him: *don't hold it so tight. Your knuckles are white. He'll see you're afraid. Relax. Just relax. It'll be all right.* But her skin had begun to prickle again, hot and cold at once. A new tide of nausea was sweeping over her.

143

29

Fragments of childhood came back to Henryk in his confusion. The paper planes he used to make for Klara and Anna, for his own pleasure as much as theirs. Experimenting with the folds. Improving the arc of flight. Let's try this. No, this perhaps. Weight it a little more here, lighten a little more at the tail. Nose-diving too soon. Veering to the left. But there, now. There. Yes, that's perfect.

High ceilings, wooden floor, littered with paper.

Curled on the floor of the church, stomach in spasm, Henryk went through his memory like a checklist. The right order, that was the thing, that was how you kept going. One thing after another, just one thing and then another thing. That was the trick of it all. You need a system. Like when you're climbing at full throttle after take-off. Oxygen: ON. Reflector sight: BRIGHT. Gun button: FIRE. Yes. That was it. Stone: IN POCKET.

And then he was back in Beirut again, last Christmas, when they weren't allowed off the boat. French soldiers were posted at the pier, a guard – for them? There were black men in uniform too, the first Henryk had ever seen, hands in their pockets, watching, listening. They were listening to the singing.

The Polish pilots sang while they waited. Carols of course. It was Christmas, remember. In the still of the night. *Wśród nocnej ciszy.* And patriotic hymns. *Pod Twą obronę.* We place ourselves in your care.

Nothing to eat for hours and hours, nothing to do but sing, and drink. Someone had a mouth organ. Zygi. Yes, that's right, it was Zygi who played the mouth organ, really quite well, considering. Where was Zygi now? He played tangos and then the Funeral March. And of course *Boże, coś Polskę. Polskę, Polskę,* ah *Polskę.* Home in their hearts and head.

But nobody could actually speak of home. They wept. They drank some more. Such longing. Henryk felt it again now. He swallowed the spit pooling in his mouth, and remembered thinking of the girls as they walked around the Christmas tree in their best dresses, just as they had the year before and the year before that. Every year the same. Could it possibly be true again? He didn't know then, not in Beirut. He could still believe it was possible.

All the storms of the journey, and then this heat. Palm trees like trees in films, like Hollywood really, with sun and snowy mountain tips behind the city to make you think of skiing in Zakopane. So hot on the coast and so windless that people were swimming in the harbour, splashing and laughing, the sea so clear you could see their bodies all crooked through the water.

And when at last it was their turn to get off the boat, how the people stared. They couldn't stop staring. Women through black veils, men in long white robes, like priests, heads wrapped in cloths, wound round and round and round. It was the way the French soldiers marched them in fours, like criminals. No wonder the people stared. Henryk remembered the shame, the guilt . . . when you don't know your own destination, you feel you are to blame for it.

There were no trees, no grass, no leaves in the town of tents they reached next. Just bare soil. By the time darkness came, some mattresses and some blankets had arrived too. The torn canvas at the entrance to the tent flapped in the wind, which came cool from the west.

A week of walking. That was it. Walking in valleys, until Sylvester Night came, and then it was time to banish that terrible old year, to drum up some hope for the next. They had to pretend to celebrate. They had to do something. And so they screamed with laughter, and cheered, and beat their mess-tins outside the tents and shouted: 'Long live Poland. Long live the New Year.' And for that moment, he believed it all possible. A free homeland. They would do it. Of course they would.

The next day the arguments began again. And two weeks after that the letters came. A great packet of them, months old, addressed in strangers' hands to the camps in Rumania.

Men stood around like statues, fists clenched by their sides, reading of horrors. Every so often there would be a gasp, or a slow sigh. Someone would let out a cry or a groan. And Henryk waited. Hoping and fearing for his turn. Checking off names in his head. He counted. If the twelfth name wasn't his, it would mean good news.

Nine. Ten. Eleven. No. No.

Twelve. The twelfth name was his. Gizela's writing he knew at once. He opened the letter and read the first words.

146

'We are quite alone now. . . . *zupełnie same.*'

Her father had received a summons, an appointment at the university. They didn't know why. Off he went. Mother – Matka – all in a fluster, looking here and there. He didn't have his suit. How could her clever husband go off like that? What would they think of him, so shabby-looking, hardly out of his slippers, no time to comb his hair? He must make an impression, a good impression. They must realise how clever he was, how important. Matka grabbed his best clothes, a freshly ironed shirt, her handbag. She put on lipstick, told Gizela what to cook for supper and jumped into a taxi to go to the university. They never came back.

And then the word went round the camp. The teachers. The professors. The writers. The musicians. They're killing them.

30

By early evening, Peggy was feeling well enough to join the birthday expedition to the cinema. Desperate though she was to make sure Henryk was all right, she couldn't let Ernest down, not after last night.

'Funny how you can feel a stranger in your own town,' she was about to whisper to him as they got out of the car. Something had changed since they'd been gone. As though they'd been away for years instead of weeks, and everything had happened without her. It made her feel detached and different, even more than usual. But when she saw how happy Ernest looked, she kept her mouth shut.

'*Contraband*,' he said, staring up at the black letters above the white-painted archway. 'What's that then?'

'Goodness. They change the programme so often now,' said their mother. 'I thought they'd still be showing *Just William*. That was going to be the surprise. What a shame.'

'It's all right, Mum. I don't mind.'

Peggy answered his question quickly, guiltily pleased not to be sitting through *Just William*.

'Contraband . . . it's illegal stuff, isn't it? What smugglers do. Like Dr Syn. You know.'

'Then why isn't it spelled 'b-a-n-n-e-d' if you're not allowed it?'

'I don't know. I suppose it should be.'

The queue was full of soldiers, of course. She'd never seen so many. Peggy didn't even know which regiment was at the Camp at the moment. The gunfire from that direction was pretty much continuous now, rattling the town's window frames over and over again. Nobody took much notice. There had never been much of a phoney war at Lydd. It had always sounded like the real thing.

'Oooh, Conrad Veidt!' said June, who had left Claudette with Aunt Myra, and put her best hat on. 'Is he a spy in this one, too?'

'He's a bit ancient for you, isn't he?' said Peggy.

'I like an older man,' June confessed, and they all tutted and laughed. 'On the silver screen, that is. Oh, leave me alone.' She took out her cigarette packet, shook it gently and frowned.

'Isn't he the one who gave all his fortune to the war effort?' said Mum.

'But he's a German,' said Peggy, hoping to distract June, who seemed to be counting her cigarettes. The tactic seemed to work.

'Doesn't mean he likes Hitler though, does it?'

June smiled and busied herself with her matches, while Ernest offered the shelter of his hands for the flame. Peggy smiled too, at the thought of the three cigarettes she'd managed to stash away for Henryk, and how pleased he'd be when she gave them to him. He was unlikely to have escaped the effects of the beans – though she hoped he hadn't suffered as much as she had – and cigarettes might make amends. He was obviously too polite to ask for anything. Thoughtful. He wanted to make things easier for her, but she didn't mind going to any trouble for him.

Up ahead, Peggy spotted Dorothy, who'd once been in her class at the Council School but must have been working for a year at least by now. Dot was hanging on the arm of a young sergeant with a shaving rash. He looked very pleased with himself. When she saw Peggy, she gave her a waggly-fingered wave, and turned back to her beau with a flounce, and then they both stared and smiled at Peggy and her family. Her heels were very high, Peggy noticed her mum noticing.

'Peg! Peg!' There was Jeannie Ashbee, jumping up and down on the other side of the road, waiting for a chance to dart through the traffic. Peggy was pleased to see her, and hurried to meet her. Jeannie didn't think she was stuck up.

'I haven't seen you for *ages*!'

'I know. I know. I've been *so* busy!' said Jeannie. 'You don't know what you're missing! Oh, sorry . . . I shouldn't have said that. I didn't mean it. What's the matter with you? You do look peaky.'

Her stomach pitched and churned.

'I ate something funny. I was sick all night.'

They inspected each other. Jeannie was wearing a dress Peggy had never seen before. Yellow gingham with short puffy sleeves, and a zigzag crochet trim at the arms and neckline. A matching belt too. She took a step towards her, and Peggy noticed her friend had also acquired a new swing to her hips. Everyone was changing. She realised how much she was looking forward to curling up in the dark in a tip-down tickly velvet cinema seat, where nobody could look at her.

'How's the Hatchery?' she asked, after admiring the dress.

'Oh, work . . . !' Jeannie managed to make it sound as though she'd been at it for half a century. 'It's not so bad. We have a laugh, most of the time. It's just a bit horrible when the chicks don't come out properly.'

'What do you mean?'

'Do you really want to know?' said Jeannie, shaking her head and keeping going regardless. 'Sometimes the eggs crack, but not all the way. And then you have to kill the chicks. They're no good, you see. Poorly. But it's got to be done.'

'What?' Peggy asked.

'Well, that's the horrible thing. You squash them. With your thumb. When they're alive. I didn't know I'd have to do that. But you do get used to it. You can get used to anything, really, can't you, if you have to? It would be nice if you didn't have to use your bare hands, but there you go.'

'I suppose it would be nice.'

'And we're all in it together. There's a conchie working there with us now, friend of the boss or something, but he's OK really, I suppose. I was surprised.'

Peggy took a step backwards. Jeannie blushed and blundered on.

'My uncle's been called up now. Lucky he'd finished making our shelter. He went last week.'

'You don't know where?'

'Can't say, can I?'

'Sorry. Didn't mean to ask. I just wondered.'

'I don't know anyway.'

The atmosphere seemed to thicken; it was getting harder to breathe. Jeannie tried to make amends.

'So, will you come to the dance this Saturday? At the Camp? They've got a proper dance floor there now, all springy. And there's going to be a live band too. The works. The food's lovely. I can't wait. Why don't you ask your mum?'

Jeannie flashed a smile at the cinema queue, eyes guarded. Peggy looked too. All those people she didn't know. She thought about it, and realised with a sudden tightening in her chest that she had not the slightest desire to whirl around anywhere with any of those eager young men. There was only one person she wanted to dance with now. It was a feeling that made her happy and desperately sad at exactly the same time.

She shook her head.

'I don't think so. I don't think so.'

Ernest called her then.

'Look . . . they're starting to go in,' said Peggy, ready to hurry off. 'You're not coming to the picture then?'

'No. I'm fed up with all this spy business. It's bad enough the way everyone talks about it all the time. Honestly!' Jeannie tossed her head dismissively. 'Talk about obsessed! Anyway, according to Mum, it's not funny men in false moustaches we need to look out for, or peculiar accents, let alone nuns. The thing about proper spies is that they just blend in, don't they? What would be the point otherwise? Everyone knows now to watch out for nuns.'

Peggy pretended to laugh, but she couldn't meet her friend's eye. For a moment she even wondered if Jeannie was saying all this on purpose, to test her. Was it possible she suspected something, that somehow she'd heard there hadn't been a pilot in that plane? Henryk didn't exactly blend in. She would have to keep her guard up here. She mustn't let anything slip. Best not linger either.

Over the road, Ernest was beckoning her urgently. She followed his gaze curiously, while she said goodbye to Jeannie. Victor Velvick and his mum had just arrived. That was why Ernest wanted to get inside so quickly. Well, they weren't going to intimidate her. Peggy walked past them haughtily. Then she stumbled. A foot withdrew, she was certain. If another pair of soldiers hadn't hoiked her up by one arm, she would have gone flying. They caught her with all the ease of a looker grabbing the limb of a passing lamb.

31

Victor Velvick cornered Ernest after the film. It was like an ambush. First a high sharp whistle through the gap in his teeth to catch his attention; then he gripped Ernest by the shoulder and held him back while everyone else moved forward in the flow of people.

He didn't say anything to begin with. Just grinned at Ernest.

'Wh-what do you want?' said Ernest. 'I've got to go.'

'What? Right away? No time for a heart-to-heart?' Without actually touching Ernest, Victor pinned him to the picturehouse wall, one muscled arm leaning across him, so that out of the corner of his eye Ernest could see the tendons flexing stiffly in the other boy's wrist. Victor seemed to have grown another couple of inches in the weeks they had been apart. The fine down above his top lip was darker now, and there were tiny holes all over the skin of his nose which Ernest hadn't seen before. His smell was different too. Stronger and muskier.

'No. No time at all.' Ernest didn't want to breathe him in.

Victor frowned and looked pointedly back at the cluster of people gathering round June and Mum and Peggy, as if to say, 'Really?' June was lighting another cigarette, and didn't look as though she were going anywhere in a hurry. It wasn't every day you got a chance to catch up with things in town. Peggy and Mum seemed more restless.

'What do you want to chat about, anyway?' said Ernest.

'Oh you know . . . this and that . . . family matters . . . thought you might be getting a bit lonely these days.'

'No. Are you?' Then he blushed. Why had he said that? Victor would take it as provocation. Nearly all the other town children had been sent away by then. Obviously not Ernest, who'd begged Mum to let him stay. And not Victor Velvick either. Mrs Velvick said she needed him for deliveries but everyone knew she couldn't face being on her own. So it was just Victor and his mother now, and a space at the table where his brother used to sit.

'Oh, I've got plenty to keep me busy, I have.' Ernest made himself concentrate on Victor's stories. 'Been doing my bit – and it looks like I'll be getting a medal for it too. Found a carrier pigeon, I did, by the miniature railway – have you seen the new armoured trains they've got? Quite a sight! I caught it too, and it turned out it had a very important message on it. I was quite the hero last week.'

'Oh. Congratulations.'

Victor narrowed his eyes.

'Are you taking the mick?'

'No, no. Of course I'm not,' said Ernest quickly, hoping desperately that Peggy or Mum might be watching. He couldn't see them now, or June either. Victor had deliberately blocked his view with his great chest.

Ernest didn't know how, but Victor always managed to make it look as if he was just being friendly, from a distance.

Something about his face, and the way he smiled, and nodded: that's what did the trick. He even punched his arm from time to time, and threw back his head and laughed, when Ernest hadn't said anything funny. Any grown-up looking at them would think they were best mates.

'I expect your dad is pretty lonely though . . .' Victor continued.

'No. No. I don't think so . . .'

Again Victor's head went back.

'No, no . . .' he gasped, pretending to wipe a tear of hilarity from the corner of one eye. 'Of course not. Silly me. Why should he be? They've probably given him a bunch of other Nazi-lovers for company, haven't they?'

Ernest's ears began to sing and burn. He felt he might explode. Ernest didn't know what Victor was getting at, and he certainly wasn't going to ask, but he knew he didn't like it. He pushed past him, muttering under his breath.

'Shut up. Shut up. Shut *up*.'

'Going so soon?' said Victor in mock-dismay. 'Ah well. Pip pip!'

Keeping his head down as he made his escape, Ernest brushed against the back of an off-duty private, and stumbled away, flinching in anticipation. But the young soldier was too busy with his girl to take the trouble to react. And Victor had vanished. Ernest rejoined the others, and Peggy gave him an odd frown. Luckily Uncle Fred reappeared just then too, and was as eager as Ernest to get back to the farm.

'Did you have a good time?' said his uncle as he held open the van door. 'You look as though you might be going down with something yourself. You won't mess up the Austin, will you?'

'No, no. I'm fine. And I had a lovely time, thank you. It was a lovely birthday.'

Once the engine had started, Peggy asked him outright.

'What did Victor say to you?'

'Nothing much. Just . . .'

'Just what?'

'Oh, he was showing off about a carrier pigeon he'd found.'

'And . . .?' Peggy wouldn't let it go.

'And what?'

'What else did he say?'

'He told me about the man at Greatstone. Blown up, he was. Between his back door and his garage.'

Mum and June and Uncle Fred began to listen now.

'They were talking about that in the Rising Sun too,' said Fred. 'Just behind the Jolly Fisherman, weren't it? They told him the shingle was mined. Any movement, you see. Any movement at all. Shift one stone, you shift 'em all, and BOOM! You've had it. Silly sod. Had to take the short cut, didn't he? Some people just won't listen.'

Ernest hunched himself back into the corner, on top of the feed sacks, and stared out of the window. Dad had always warned him not to take too much notice of people like Victor. Some people were just like that, he said, always trying to insinuate something. You ought to feel sorry for them, really, instead of feeling sorry for yourself. But it was very hard.

Another story followed: an attempted arrest the other side of Hythe; that turned out to be a scarecrow 'signalling' to the Germans. Fred was really getting into his stride now. His next tale was of the LDV on a nightwatch, up the watertower, listening in the dark. Footsteps on the shingle down below. To and fro. To and fro. Scrunch. Scrunch. Scrunch. Ernest could feel the fear edging up his neck as his uncle built up the yarn, with a kind of glee that made him suspicious. Eventually the men decided to go down to investigate. Ernest held his breath. Germans? No, rabbits. Tens – maybe hundreds! – of rabbits, circling the ladder, hopping around, nibbling away. Fred roared with laughter.

Ernest's mind kept flicking back and forth, from parachutes to washing lines, from spies to rabbits.

The lanes got narrower and bumpier, and the car got slower.

His head throbbed in the rhythm of those horrible words: Nazi-lover, Nazi-lover, Nazi-lover, Nazi-lover. Whatever Dad said, Ernest didn't think he could ever feel sorry for Victor Velvick.

32

This time Henryk had seen her coming. How could he fail? He hadn't stopped watching for Peggy from the moment the first faint trace of pink appeared at the window. Long before that he'd made himself ready, creeping out and washing under the moonlight. He wanted to be clean and fresh when she came, as fresh as possible.

Just inside the porch he stood, with a sense of ownership he identified with grim irony. *An Englishman's home is his castle* ... one of the sentences they'd recited when they first reached Liverpool. Until he came to this church, he hadn't slept alone in a room since leaving Poland. Tents. Barrack rooms. Camps. And now he had all this to himself. And such a sky to go with it too.

She came early, when trails of mist still hovered low, just above the glassy water, dissolving as he watched. He swung open the door the instant Peggy rounded the corner. Henryk watched her catch sight of him, stop, smile and then hurry on. He could hardly believe how much he had missed her. He had let himself depend on her return.

'You come back.'

Henryk could have been making a statement or asking a question. It might have been a plea for the future. He wasn't sure if he had said it quite right. It didn't matter. There she was. She had come back. He could almost touch her now.

There was something insubstantial about her, ethereal. It was partly an effect of the thin dawn light. Paler, she seemed, more frail. In just a night, a day, and a night. And from the way she stared, perhaps he had changed too.

'Were you awfully sick?' she said. 'I'm terribly sorry. It was the beans, you know.' She thrust out a hand, which made him jump, but it was full of flowers. All colours, papery petals on stick stalks, and such a smell.

'Sweet peas,' she told him. He buried his nose in the peppery sweetness, and thanked her. As he took the bundle of stems, his fingers closed round hers, just for a moment. Warm and dry and electrifying.

'So stupid of me. I can't tell you how . . . I had no idea.'

'No.'

He had worked it out in the end, once the worst had passed. And then, as his capsized stomach struggled to right itself, he held on to the memory of her sitting next to him, nonchalantly nibbling. Of course she hadn't known. Just as she had no idea how lovely her mouth was. Nor that he had actually begun to envy the beans as she ate. Or how much he wanted to be feeling her slightly off-centre teeth against his own skin. But these were thoughts he had to banish.

'I am fine now,' he said.

'But still . . . I just can't believe I was so stupid. Such an idiot.'

'But now it is finished, and we are both better.'

He could take her hand properly and lead her inside. Except somehow he couldn't.

'Yes, much better, thank goodness. And I would have come sooner . . . I should have . . . but we all went to Lydd – to town – for my brother's birthday. To the cinema. A treat. My uncle had feed to pick up so he drove us in. And they made me go straight to bed as soon as we got home. I wanted to come before. I really did. I couldn't sleep for worrying.' She looked at the flowers. 'I wonder if we can find a jam jar or something. Should have brought one with me. I didn't think. Just, you know, at the last moment, I saw them. To make up for the beans.'

'Yes.' Reach out now. Go on.

If she were coy, and simpered, and expected it, it would be easy to kiss her hand, and think nothing of it. But there was no trickery like that about Peggy, not that he could see. He didn't know the rules for a friendship like this.

'I was worried,' she said.

'You must not worry. Come. We must shut the door.'

He backed into the coolness behind, not wanting to take his eyes off her.

'The film was good? How old is your brother?'

'Oh, he's twelve now. Though you wouldn't think to see him.' She held out a hand, to show his size, and smiled again. 'Do you have a brother?'

'No. Only sisters. I had only sisters.'

It frightened him that when he thought of Gizela, and Klara and Anna, he could no longer recall exactly how they moved. How their bodies fitted together and worked. They had become like photographs in his mind, trapped and silenced and far away. When he tried to animate the images, their actions were jerky

161

and strange. Arms and legs like puppets, faces colourless and immobile. He could no longer hear the sound of their voices.

'Let's sit down,' Peggy said, making straight for 'their' pew. She settled herself like a guest in a parlour, knees together, bag on her lap.

'Guess what?' she said. 'I've got cake for you. No icing this year, but cake! Isn't that wonderful?'

'Wonderful,' Henryk agreed, sitting next to her. 'Cake is wonderful.'

English cake was plain and yellow, with never a poppy seed in sight. They used to have cake like that at the aerodrome from time to time, with tea, in green cups and saucers. The wireless operators would bring it in, baked by their mothers for 'our boys'. Someone had decided that cake was good for morale. Just the ticket, old bean.

She had other food for him too. Milk, and strawberries and a tin of pilchards, and some cold boiled potatoes. She pointed out that the skin is very nutritious. The one good thing about the bean disaster was that he had been left temporarily without hunger, but the sight of more food prompted its return. Henryk was careful not to appear desperate. He hated the idea of being a burden to Peggy.

'Can you stay for long?'

It was her company he craved, anyway, more than food and drink. She brought hope when she came, unloading possibility with each small offering she brought, a sense of a future worth having. When Peggy was there in the church, talking and smiling and busying herself around him, for just that short length of time, he even felt safe.

33

Ernest opened the back door as quietly as he could, and looked out. There was absolutely nothing to suggest where Peggy might be. No tell-tale dewy footprints. No broken grass stems. Just an empty bed, when everyone else was still asleep, and a half-heard click of the latch, which was probably what woke him up.

Still no rain, which was good. The early morning air had an earthy freshness: you could feel the beginnings of the heat that would soon take over, but right now there was no shimmer to it at all. Ernest stepped out and tuned his ear to the dawn. The crazed call of a sedge warbler came from the reeds fringing the ditch that separated farmyard from field, a small yellow bird in frantic argument with itself. So easy to hear, so hard to see.

A thought struck him. It sounded like a random ramble of sounds: a relentless, tongue-clicking monotone, remarks that were constantly interrupted by whistled contradictions. But supposing it was actually a complicated series of dots and dashes, as precise as could be? A code of some kind? This warbler might be sending out a secret message. If only he knew how to work it out. Or maybe – and Ernest's heart beat a little faster at the thought – maybe it wasn't a living bird at all, but a carefully disguised machine. A secret device, pretending to be a bird, waiting for a passing Fifth Columnist. The enemy within, hidden in the reeds.

He tried to laugh at the thought. He wanted to make light of things, he really did. It almost felt his duty. But with so many new instructions all the time, it was only getting harder. Even June, who'd handed over her coat hangers for the aluminium effort last week with good enough grace, had started to grumble about not being allowed to grumble. *Who do they think they are? The mind police?*

Again Ernest thought of the parachute. He couldn't go on pretending he'd never found it. He simply had to go back and look properly. He needed to be absolutely certain. If it hadn't been for her empty bed, he'd have woken Peggy up to tell her about it today, offered to take her to the spot to show her, and there seemed a good chance they might laugh together about his mistake. But maybe not. Her disappearance brought his doubts oozing back. He had to find her.

Ernest dashed inside to equip himself. Binoculars. While he still had them. Hardly a day went by that Myra didn't remind Uncle Fred that he was supposed to have handed them in. And yes, he would take his new gun too. The decision make Ernest feel a little taller, and older. This wasn't just a game.

He had to get a chair before he could reach for his new air rifle. Uncle Fred had hammered up some hooks before they went to the cinema, and the gun already had a place of its own, under Fred's own shotgun, near the front door. Ernest dragged the chair into position, and climbed up.

Beginning to wobble immediately, he looked down to see

that one chair leg was on the doormat, sending him off-balance. Also on the mat was a yellow envelope, addressed to Mrs Elizabeth Fisher in unfamiliar handwriting. No stamp, which was strange. He put it carefully on the hall table where she was sure to spot it and then pulled open the drawer and found the tin of pellets. He had to open the lid carefully, so they didn't rattle too much. How many would he need? He held one up to inspect it, turning it a little, and watched how it glinted, without menace, the light catching the dull silvery ridges on its skirt. So small. He picked out a handful and shoved them in the pocket of his shorts.

34

Peggy sat and looked at her hands in her lap and his hands in his, and she remembered the scene on the train from the film. Nothing spoken, but so little need for words. Just one person's hand, slowly, firmly, moving towards another's, and staying there. Henryk's hand trembled from time to time, but it did not move. He had been so much in her mind all the previous day that she'd convinced herself he must be thinking of her with equal intensity. Now she wasn't so sure.

She asked him more questions, steering away from family matters, and he talked of what had happened in Rumania and Bulgaria, of passing Constantinople and arriving in Beirut. The Marsh seemed suddenly very small. When he told her about the letter from Gizela, her hands flew to her mouth and Peggy felt herself going white. Cloud white. She thought she might float away, and she gripped the wooden edge of the pew until Henryk gently uncurled her fingers and placed them back in her lap.

'Tell me more about Gizela,' she said at last.

'Yes, I will. I would like to tell you about all my sisters.'

Peggy's bones unlocked. So she must have misheard earlier; she had misunderstood. His sisters were still safe, after all.

'Gizela is the oldest. Seventeen. No, eighteen. No, seventeen.' Henryk stopped. How could he possibly not know? He stared at the herringbone pattern on the floor, and then sought help from the beams above, eyes blinking rapidly.

'And after Gizela . . .?' Peggy prompted in a whisper.

'When I left, Klara was thirteen. The month before. A summer birthday, like your brother.'

Henryk swallowed. She waited, intent on the movement of muscles in his cheek and jaw as he began to frame his first sentence, wishing she could speak Polish. Maybe she would one day. Why not? If he could learn her language, she could learn his. It seemed very hard though. The little she had heard him mutter sounded like zips opening and shutting to her. But really she ought to try, and then, when the war was over, perhaps he would take her back to Poland, and she could talk to his sisters in their language. And they would like her more for that. His mother too . . .

'And then little Anna,' he said. 'We always call her little Anna, but she is getting big now. Eleven years old. But our baby.'

There was more. Peggy knew there was more to tell so she kept very still. He wanted to tell her. She wished she knew how to help.

'Her hair . . . what colour . . .?' she prompted.

'Still fair. Not like me. And each day a different colour ribbon. Red her favourite.'

'Straight or curly?' Peggy gestured with her finger, a little circling movement, to help him along.

'Oh, straight. Very straight. In two . . .' And he mimed two long plaits, his hands almost brushing Peggy's ears.

'Sometimes like this . . .' Then he showed how the plaits crossed over the top of her head, and Peggy's scalp tingled.

'I know what you mean.'

He nodded slowly, and looked at her legs. Almost absent-mindedly, he touched her, very lightly, on a kneecap that was scarred from a playground fall five years earlier.

'Always falling. Always a hole in her stocking. And then always trouble.'

Peggy didn't move. Her lips stuck together as she tried to open them for her next question. One finger went on circling the scar on her knee, sending inexplicable darts of sensation through all her limbs.

'No picture?'

'No. No picture. I have no picture.'

Her mind went back to the letter. She struggled towards safer ground.

'How did you get away from the camp? From Beirut?

'A few days later another boat came, to take us to France. But we weren't allowed to fight there either. We were like prisoners still.'

'I don't understand,' said Peggy. 'Didn't France need your help?'

'We didn't understand too. Of course they needed us. We are the best pilots.'

Henryk straightened his back, and Peggy smiled. If anyone else had said this, she'd have thought it boastful.

'Yes,' she said.

'But instead they put us in another camp. Many, many people were there already. We could not understand them at first.

Another language I did not know. Then somebody told us they are refugees from Spain. From the war there. Thousands of them. Whole families and broken families. Children with missing arms and legs. Scarred by burns and bombs. Orphans and widows and old men. Men who had fought to save their country and failed. All with no homes, no country.'

'But why were *you* there with them?'

'We had no idea. No idea.' Henryk looked grimmer than ever. 'Oh, Peggy. We were desperate. In despair, that is what I mean. It is the same? And angry. Truly. We had no uniforms. No coats. No money. Everything tatters, our shoes falling apart, so cold. And still all we heard was that our officers lived in luxury while we starved. All we could fight was each other. While we longed for spring to come.'

Peggy could feel the fury in Henryk, as though the tension in his limbs had affected the air between them. She wanted to say something reassuring, some tender lie: *That's all over now. You're safe. I won't let you go hungry or cold ever again.* She tried to speak, but her throat was too dry.

'Sorry.' That was all she could get out. 'I'm sorry.'

'It was not your fault. It didn't last forever.'

Of course not. What lasts forever?

'No.'

'After months and months of waiting we were given planes, at last. Terrible machines . . . no good at all. A Caudron against a Messerschmitt? What a joke. But our joy when we flew again – you cannot believe it – we were like birds escaping from cages. At last we had our chance for revenge and so we took it. But that happiness did not last either. No time at all.

You see, we could not understand them and they could not understand us.'

'You mean they didn't speak Polish? And you didn't speak French?'

'No. No. It was not the language. Many of us speak French. It was . . . everything else . . . the way they thought, the way they acted. They were not like us. I cannot speak of it. And when the Germans came, well, it was as we feared.'

'What happened?' What had it been like, over there? What would it be like, over here?

His chest filled. She edged a little closer.

'You . . . you don't have to say,' Peggy quickly told him. Part of her didn't want to know. There was a long silence, and the heaviness of defeat settled around them.

'To give up like that,' he murmured. 'Just give up. So easily. To burn your own aircraft. We could not give up like that. We knew we had to come to Britain.'

There. They had reached the question Peggy couldn't bring herself to ask, the subject they had skirted all this time. It was like being drawn to the very edge of a cliff: you feel compelled to look down but it's making you dizzy, and you're terrified of falling. After all that, what had made Henryk give up now?

He closed his eyes. Woken by the light, a fly began to buzz at the window, banging and bouncing against the glass. Then Peggy noticed that the inner door was moving, swinging towards them with a mild groan. The long barrel of a gun pointed towards them.

35

Crouched between the two doors of the church, Ernest fought the urge to flee. The voices stopped almost right away, though not before the man's accent had given the game away. Ernest forced himself upright, rifle at his shoulder, and his binoculars immediately swung forward and back again, crashing into a gut already taut with fear. A little *oof* came out before he could stop it, and he realised with horror that his rifle was already poking out past the edge of the door.

'Handy Hock!' he shouted, moving forward, wishing he had a choice.

Ernest closed one eye and then the other. The church bounced and jerked back and forth, back and forth; he saw moving hands and faces, and his finger trembled on the metal trigger, but Ernest couldn't remember the next bit. Then it came to him. Almost. 'Oom kay . . . oom kay . . . oom kay something march something.' He waved the gun in little circles.

The stranger must be so strong, to have dragged Peggy all this way. And cunning – waiting for days, hiding in the outbuildings and watching the house all through the late evening air raids. And then finally, he must have gone creeping up the stairs, the bannisters' shadowy cage spilling out across the staircase wall as he passed with his torch. Breathing in a harsh German way over Ernest's own bed perhaps, checking him out before rejecting him, then gagging Peggy's cry with a tight, efficient cravat. Silk, of course. Always silk.

'Ernest, stop!' ordered Peggy. 'Put it down!'

From the tone of her voice, he could have been one of the dogs, worrying a shoe.

'Now, I tell you.'

Ernest lowered the rifle. The wrought-iron chandelier, the lectern and the altar all stopped moving. The man stood still too, silently watching him. Peggy moved a little in front of the man, one hand out and slightly behind her, as if she were guarding him, instead of the other way round.

'It's all right,' she said. 'It's all right.'

She was speaking to the stranger. Then Ernest noticed his clothes. He stared at the clay-encrusted jumper and the corduroy trousers. Their ridges were worn smooth at the knees and there was a rip beginning at one pocket, just as he remembered.

'Who are you?' he shouted, panic flooding through him. 'What have you done with Dad?'

The two of them just looked at each other. He shouted again, louder this time.

'What the hell have you done with Dad? Where is he?'

Ernest rarely rises to the occasion, his school report once said. And now here he was again. Stupidly, so stupidly, he began to cry, noisily and messily. He couldn't see anything. He was useless. Keep your head, he told himself, keep your head. *IF YOU KEEP YOUR HEADS, YOU CAN TELL WHETHER*

A MILITARY OFFICER IS REALLY BRITISH OR ONLY PRETENDING TO BE SO. He had a vague and alarming sense that the man was getting something out of his pocket, and walking towards him. Ernest backed into the font. He wasn't keeping his head. The held-out handkerchief dissolved and reformed before his teary eyes. He took it, wiped his nose, and smelled his father in the cotton. Ernest glared at the man, who finally spoke.

'I'm sorry, Ernest. I don't know your father, and I don't know where he is.'

He spoke in a funny, deep voice. It sounded sincere, but he would have been trained to sound as if he was telling the truth. The man came a step closer. Ernest had nowhere left to back away.

'Stop. Just stay there,' he said. This had gone all wrong. He hadn't rescued Peggy at all. He could have run for help, as soon as he'd noticed the church's open door. He should have told the authorities, like the leaflet said, just as he should have reported the parachute, but here they were instead: both trapped.

'Please don't come any closer,' ordered Ernest shakily.

He wondered miserably when they would be tied up.

The spy wasn't what he had expected. That raggedy beard made him look older, his height adding to the impression, but when you looked closer it was clear he was no bruiser. His youth and slight lankiness must be part of the great deception. What did they call men like this? Intelligence. That was it. Which meant he was clever and tricky and he knew how to put you off your guard and on the wrong foot or the back foot or something.

'This is Henryk, Ernest.'

A huge hand was coming towards him with long fingers and flat, broken nails. He was bowing too, in fact, actually bowing, and doing a funny kind of salute, all straight and jerky, while he snapped his heels together like a tin soldier. His heels, in Dad's workboots.

Ernest wanted to spit on the floor of the church.

'Pleased to meet you, old chap,' said Henryk.

He wouldn't answer, decided Ernest. He didn't have to. *Do not tell him anything.* He kept his eyes low and surreptitiously measured the distance to the door. He'd have to choose his moment. He could only run if he wasn't being watched.

'Listen, Ernest. *I* gave him Dad's clothes,' Peggy said, moving between him and the door. Ernest's thoughts crashed around his head. She's going to make a run for it too. We can escape together. I must keep hold of the gun. Maybe I can hit him over the head with it. He tried to give her a sign. A jerk of the head. She just stared at him. She must understand. She must.

She didn't. He mouthed the words:

'On the count of three.'

She shook her head.

'We're not running away from here,' she said. Out loud, for Pete's sake. Just like that. Ruining everything. Then it dawned on Ernest that Peggy had moved deliberately, to block his exit. It seemed incomprehensible.

'Why did you give those clothes to him? They're Dad's. He'll need them when he gets back. We've got to look after them for him.'

'He needed something to wear. He had lost his boots.'

174

Ernest looked from the boots to Henryk's face. He gave an apologetic shrug.

'Did he make you give them to him?'

'No, he didn't, actually,' Peggy said. This time she didn't look at Henryk for confirmation, so Ernest was even less sure what to believe. 'I offered. It was my idea.'

'You're a collaborator!' That was the word.

'Peggy. Stop,' said Henryk. 'I will explain.'

He sat heavily on the harmonium stool without looking at either of them and stretched both hands across the keys, knuckles spreading, as if preparing to play a crashing chord. Then he thought better of it, and curled and uncurled his fingers, several times. Stranglers' hands, Ernest thought again. The hands of doom. Except they were shaking. All three of them could see quite clearly how much Henryk's hands were shaking.

36

Peggy watched Henryk's spine collapse and his shoulders cave in: a broken man with broken English. She could feel his shame.

'No, no, there isn't time,' she said quickly, determined to protect him from Ernest's questions. 'It's getting late – look! We have to get back to the farm before Marge starts making a racket. But Ernest, you're not to say a word about Henryk. We're not leaving here until you swear.'

She could hear her bossy big sister voice, rising, commanding. It was so tempting to play the games that worked. She could grab Ernest by the wrist, force him into submission with a Chinese burn and a hissed threat of worse consequences. A few years ago, she would have done it without a second thought.

Henryk stood up, slowly, like a creaking old man.

'But I think it is too late. I cannot stay longer.'

'No!' Peggy cried out. 'You mustn't go just because of Ernest. You mustn't worry about him.'

'Where?' said Ernest. 'Where is he going? Back to Germany?'

'No, you idiot. Henryk's not a German – do you think I'd be here if he was? He's Polish. He's in the RAF. But he's a deserter.'

There. She had said it.

She felt Henryk flinch, and glanced at Ernest. He really did look like an idiot now, with his mouth open wide and his forehead all crumpled, understanding dawning fraction by fraction. Then he said those letters again. He knew exactly what she was talking about.

'Oh. LMF. That's what you mean.'

She nodded. Couldn't go further than that. It felt so cruel in front of Henryk. Then Ernest made things even worse.

'But I thought . . . I thought Poles were fearless.'

The church was silent with the nothingness that follows an accident, or resounds after a ball has crashed through glass, after a metal pan has smashed against a stone floor, after a gun has fired.

'Not all Poles,' said Henryk quietly. 'Not this one. Not any more.'

Ernest's expression changed.

'Come on,' said Peggy quickly. 'Let's go. We'll leave Henryk to have his breakfast in peace.' Ernest hadn't spotted the cake yet. 'And look . . . I almost forgot . . . I brought you some cigarettes.' One had broken in her pocket, she discovered, and was spilling tobacco from its split paper. She blushed as she held them out. Ernest would know she'd stolen them from June.

'Thank you.' Henryk smiled. 'But there is no need. I do not smoke.'

'But I thought . . . Oh, well in that case, I'll put them back . . . I'll see you later. Don't worry. And you mustn't think for a minute you have to go now, just because of Ernest. You're not ready to leave. I really don't think you're ready.'

She wasn't ready.

37

Peggy was too furious with Ernest to wait for him, and he had to keep breaking into a run to keep up. His questions never stopped, and she simply didn't know all the answers.

'But you don't speak Polish. Or German. How do you *know* he's not just pretending?'

'It's on his uniform. His R – A – F uniform,' she spelled out sarcastically. 'You can see for yourself if you insist.'

'What if he's stolen it?' Ernest asked.

'I don't think that's very likely.'

'But you don't know.'

'Isn't it obvious?'

He didn't reply – just puffed along behind her for so long that Peggy began to get nervous. It wasn't as if she hadn't worried about the same thing herself, at their first encounter.

'I don't know that it is,' panted Ernest, catching up with her again. 'The leaflet said you can tell if an officer is really British or not. If you use your common sense, and keep your head, that is. It didn't say anything about Polish officers. Why didn't it say anything about them?'

'Because . . .' Why was it? They hadn't thought of it? 'Maybe there weren't any here when they wrote it. I don't know. It would have been useful if it had. Wouldn't it?'

'Yes. Definitely.'

Peggy lengthened her stride and Ernest fell behind again. She should have been more careful. Now how would she keep him quiet?

'Wait, Peggy, please!' he called out. Then, 'I wonder if there are any Polish words in the Pears Cyclopaedia. Then we can test him. Then we'd know.'

'Shh . . . don't shout!'

'Then slow down, so I don't have to.'

She stopped but didn't turn round. *Shhhh. Shhhh.* The wheat, riper and drier, made a different sound now. Its gentle rustling had become harsher. It rattled when you ran your hand along across it. *Why should you never tell secrets in a cornfield? Too many ears about.*

'Anyway, there aren't,' she told him.

'What?'

'Polish words in Pears. I looked. I found where he's from though. Cracow.' That wasn't how Henryk had pronounced it, but she thought it must be the place he'd said. 'I found it in the *Gazetteer*.' *c. of Poland*, she remembered. City, that must mean. *Strong fortress, university, impt. manuf.; p. 176,463.* At least that was the population in 1929 or so. She had no idea what 'impt' was but she'd looked at the maps and seen how close the city was to Prussia's spreading pink.

'But how do you know he's really from there?' asked Ernest yet again. It wasn't an accusation, but Peggy felt accused. The truth was she didn't know. She simply believed Henryk. From the time she had first returned to the church, doubt hadn't re-entered her mind.

'Anyway, if he's really Polish, why do you need to hide him?' he asked next.

Peggy started walking again, more slowly. She didn't want to have to face him as she answered. It was a simple question. She ought to know how to reply. But there were lots of different reasons, and some of these might take them in directions she didn't want to go.

'Because he can't fight any more, because . . . Oh, it's so hard to explain. He needs . . . he's worn out, you see. He's been fighting for so long. He needs some time . . . someone to look after him.' Her voice was wavering more than she wanted it to. 'He needs me.'

'Is he hurt?' tried Ernest. 'I didn't see. Why doesn't he go to hospital?'

'He twisted his ankle. But that's better now really. He's hurt in another way though. Not the kind of hurt they can do anything about in hospital, I don't think. It means he can't fly. And if he'd gone back when he first bailed out, they would have made him fly.' Peggy found it hard to say the next thing she had to tell Ernest. 'The trouble is that if they find him now, I don't know what will happen.'

'I see,' said Ernest and looked at her in some wonder. He was used to her know-it-all certainties, she supposed. That was her job: to be right at all times and do things properly. They all knew that. Ernest rarely seemed to resent it, and she didn't usually admit to fallibility.

He nodded gravely.

AWOL. Deserter. Lack of Moral Fibre, she could see him thinking.

180

'So do you believe me now?'

'I think so.'

They had reached the lane.

'And you won't say anything?'

'No, I won't say anything.'

Peggy glared at him, to make sure he meant it.

'You have to promise,' she said fiercely.

'OK, OK . . . I *do* promise.'

She almost wanted to demand physical proof, to seal it in blood, but they were both too old for that.

'I'm sorry we frightened you,' she said instead.

Any other boy would have denied it. That didn't even occur to Ernest.

'I'm not so frightened now. And you didn't mean to. But I wish you'd told me.'

They were approaching the gate where they could take a short cut across the pasture and round to the back of the farmyard. The fields were alive with rabbits. Ernest's hand tightened on his gun, and he glanced at her, and began to shake his head.

She held her hand out for the rifle, eyebrows poised commandingly. Ernest looked from her to the rabbits, and back again, and he handed it over with a sigh. The butt was warm from his hands.

'If we come back with a rabbit, there'll be no questions asked,' she said firmly. 'And we'll have meat for tea.' And if I can bring in food, I can take food, she added silently. 'Loaded?'

Ernest nodded, and closed his mouth. She looked at the gun with more respect, and swung it away from them both.

'Stay here. Don't move.'

181

RULE FIVE: BE READY TO HELP THE MILITARY IN ANY WAY.

38

For a good week Ernest did keep quiet. He covered for Peggy when she slid away, and even took the blame when Myra noticed food disappearing. Half a loaf of bread took some explaining.

'You can't expect a decent pile of sandwiches if I've nothing to make them with,' she said as they stood at the edge of the field, weedhooks in hand. 'I'm not a magician. Actions have consequences, you know.'

'He's a growing lad.' June pulled on her gloves. 'And he'll be hungrier still before this day's out.'

Peggy said nothing, while Fred sighed and said it was time to get on with it. The longer you left it, the harder it would be. Anyway, they'd have the War Ag on their backs if they didn't watch out, for the thistles were coming through the earth with more strength than the barley.

The newly ploughed field could not forget what it had been, thought Ernest. Just as in other years, in a certain light, in a certain season, with the wind streaming across it, meadowgrass seemed to transform itself back into the sea from which it had been claimed.

'Is it true that they'll flood the Marsh when the Nazis

come?' he asked. It wouldn't be difficult.

'If,' said Fred, with a tight smile. 'Come on. Let's get moving.'

There had been talk of setting fire to the sea too. Ernest didn't think he'd get a straight answer about that either, so he didn't bother to ask.

Their efforts to root out the thistles out were interrupted so often that day that after a while even the children stayed out when the planes came over, retreating only to the nearest ditch, which suited Ernest. He hated the cellar, hated the thought of being buried alive. Hiding in ditches, heads down, listening, they felt the sun hot on their backs. The first warnings came from Lydd or Rye, depending on the wind direction. It changed so often on the Marsh. The sirens' faint moanings penetrated your consciousness like a half-remembered dream, the all-clears often running into the alerts. Sometimes you only became aware of the change when you saw another worker suddenly stopping, half-bowed over his hoe, or mid-swing, hoiking weeds onto a shared pile. It was like a game of musical statues. Between sirens, they took it in turns to read the sky-writing, endlessly trying to interpret the loops and swirls that now punctuated the heavens.

When they stopped to eat, Ernest sat apart from the others. He picked the tiny bristles from his fingers one by one and studied the leaflet again. He kept coming back to one sentence in particular. It had not struck him much before. *You must know in advance who is to take command, who is to be second in command, and how orders are to be transmitted.*

He should go back. He had to see this Henryk on his own, without Peggy, he decided. You just had to work things out for yourself. That was the point. You couldn't take anybody else's word for anything.

TRY TO CHECK YOUR FACTS, the leaflet said.

Timing his chicken-feeding to catch the end of evening milking, he caught Peggy in the cowshed later. She was wiping down Marge's udder, and didn't look up at first. Slowly and deliberately, she hung the cloth up to dry, moved the bucket of milk out of kicking range and leaned against the cow, arms folded, waiting for Ernest to speak. Marge turned her head and watched him curiously too.

Ernest looked at the enamel dish in his hands, now empty. He began to feed it round like a steering wheel, while he decided where to start.

'I was just wondering . . . What have you got for Henryk to eat today?' he said.

'I hid some of my rabbit pie last night. I thought you'd noticed. Why?'

'I can hide some of my breakfast tomorrow. I'm never that hungry anyway.'

Peggy's face softened.

'Thank you. And thanks for saying you'd eaten that bread.'

'It's OK. ' Ernest paused. 'It must be hard, finding enough food,' he said.

'It is. I'm always hungry.' On cue, her stomach let out a high spiralling groan. Just thinking about food was enough to set it off.

'I'll ask for seconds then. It's easier for me. Like they keep saying, I'm a growing boy.'

Peggy laughed.

'Shame you're not.'

She meant it in a friendly way, so Ernest didn't mind. He'd like to be taller, but it wouldn't make *that* much difference to things. And he thought he'd probably get there in the end. Some people just took longer.

'Let's get a move on then,' said Peggy. 'You let Marge out, and I'll take the milk.'

Ernest knew this chain of command. He unlatched the half-door and gave the cow a friendly slap on the rump. She was a good sort really. He liked her eyelashes. She didn't make trouble. Just mess. Peggy looked from the splattered cowpat on the stone floor to the scraper, and he got to work.

'I suppose we'll have to get more rabbits soon?' he asked, as she bolted the door.

'I think so. It's no good being squeamish. Some things just have to be done,' said Peggy.

What is it like? Ernest didn't ask that either. Some of the boys at school used to catch rabbits with their bare hands down on Denge Marsh.

'I think I'd rather start with target practice,' he said instead. 'So I can be certain of getting it right.'

'Yes, it's better to be certain. Yesterday was sheer luck. I need to practise too. We can do it together.'

Ernest knew he had to get the important question out before they got to the back door.

'By the way, you know Henryk?' Obviously.

'Yes,' Peggy replied slowly, her face closing again. 'I do.'

'Do you ... do you think I could take him his food tomorrow?'

She stopped. She scrutinised Ernest, chewing on her lower lip, weighing things up. He had counted to sixteen by the time she spoke again.

'Yes. Why not?'

39

The handbag's silvery jaw snapped shut. Peggy looked up. Too late.

'So it *is* you . . .'

June stood in the doorway, languorous as ever in duck-egg blue, but looking more amused than angry. Peggy pushed the bag across the hall table as if it might contaminate her. The rising heat in her body made her think of the word 'red-handed'.

'I was afraid it was Ernest who'd taken them. You only needed to say, you know,' June went on. 'You didn't have to stoop to this.'

Peggy mumbled something about a mistake, and June's mouth twisted thoughtfully, while her hand reached for the bag.

'And this explains your late-night wanderings too, I suppose. I had a feeling it wasn't sunsets you were after. How many have you left me this time, then? I'm gasping.'

And now she was checking the packet. Peggy went from hot to cold. She was glad the hall was dark. But she could hardly have miscalculated more badly. If only she hadn't finally put those battered cigarettes back – or if she'd done it sooner – she might have got away with it. She hated stealing from June, of all people.

'It was a mistake. I – I just tried one. I was putting the others back.'

'So I see.'

The broken one she'd dropped by the sluice, and watched float away. The others had been forgotten in the pocket of her cardigan.

'But it was horrible. Really horrible.' Peggy repeated what Jeannie had told her a few months earlier. 'It made my throat burn. Stupid really.' She tutted herself. 'I don't think I'll ever be glamorous enough to smoke properly.'

There. That was quite convincing, wasn't it?

'Oh, sweetheart!' laughed June. 'No need to be defeatist. I'll teach you – if you really want me to.'

'Will you?' Should she? Peggy wasn't actually sure how impressed Henryk would be if she suddenly turned up and started blowing smoke at him as if she thought she was Greta Garbo.

'Maybe. I can't keep us both in fags on my own, and we'd better not tell your mum, but I dare say I can find a way.'

Hand on hip, June looked Peggy up and down. Then she reached forward and adjusted a hairgrip.

'Look, you just need to roll it back properly at the front. Like this. Actually, if it's glamour you're after, I've another idea. Come with me.'

Peggy followed June upstairs and into the bedroom, inching past Claudette's cot to sit on the bed. The room smelled sweeter than hers and Ernest's, of powder and rosewater and other mysteries. She leaned forward to straighten the little row of pots on the dressing-table. June was already on her knees, rummaging through the bottom drawer of the wardrobe.

'I'm sure they're in here somewhere . . . don't know where else I'd have put them anyway. Aha!'

A small package landed on Peggy's lap, flat, light, and wrapped in tissue paper.

'You might as well have them. My figure just hasn't been the same since Claudie,' said June, her own hands encircling her still slender waist. 'Don't suppose I'll ever get them on again. I'll make myself some bigger ones as soon as I can get my hands on some more silk.'

Knickers. Two pairs of swirling gossamer knickers – handstitched, cream-coloured, as French as you like – beautifully ironed and giving off the faint, prickling scent of mothballs.

'Oh, June . . . can I . . . do you really . . .?' Peggy held their softness to her face, and couldn't believe her luck.

'Have them . . . they're a piece of cake to make, as a matter of fact. Look . . . it's just a big circle really, with another cut out from the middle. That's how you get that nice floaty effect. On the bias. I'll teach you that too, if you like.'

Peggy gave June a huge kiss, and she laughed again.

'It's just a couple of pairs of knickers . . . hardly the crown jewels! But I'm glad you like 'em.'

'Oh I do. I really do. I can't wait to try them on.'

She couldn't believe her luck, on every front. It had to be a good omen, didn't it?

40

Crossing the grassy causeway to the church, Ernest felt quite jumpy. Several times he had the feeling of being watched, and found himself looking around nervously. But there was never anyone in sight. The sky was clear again too, the clouds high and wispy. Only the scribbled trails of planes, and a few slow crows gathering. Perhaps the church was empty now too? But no.

'Hello,' said Henryk, ready at the inner door to usher him in. He must have been watching for him. Nothing much else to do. 'How is tricks?'

'Fine, thank you,' Ernest replied, sensing his arrival had been a disappointment, although Henryk was hiding the fact quite well. Something else struck Ernest. *You are pretending to trust me and I am pretending to trust you.* 'Peggy sent me. Look.'

Henryk perked up at Peggy's name. Ernest followed him inside and began to unload his pockets, while Henryk held out his hands to catch the food before it fell, and helped arrange it all carefully on the edge of the font. He seemed to arrange his words with equal care.

'This looks jolly delicious.' He flicked a little fluff from the buttered toast sandwich, and glanced at Ernest, obviously hoping he hadn't noticed. 'I like toast very much indeed. Do you mind if I eat it now?'

'No, no, not at all.'

'Splendid.'

It was like the parties Dad used to have at the gallery in Rye, when he had a new exhibition. Everyone standing around, nibbling, looking, being polite. Perhaps the man's hunger would make him drop his guard. Maybe Ernest could learn something from watching him eat.

'I suppose you know where you are?' said Ernest.

Henryk looked up, one hand over his mouth. He did not want to speak through a mouthful of toast. He seemed different today. More willing to talk, though the way he spoke was confusing. His accent was very strong, but each word was separate and precise. Perfectly ordinary words sounded strange from his lips.

'I am in England.'

'Yes, but don't you need to know where?' Not that he would tell him, thought Ernest, if it wasn't too late already.

'Not exactly. Not the co-ordinates.'

Ernest waited.

'Kent,' said Henryk. 'I do know that.'

'Did Peggy tell you?'

'No. I didn't ask. I didn't need to. I am a pilot, remember, Ernest. I know the maps. It is . . .' He hesitated. 'It is my job.'

Ernest thought about this business of maps, and the carefully hidden Cyclopaedia. It all suddenly seemed rather pointless. Why would you send a spy without a map?

'Do you know the name of the nearest village?' he asked.

Henryk's jaw stopped moving. Then he chewed thoughtfully, and swallowed, and looked at the last piece of toast as if disappointed.

'No.'

Ernest had another idea.

'I found your parachute, you know.'

Henryk choked.

'What did you do? Did you tell anyone? Do you think –'

'I covered it up again, when I was coming here. I thought I'd better check . . . it's all right, here, gosh, are you OK?' Ernest hammered Henryk on the back, while he spluttered. 'I haven't told anyone else. But what about your uniform? Where is your uniform?'

'You want to see uniform?'

'Yes.' Of course I do, thought Ernest triumphantly. He stood with his shoulders back and head up, watching. Henryk silently walked over to the pew by the pulpit. Ernest watched while he unlatched the white wooden door, and then knelt at the bench, with his back to Ernest.

Neck strained, heart beating faster, Ernest watched him reaching behind the panelling, fumbling for something. His heart began to race a little more. *Be ready*, he told himself. *Just be ready*.

Backing out again, on hands and knees, Henryk pulled out a flying suit, dragging it along the parquet with a slow soft shuffle. Then a jacket, in petrol blue.

'Come here.'

Ernest was still wary. He could be hiding anything in there. But he went.

'Look.'

RAF wings. Silvery thread. Another embroidered badge below, with the word 'Poland' in capitals, white on black. Henryk twisted the cloth so that Ernest would not have to read it upside down. Then he looked at Ernest, waiting for a response.

'Yes. I see.'

Henryk folded away the heavy garments and pushed them out of sight again. He looked so crushed that Ernest hardly had the heart to inspect or interrogate further. He was too used to humiliation himself to want to inflict any more on this man. But if you were going to disguise yourself as a Polish Airman, that, surely, would be exactly what you would wear. He would have to think of something better.

'Will you tell me about your squadron?' he asked. It was the kind of thing any boy would ask. Warming to his theme, he added, 'What's your squadron leader called?'

Henryk looked a little surprised at the question.

'Yon Barnes,' he replied. 'Do you know him?'

'Yon? No. Oh, you mean John. No, I don't know him either.' This wasn't going very well. 'You've made a mistake.' He tried not to sound too jubilant.

'Awfully sorry, old chap. In Poland we say Yan. Sometimes I am confused.'

Clever, thought Ernest. Well-trained. And so spontaneous it was almost convincing. It gave him another idea. As casually as he could manage, he said, 'How interesting. And how do you say John in German?'

Henryk narrowed his eyes and smiled uncertainly.

Again Ernest waited. He became aware of a pulse at the back of his knee. It was throbbing, faster and faster, as though it wanted him to run.

'You are testing me, perhaps, Ernest,' said Henryk steadily. 'You think I will give myself away?'

Ernest hoped he wasn't going to blush like a girl. Henryk brushed some crumbs from the font into his cupped palm, and spoke over his shoulder.

'But you see that question is easy. In German John is Johann – like Johann Sebastian Bach or Johann Strauss. You know? They are very famous composers. And you do not have to be German to know that.'

'Oh.' Ernest hadn't known. He knew about birds, and glazes, a little, and how to throw a pot, and keep it centred. He knew how to stay out of trouble a lot of the time. But nothing at all about music. He could check later, if he could make himself remember. Strauss. Bach. He purred the second composer's name at the back of his throat, as Henryk had done.

'Sit down, Ernest. I will try to explain.'

Man to man? Ernest took a step back.

'I'm fine. I'm fine standing.'

'Then I sit down.'

Henryk sat on the harmonium stool, his back to the instrument. Everything about him sank at once, as if gravity were pulling him down, and Ernest was reminded of their first encounter. How he had looked suddenly so old and heavy and weary, as if it were an effort simply to stand.

'If you trust your sister, you must trust me also.'

Ernest thought about that, and nodded, and Henryk waited

patiently before continuing. The next thing he said was rather surprising.

'I know what you are thinking.'

'Really?' said Ernest.

His mind became tangled up in possibilities all over again. Bluff, and double bluff. Surely only a master agent could read another person's mind . . . Could this wreck of a man actually control his thoughts?

Another test, then, for both of them.

'Go on then. Tell me.'

And he looked at Henryk, expectantly.

'No. Not like that. I am not a . . . a reader of the mind.'

'Oh.' Ernest let out his breath.

'But I can guess. This is what you are thinking. You think I am pretending. If I am who I say I am, why am I down here and not up there?' Henryk gestured to the rafters. 'And so I must be the enemy. It is jolly obvious.'

Was it?

'I tell you stories. I give you my word. But I cannot prove anything to you. All I have is who I am. It is your choice. Believe me or not. So I put my life in your hands.' Henryk's green eyes caught Ernest's. 'You are a very brave young man. You must be, or you would not be here, now, alone with me. You do not know who I am or what I might do. But you came to find out. That is courage.'

He paused, as if he had to work out how to say the next bit. Eventually he was ready. It was a long, slow speech.

'I think about courage now. All the time. I have much hours to think. And now I think maybe it is like a bank, a little. You have money in the bank. When you need it, you get some money out and you spend it, and there is a little less in the bank. Each time. You spend it, and you spend it, and then one day you come to the bank and there is nothing left. It's gone. You have used it all up, and that is the end of it. How did that happen? Where did it go? All gone, and you did not notice. Never mind, you think, I will get some more. But getting money is not so easy. You have to find a job and earn it. Somebody needs to give it to you, for something you have done. You cannot just make it on your own.'

'And courage?' said Ernest.

'I don't know. That is what I think about now. Can you make it from nothing? I don't think so. I think perhaps . . . I think you get courage from other people. But when they go, it gets harder and harder. And when you know you have just a little left, and just a few people, it seems to go faster and faster. Until you are like me. Ernest, I have to tell you . . . I have none left. Not even the courage to die when I wished it. So I am still here. Waiting to see.'

41

Ernest had counted on getting back to the farm undetected. He was sure nobody had seen him come over the fields. But when he reached the lane, he spotted a bicycle heading towards him. From the distinctive squeak one pedal kept making, he had a pretty good idea who was riding it. The squeak of doom.

It was too late to hide. The lane was long and straight, and Victor Velvick was in no hurry. Ernest would just have to keep walking. At least the pockets of his shorts were no longer bulging. There was nothing to betray him, nothing visible. Head up, don't look for cover.

Ernest could tell when it happened, the exact moment Victor Velvick first recognised him. His old enemy began to freewheel . . . click, click, click, click . . . the bike gliding towards him, taking its time . . . and then Victor started to whistle.

Roll out the barrel, we'll have a barrel of fun.

Roll out the barrel, we've got the blues on the run.

Loud and slow. Who'd have thought a song like that could be so taunting?

He would look straight at him as he passed. He could actually say 'hello', or even 'hi', and make sure he got the first word out. It was all a matter of confidence, you see. That's what

Peggy said. Look him in the eye. Stare back. Don't let him see you're afraid.

I'm not afraid, thought Ernest. Why should I be afraid of you? You're nothing to me. Nothing. Nothing.

Zing boom tarrarrel, ring out a song of good cheer.
Now's the time to roll the barrel, for the gang's all here.

Victor Velvick didn't have a gang any more.

As he drew near, Ernest gave him a swift salute, hand firm and arm stiff. Though he kept his eyes firmly ahead, he was aware of Victor turning in his seat as he passed, then staring after him as the bicycle glided on. Ernest kept walking firmly forward, counting to twenty before he let himself look back over his shoulder. Victor had stopped. Feet on the ground, his gaze was still on Ernest, his expression unreadable. Then he set his pedal and the squeaking resumed.

He'd got away with it. Buoyed by the narrowness of his escape, Ernest gave the other boy a wave. It probably looked cheery enough from this distance.

42

When Ernest had gone, Henryk's limbs began to twitch once more. He found himself gnawing at his nails, and the rushing in his head returned. He could be calm and rational and reasonable with Peggy there, and even with the boy. He had made some sense, he felt, and kept the tide of terror at bay. But then the panic always returned.

And the deluge of other memories began: all that he had seen from the air, all that he had heard. Lanes blocked with people and handcarts, mattresses piled on motorcars, prams full of random possessions, and others discarded on the roadsides, worn-out people and worn-out bicycles with them. Unmilked cows groaning and staggering under the weight of their swollen udders.

In France, as you passed overhead, a steady flow of rising faces caught you in their empty gaze, a dazed indifference. Sometimes, if you flew low enough, you'd glimpse a look of confusion in a child's eye. These were children younger far than Ernest. Henryk felt responsible for their fear. At railway stations it was worst of all: you could measure desperation like air pressure.

It was just a matter of time before England was the same. It could hardly be much longer. Henryk didn't know whether to warn Peggy, or protect her from the knowledge of what was coming. The English could be so strangely innocent – they seemed so unprepared, as if they didn't really believe what was happening. But if Peggy didn't know what these invaders could do, she risked making the same mistake as his sisters.

Amazing that the news had ever reached him at all. A kind of miracle. Sometimes he wished the unsigned letter had never come. Now it lay at the bottom of his locker at the airbase, one postmark overlaying another, address after address scribbled out in the handwriting of one stranger after another.

Except they would have given up on him by now. He'd have been cleared out, another name to duck away from. It would never do to show you cared. Someone else would be sleeping in his narrow bed – or failing to sleep, more likely. Henryk felt guilty as he remembered Pikey and the picture he kept on show beside his own bed: a silver frame round an open smile and shining curls. He hardly knew her, Pikey was happy to admit, this new friend of his sister, but she liked to write from time to time, and Pikey was always optimistic that she'd be persuaded to come to a dance eventually. Pikey or Taff must have had the task of tidying up Henryk's things. Not much to sort out: a few pairs of socks, a spare vest, no other letters. No diary, or bible, or books.

Right now, in the dorm, somebody else's pyjamas must be neatly folded on the pillow, and perhaps their owner would return. Perhaps not. A young pilot, younger even than Henryk, and eager for action, or frightened, or both. Less experienced, without doubt, and unlikely to last as long. The new recruits were sent out before they had a chance really, scrubbed and fresh and so very English, but without half the training he had under his belt. Other than the kind they'd had from birth, that excellent training in how to hide their feelings, which even Henryk had begun to practise.

He had been the only Pole in his squadron, though others were due soon. So what would they do with that unreadable letter, in its uneducated handwriting and foreign markings? He couldn't blame Mrs Kosowicz for not putting her name to it. Bravery to write at all. If she had. If his guess was right. The whole thing could hardly have been easy for her. Every time she glanced up from the counter, every time the shopbell rang, to look past the loaves piled up in the plate-glass window, past the hunger on faces looking in, the hollow eyes, over the heads of the queues. And every time to see the four bodies hanging there in the square.

She'd watched each of the girls growing up, after all. Ester too, since she was always with Gizela, far tighter than a sister. Mrs Kosowicz used to wait for them to choose their Saturday treats week after week, with never a hint of impatience. Éclairs for Anna, always. Usually chocolate, though more recently she'd tried coffee. More grown-up. Klara was more changeable, less predictable. A wafery piszinger one week, a slice of cheesecake the next. As for Gizela, she'd almost grown out of her sweet tooth. Except when it came to birthday cakes, that is, and then she could always be tempted. How many birthday cakes had Mrs Kosowicz baked for the family over the years? Henryk didn't want to count.

It must have been common knowledge. Perhaps Mrs Kosowicz had witnessed everything. Perhaps that was how she knew. Or it had been whispered in the bakery, one customer to another. Maybe these things were becoming so frequent it was easy to guess. And it was easy to think how it could happen: Gizela refusing to use the pavement, while Ester was forced to walk in the road. When had Gizela ever cared about drawing attention to herself? She was always too angry to be frightened, too full of outrage to be silent. She never could stand compromise, or injustice. And so one day all three of them had been walking angrily in the road, Ester in the middle, blue star on her white armband, Gizela on one side, Klara on the other, Anna having to run to keep up with their furious strides.

They called it *Łapanka*. Henryk wasn't sure of the word in English. Once it was just a playground game. Everyone running, running out of reach of the catcher, screaming with glee as they twisted out of the way.

But that first time the Nazis played the game in Cracow, Ester had not been fast enough. They had come too quickly. It happened so suddenly. Surprise! This street is blocked. And this one. Here, and over there now as well, and that alleyway too. That was how the round-ups worked, the letter said. Henryk had heard something like this from others too, just before the pilots left France.

And when every exit was cordoned off, or under guard, then it becomes simple. All they have to do is keep on moving closer.

'No! You can't take her! You'll have to take me too!' Gizela had screamed, dragging Ester onto the pavement. So they did. They took all four.

43

Before long Peggy was wishing she'd never let Ernest go, though she knew how selfish it was. The very next day, when they were safely out of earshot by the woodshed, he asked if he could go back to the church with her again.

'He's interesting. I like him. And I can be your, your . . . what's it called?'

Even if she did know the word he was looking for, Peggy wasn't going to help Ernest. She ran one hand through her hair and shook out the sawdust. It stuck to her skin, sticky with heat and effort. Damn. Should have worn a scarf like June told her to. Next time she would.

'Your alibi,' Ernest said. 'I can be your alibi. Plus, if we're together, I don't have to answer questions about where you are. And if we take the gun . . .'

She looked at him. Criminals needed alibis. But they also needed to be able to trust them, completely. She still wasn't sure if she could trust Ernest. At least she could keep an eye on him if he was with her. It was better than him sneaking off on his own.

'Pass me another log.'

Peggy thumped it down on the chopping block. She let the wood finish rocking before raising the axe above her head again, then brought it down with all her strength. The log split in two, splinters flying.

'Come on, Peggy,' said Ernest. 'You asked for three reasons why I should come with you and I've given you . . .' He stopped to count on his fingers: ' . . . four, no five. It's not fair. You let me come before.'

Peggy eased the axe-head out of the block, picked up the larger chunk of hawthorn and set it back in front of her.

'I haven't said no, have I?'

She knew exactly how annoying she was being. But she didn't speak again until the wood in front of her was in three more pieces, and Ernest had set them in the right-sized piles.

'Well?'

'Tomorrow you can come with me. After supper. We'll both go. If there isn't an air raid.'

Peggy looked hard at Ernest, then gritted her teeth and kept chopping. Thunk. Thunk. Thunk. She thought it would help, but instead of working out her frustration, she seemed to be working herself into a fury.

Why didn't he . . .? Thunk.

Why didn't he . . .? Thunk.

When would he . . .? Thunk.

Every blow juddered up her arms.

Perhaps he never would. Perhaps she had misinterpreted everything. Perhaps there was nothing between them at all. Stop dreaming, she told herself angrily. Forget all this nonsense. She was nothing more than a meal ticket, and it was no use expecting anything else, and she may as well take Ernest because nothing else was ever going to happen.

But oh, she couldn't help wishing.

Peggy turned to Ernest for the next log.

'What?' she said, scowling at him. All this time he'd been talking and she hadn't heard a word.

'How long do you think, I said.'

'How long do I think what?' Peggy replied, impatiently. 'What are you talking about?'

'How long do you think we can keep Henryk in the church? He can't stay there forever, can he?'

'No. No, of course he can't.'

'So, don't you think . . .?'

'What?' said Peggy, while Ernest squirmed.

'Well, I just thought, maybe . . . it might be easier if we just told –'

'No,' said Peggy very loudly, raising the axe again.

'I just meant . . .'

'I'm not telling anyone, and neither are you.' She stopped chopping, and stared at Ernest.

'Are you sure it wouldn't be –'

'Listen, Ernest . . .' Peggy tried to stay calm. Suddenly aware quite how threatening she must look, she slowly lowered her axe. No good flying off the handle. No point in trying to scare or bribe him, tempting though it was. Once Ernest got to know Henryk, he'd understand the problem better and be easier to manage, so she'd better get used to sharing him. 'The thing is, you see, we can't push him. He needs . . . I think he needs . . . I mean, wouldn't *you*? Don't you think he just needs to feel safe for a bit?'

She watched Ernest think this over.

'And then will he go back to Poland?'

Her patience was exhausted.

'Oh, don't be so ridiculous. Of course he can't. How can he possibly go back to Poland till the war is over?'

'Sorry. You don't have to shout.'

She went back to work.

'So what will he do?' Ernest persisted. He had his back to her. He was stacking the rest of the cut wood now, taking ages to decide which section each piece belonged in, hesitating as he looked back and forth from his hand to the pile, then finding exactly the right spot for the wood to nestle, where it wouldn't roll off, or have to balance, or leave too much of a gap.

'Oh, hurry up with the next log. We haven't got all day.'

There was always someone waiting for something.

'What do you think he'll do?'

She didn't answer.

'And what about when the Germans get here? What will we do with him then?'

'How should I know?'

Thunk. Thunk. Thunk. Her blows were faster and more furious. The blade of the axe went slightly further into the chopping block with each one, and took slightly longer to ease out. Using the back of her wrist, Peggy wiped away the tears that kept brimming over, their salt mingling with the sweat on her face.

'What's the matter?' said Ernest.

'Nothing. I've got sawdust in my eyes. That's all. It hurts.'

Without a word, Ernest passed her the hanky he still had in his shorts pocket.

'Thanks.'

It was pretty filthy now. It didn't smell of Dad any more. It didn't smell of anyone in particular. She blew her nose.

'Bit of hayfever.' One excuse too many.

'Bad luck,' he said. 'Oh, by the way, you haven't seen my binoculars, have you?'

'No, not for a few days. You had them when you met Henryk, didn't you?'

'I know, but I can't find them now.'

'You'd better try and think back to exactly where you were when you had them last.'

'Well, that's just it. I specially hung them up in the stables where the bikes live now, out of sight, because I didn't want Uncle Fred or Auntie Myra to change their minds about handing them in. But maybe they have.'

'I'm sure they wouldn't do that without telling you,' she reassured him. Ernest was always losing things. The binoculars were bound to turn up. 'Come on, we've got a lot to get through.'

She kicked a chunk towards the woodpile, and rested on the axe handle, while Ernest went for the next big log. Before he could set it on the chopping block, there was a crash and a scream from the house.

Ernest ran first. Peggy had to decide what to do with the axe. She looked around, realised there was no time to hide it, thought about burying the blade in the block, and, at the last moment, took it with her.

It was quicker to run round to the front of the farmhouse. June stood in the porch, hand over her mouth, staring with huge blank eyes at the telegram. Only the uneven squeak of the delivery boy's bicycle could be heard, disappearing up the lane. A pudding basin lay shattered on the front step, one half a perfect break, the other in cream-coloured pieces in a yellow pool of beaten egg. June began to sway, and put out a hand, bracing herself against the doorjamb.

'Quick, Ernest,' said Peggy. 'Go and get Aunt Myra. She's clearing the barn with Mum.'

Ernest looked glad to go. June turned away when Peggy approached. She put down the axe and briefly touched her cousin's arm, but there was no response. So Peggy quietly bent and gathered up the whisk and broken china, and scuffed at the spilled egg with her foot.

'I'll just . . .' she started to say, gesturing vaguely with her full hands, and then she remembered Claudette, and hurried to the kitchen. A phrase from the wireless came into her head – they always said it at the end of the news: *The next of kin have been notified.*

June had left the baby on the rag-rug in front of the Rayburn. She sat there, calm and straight-backed, and when she caught sight of Peggy, she beamed and put her arms up.

'Come on, you,' said Peggy, and sat her on her lap on the floor, loving the solidity of that little body against her own. She bent her head and wiped a tear away on Claudette's wispy hair, and breathed in her baby smell. She didn't want her to see her face. She didn't want her upset: it would be a long time before Claudette could understand any of this.

'Here!' Peggy reached over to retrieve the humming top, which had rolled out of the baby's reach. She used to pump that screw-formed handle for Ernest when he was little. Over and over again. Now the red paint had almost come off the knob on the handle, and the wood was showing through.

She pushed it down, hard, a few times. The carousel horses on the tin body began to move, with a rising hum, resistant at first to her pressure. Then they were off, galloping into invisibility, spinning and spinning and spinning, faster and faster. The reds and blues and greens merged into a single muddy streak of colour, and it sang a high-pitched moaning song that reminded Peggy of the sound of sirens coming over the Marsh from Rye.

She didn't touch the top again. Just let it whirl itself out, while they both watched, mesmerised. Slowly, the horses reappeared. The toy did a few last turns, tried to keep its balance, and tottered before toppling with a rattle onto the flagstones.

44

Haymaking wasn't the same without the usual gang. It was just the family this year, and a couple of farmhands from a neighbour – they'd be returning the favour soon. Every so often Ernest would catch Peggy gazing in the direction of the church, as if she couldn't help her eyes drifting, even though it was out of sight.

'What are you staring at?' she snapped, when she caught him looking at her.

'Nothing,' he mumbled, and went back to his trudging, fork in hand, engulfed in the sweet smell of hay . . . turning, turning, turning. And sneezing occasionally as the dust or pollen got up his nose. At least the weather was still on their side, Uncle Fred said after breakfast, jangling a few coins in his pocket as he looked up at the skies. No need to cock the hay this year.

Ernest had got in the habit of watching people the way he watched birds. Quietly observing. You could tell a lot from what they didn't say. Take June, forking away mechanically on his left, further up the field than either Peggy or Ernest. A steady, silent walk, back slightly hunched. She always used to sing when she worked. Well, it had barely been a week since the news. Mum said she was in shock. She said it was hard to know what to do with such uncertainty. You couldn't mourn if you didn't know for sure.

Ernest kept up the rhythm of his work by muttering lists of initials. M.I.A. had been hammering through his head like a runaway train ever since the telegram. Missing in Action.

L.D.V. A.R.P. R.O.C.

He wanted to keep on top of them, didn't want to get caught out.

S.W.A.L.K. June had once showed him that one, only a fortnight ago, on the back of an envelope. It wasn't one he really needed to remember, but somehow he couldn't forget it. Sealed With a Loving Kiss.

L.M.F. He had a feeling not many people knew that one.

June stopped at the end of the row to straighten her back, but she didn't respond to his smile. He might as well not have been there. Ernest followed the direction of her gaze. Just a dog in the distance, nosing around, looking for rabbits, half an ear cocked for its master's whistle, no doubt. He went back to his turning, aching from the repeated twist.

She was duller now. June didn't sparkle any more. Ernest wanted to put her in vinegar, like they did each year with the Christmas pudding sixpence. Bring back her shine.

45

Peggy hurried away as soon as the first shouts went up.

'Myra's here! Dinnertime!'

If she said nothing, it would look as if she'd slipped away for a pee. Saliva collected in her dusty mouth, and her stomach growled, but Peggy strode on. There was something else Henryk wanted to tell her, she was sure of it. She had managed to sneak away for nearly an hour the evening before, after Ernest had gone to bed, and Henryk had come so close to saying something. His breath on her face. His lips about to open. And then he had drawn back.

Her stride lengthened. As she moved, the cool flow of silk under her cotton frock and between her legs made her feel fluid and lithe. One thing on the outside, another underneath. She smiled, enjoying the sensation. You couldn't tell anything just by looking, could you?

It was easier than you might think to stay out of sight on the Marsh. Peggy knew all the different paths you could take to the church now, every crossing point of every dyke and every field. She could get there almost unseen from just about any direction. If she was quick enough now, she could be back before the afternoon work got under way, with nobody the wiser. June didn't notice Peggy's comings and goings any more. Sometimes when you spoke her black-smudged eyes would just stare at you, as if you were speaking Latin.

If she looped over towards the Looker's Hut, Peggy could walk along beside the big dyke, sheltered by the reeds on one side, and then cut back across. Perhaps she should have a quick look inside while she was so close. She kept meaning to. It might be a better place for Henryk to hide in the long run. At least it had a bed, as far as she could remember. It must have a bed, mustn't it? Maybe not a key, though. She'd have to check that.

Then she stopped abruptly. A howl went up, unlike any other. It sounded like a new kind of siren, but what could be the point of a warning system nobody knew anything about? She certainly hadn't seen any leaflets on the subject. The noise started high, and dropped chillingly in pitch and volume, frosting her skin in creeping waves of ice.

A few steps further, and she understood.

On the slight rise of the bank ahead, nose to sky, a sheepdog was calling. Next to the animal there was a man sitting on the grass, his body slumped forward, his head almost between his knees, like somebody trying hard not to faint. When the dog caught wind of Peggy, it looked at her, nudged the man gently, and then went back to its howling. Her first instinct was to turn back, creep away before she could be seen.

Then she recognised the dog's owner. It was the looker, the old man who'd stood with them at the station and watched the sheep depart. It felt like months ago, but it was barely more than a few weeks. He had looked sad enough then, she thought, with that terrible distance in his eyes. Now he was a picture of misery, refusing to respond even to his own sheepdog, whose attentions had almost knocked his cap off. He clearly didn't want to be disturbed. But Peggy felt uncomfortable about leaving him. She couldn't just walk away from that white hair and unkempt whiskers, or the desperation of that dog.

'Hello?' she called out, wishing she'd gone the other way, wishing she was in the church now, instead of wasting the precious minutes she could be spending with Henryk. She walked towards them. Right in the middle of a downward moan, the dog broke off, and looked at her expectantly.

'Hello?' Peggy said again, from just behind.

He still didn't move. How awkward this was. Cautiously, she began to circle the pair. The smell of the blood hit her at exactly the same time as the sight of it: rusty, salty, raw. The front of the looker's smock was drenched, and one hand was bloody too, smeared like the clasp knife dropped beside him on the grass. There was a white cotton handkerchief caught under his boot, and that was stained too, red and implausibly gaudy. It reminded her of the dark viscous gore oozing along the channel of the dead rabbit's ear when it finally lay still, and the feel of the animal's fur against her bare leg, the extended spring of unstiffened sinews. She couldn't touch the looker now. She couldn't ever touch him.

The dog reduced its howl to a low anxious whine, but kept a steady gaze on Peggy, as if she had brought an answer, a solution, and any moment might bring its owner back to life. Peggy suddenly found herself too shaky to stay upright, but neither could she sit, not there, not so close.

She ought to make sure. That was the first thing, wasn't it? She had no idea if you could have a pulse if you had stopped breathing. Her own was throbbing so violently she felt it would drown out everything else. She couldn't really see if the blood was still flowing or not, and didn't even know if life or death would make it stop. She didn't want to look too closely. She couldn't bear to see the wound.

Peggy glanced at the dog, and its look of eager hope gave her hope too. Maybe it wasn't too late. As she leaned forward the dog suddenly darted across, nosing after a crust of bread under the limp handkerchief.

'No . . . stop . . . you can't eat that!' Peggy's voice faltered. The dog licked up the last crumbs from the grass, and settled back to looking, and waiting.

Peggy knew then that she couldn't be alone with this body for another moment. She turned and ran, back towards the haymakers. The dog barked twice – short, angry barks – and then took off after her, determined to round her up. It sped towards her, sleek and low, nipping at her heels in no time, before finally taking a mouthful of Peggy's frock.

'No, no . . . go away!' Peggy gasped, horrified, as the cotton tore. 'Back! Go back!' she ordered, as loudly and fiercely as she could manage. She marched firmly away, looking back just once, to see the dog slinking back to its dead master. When Peggy felt sure it wouldn't come after her again, she ran as fast as she could.

46

Uncle Fred caught her by the elbows, just as she collapsed, though Ernest wasn't far behind. He could hardly hear her words for snot and sobbing.

'He's dead.' She took another gulp of air.

Ernest actually clapped his hand to his mouth to stop himself from spilling out Henryk's name.

'Who, Peggy? What are you talking about?' said Fred, and the way her legs trembled and her shoulders heaved and juddered made Ernest feel sick. No. Oh no.

'The looker. The old man. You know.'

'She means Frank,' said Myra. There was a clatter as she dropped the dinner things she'd just been packing up. 'Is it Frank?'

'I don't know. I don't know his name. He's dead. I'm almost sure of that. His dog . . . there was a knife . . .'

'Where . . .?' The questions sped up, shouting and urgent and all at once. Was she sure? Frank often slept out. It was his way. How did she know he was dead? 'Blood,' said Peggy, becoming less coherent all the time. 'Lots of blood. A knife,' she repeated.

'Mum,' she said, her legs twisting under her again. 'Mum, it was awful . . . so awful . . . I can't tell you . . .'

Aunt Myra brushed Mum aside and shook the answers she needed out of Peggy, before dispatching help in all directions. Fred and the two farmhands were to go over to the Hut with the horse and cart to find the body, and bring it back if there was any hope. Ernest was to cycle to the pub, and make them telephone the police. June sat Peggy down on the stubble with a mug of cold tea, sweet, 'for the shock'.

'Take your pitchforks,' ordered Fred, over the jingle of harness. And then Ernest, on the point of rushing back to the farmhouse, overheard the word 'manhunt'. From the dart of fear in Peggy's eyes, he knew she had heard it too.

'Claudie!' screamed June, standing up and going grey. 'Why did you leave her, Mum? How could you leave her?'

'She was asleep. She'll not wake for another half an hour. She never does.'

'I'm going back to the house with you. I can't stay here,' said June, and set off at a run. 'Ernest, come on . . . hurry up . . . what are you waiting for?'

Ernest felt his skin twist as Mum grabbed his arm. She looked uncertainly from him to Peggy, making a decision.

'No. You stay with your sister. Look after her. I'll call the police.'

Mum doesn't trust me, he thought, even though I was right about the plane.

'Don't worry,' he said. 'We'll be fine. You don't need to worry about us.'

It wasn't exactly worry he could see in her eyes. It was fear. He didn't want to think about the change. No time anyway, as Fred was urging her away, and then calling her back to whisper something else in her ear. She nodded, twice, and they all went their separate ways, leaving Ernest and Peggy alone under a burning sun in the half-mown field.

Peggy was shivering, her teeth actually chattering, clicking away like the telegram machine at the post office. Ernest looked around for something to keep her warm, and spotted Mum's cardigan, tossed to the edge of the field.

He went to get it, put it round Peggy's shoulders, and her eyes unglazed.

'Are you hungry?' he asked.

Peggy shook her head, and looked at him properly.

'It was awful,' she said again.

'Because of the blood?'

Peggy nodded, and seemed to go pale again.

'How . . .?'

'Throat cut. I think . . . he was sort of slumped forward, like this . . .' Peggy demonstrated, chin on chest. '. . . and I didn't want to look . . . not at the actual . . . the wound.'

'They mustn't move the body. You don't think they'll move it, do you?'

'What?' Peggy frowned.

'It's all evidence. Clues. They'll have to find a motive. You didn't touch anything, did you? You didn't leave any fingerprints?'

'Stop it, Ernest. This is real. It's not a story.'

'I was just trying to help.' Ernest refused to take offence. He couldn't let her upset him when he was meant to be looking after her. 'So what do you think . . .?'

'I think he cut his own throat. Oh, Ernest . . . can't you see?

He was old. He knew about war. He didn't want to wait to be killed by the Nazis. And he's not the first to think that way, I can tell you.'

This was news to Ernest.

'But what if he *didn't* do it himself? What if . . . ?' No . . . surely not. But Ernest couldn't get the idea out of his head. The old man opening the church door. The shock on Henryk's unprepared face. And then what? Did he threaten him? Did he follow him? He had killed before, after all. He had seen a plane hurtle from the sky in flames and known he was responsible. Maybe there's not such a difference when all you're trying to do is save your own life. 'What else did you see? What can you remember?'

Peggy sat up. Her expression had suddenly changed, as if she were seeing something inside her head too. Her eyes dropped, and then she looked at Ernest again.

'His sandwich. The dog finished his bread. Just the last crust.'

'The dog? There was a witness?'

'That's not what I mean.'

Peggy seemed reluctant to say more.

'Why would you bother to eat if you know you're going to kill yourself?' he said, slowly realising what she was thinking.

'Maybe he hadn't decided then.'

'Or maybe it was seeing the knife when he got it out to cut the bread that made him think of doing it.'

Ernest hadn't even convinced himself. But he didn't want to think about Henryk's hands on that knife, and he certainly didn't want to suggest the possibility to Peggy. Her eyes had glazed over again. Suddenly she made a noise as if someone had punched her in the stomach, and scrambled to her feet.

'Ernest . . . a manhunt. Everyone will be out looking. I've got to go and tell Henryk. I have to warn him. What if they search the church?'

'But Peggy –' started Ernest, grabbing her before she vanished again. He still couldn't quite put his suspicions into words.

'What?' she said, shaking him off.

He'd have to say it.

'You don't think Henryk . . .'

'Of course not,' she said indignantly. 'Not in a million years.'

Ernest took one look at Peggy and knew he'd never stop her going.

'No, of course not,' echoed Ernest.

'You'll help me, won't you? You promise you'll help me keep Henryk hidden? You won't let them hurt him?'

Ernest shook his head. He stood there, chewing his lip, looking after her, looking all around, thinking as hard as he knew how.

47

The banging didn't sound like Peggy. When it started up, so loud, so urgent, Henryk believed the end had come. This was it. It was bound to happen in the end. And now he had just a few seconds to decide – give himself up right away, or put it all off for a few more days, or hours, or maybe only minutes? Then he heard her voice, calling his name, and he unlocked the door.

'Quick . . . they're coming, they'll be here any moment.' Peggy grabbed the key, and stuck it on the outside of the door. 'Why did you lock the door? It's no good locking the door. It just looks more suspicious. You have to hide. Get under the pulpit right away. Go on. I'll explain later.'

Pushing him away with a hand over his mouth, she just shook her head and shushed him as he tried to question her. She was hot with speed, her dress torn, hair wild, eyes bright and restless, casting round the church for anything he may have left out that could give them away, while she fumbled with the latch of the pew.

'The milk churn.' Henryk pointed, and then dived for the pew, dropping to his knees to open the hidden door under the bench, before worming his way in backwards. Whatever happened next, he wanted to be facing it. Peggy grabbed the empty can, saw the jam jar of faded flowers on the windowsill and bent to thrust that in after him too, then glanced again through the window and gasped.

'They're coming already. Oh no. I can't get away. There's no time.'

Henryk reached out a hand. His fingers closed round her bare ankle and he pulled gently.

'Come . . . quickly . . . there is space.'

It was almost true. He pressed his back against the brick at the side, squirming out of her way, and helping to pull her in at the same time. One hip jammed against the wooden beam above. He shuffled his uniform across, so that at least she could lie on that. It would take the edge off the hardness for her. But there was only one way they could both fit in: he would have to curl himself around her.

'Shut the door now,' he whispered, trying to keep his upper arm back and away from her, trying to give her room. They had never been so close. He felt her urgent movements, heard the swish of the hatch, and everything went dark. Water from the spilled jam jar soaked into his sleeve. The blackness filled up with their breathing. She must have run all the way. He could feel her fighting to control each exhalation, the rise and fall of her ribcage. Her back burned through the thin dress. He felt the darkness glowing with the heat and life of her. She was his flarepath.

Together, they listened. Nothing, at first. Henryk's spine stiffened as he tried and failed to keep his face a safe inch or two away from the warmth of her neck. Damp tendrils of hair.

The smell of new-mown hay and dust and earth. There was a moment when he felt the give in the tension of her body, as if she couldn't keep herself separate from him forever, and didn't want to either, and then he felt her weight and warmth against him like an unexpected gift. Still he didn't move.

Longing kept surging through him: it was dizzying. Like diving in a Hurricane, a corkscrew dive or a roll, red flecks in your eyes and the crush of acceleration on your chest as you plunge. A second away from unconsciousness and no knowing where you will find yourself when the blackness clears: plunging towards waves, or soaring into blinding sun. Control. He needed to keep everything under control. She must not know how much he felt for her. It was too much.

Voices outside. Deep, male voices, loud and confident, such as Henryk hadn't heard for days and days.

'Do they know about me?' he said right into her ear, so quietly he wondered if she would hear. She twisted her head towards him. He felt the flutter of eyelashes on his forehead.

'No. They're looking for someone else. For a murderer.'

Henryk's questions had to stay unsaid. The shouting was getting louder. Impossible to make out words through brick and wood and stone and air, and the pulsing terror in their own heads. There was a crash, and then another as the church doors were thrown open, first the outer, then the inner. Peggy winced and braced herself against him with a muffled whimper.

'We know you're in there!'

Did they? Henryk felt Peggy shake her head, moving just a fraction, so he would know it wasn't true. At last he laid his arm around her, very, very gently, holding her to him, as much to comfort himself as to keep her still and silent and safe.

Another voice.

'Do you see anything? What can you hear?'

'Look behind the altar.'

'Shhh. Just listen a moment?'

Another stranger. More banging. Doors. They must be checking the vestry. Henryk was pretty confident he'd covered his tracks well. They would find the cassock hanging from a peg, just as he had. The hymnbooks piled up. Some spare altarcloths.

The next voice was full of authority.

'We've got the place surrounded. You may as well come out now.'

Henryk heard Peggy swallow. Again, a tiny movement of her head. Hot darkness. Her trembling against his hips.

He began to count. Footsteps. Striding closer, then shuffling away. Stopping and starting. The loose benches beside the altar scraped against the brick; he heard a grunt, as if someone had leaned over the altar rail to lift the cloth. And then the steps and voices came back their way. Steps, and a low, irregular thud – perhaps the wooden handle of a pitchfork, perhaps the butt of a rifle. Someone was mounting the pulpit. He was right overhead. It felt crushing.

Henryk and Peggy shrank as one from the boards above them, squeezing themselves away from the thunder of boots. He gripped her hand and felt his pressure returned. He had never been so glad not to be alone.

They waited.

'Don't know when I was last in here,' said one man. 'Hard to tell if anything's been disturbed, isn't it?'

A different kind of grunt. Muttering about cobwebs.

'If someone has been here, they knew how to cover their tracks, I reckon. Hmmm . . . not sure about this though . . .'

And then the door banged again, and they heard a new voice – familiar – young. Ernest.

'Hey! I've found something! I've found a parachute.'

'A parachute? Where?'

'In the bank . . . Gut Sewer. Come with me . . . quick . . . I'll show you.'

'What did I tell you, Ted? Didn't I always say it had to be a parachutist?'

The voices retreated. Peggy collapsed against Henryk a little more, and a gasp escaped him.

48

They were alone again. Peggy's racing heart gradually reined itself in. She felt as if she'd been knocked down, winded.

'Why did he do that?' she finally said. 'I can't believe it. I'll never forgive him.'

'Shhhhh,' said Henryk. 'You must not say that. You don't understand. He has saved us.' His whispered words dusted her cheek.

'What?'

'It would have been easy to give us away – me and you. Just to say "look – they are there. I have seen him". But he didn't, did he? He has led them away from here. That is why he came.'

He was right, of course. One more minute and the men would have found something that betrayed them.

'I wonder if he has really found your parachute,' said Peggy, reluctant to move.

'He did. But not today.'

'What? When? I didn't know.'

'He told me, the first time I saw him alone. I believed him.'

Peggy didn't like the idea of Ernest and Henryk sharing a secret, without her. She was glad he couldn't see her face.

'He didn't tell me. I don't know why not,' Peggy admitted. 'He can be funny like that. You don't always know what he's thinking. Like June always says: a queer customer.'

'A "dark horse"?'

Henryk shifted a little, separating himself from her just a fraction, as though re-establishing proprieties, and they lay there for a while, in the darkness and the dust. Peggy could feel the texture of his trousers at the back of her bared thigh, his knees nestling into the back of her own. Her dress must have ridden right up as she wriggled in. She couldn't tell if he had noticed – surely not, in the dark, and rush? She wondered if she could adjust her clothing without drawing attention to its waywardness. Her new underwear made her feel terrifyingly, deliciously naked.

He sighed into her neck.

Her body seemed to be fighting itself. Strange aching waves flooded from her very centre, though the arm she had been leaning on was numb and lifeless. Peggy didn't dare shift position, for fear Henryk would think she wanted to get away, and she really didn't. It was the very last thing she wanted. Despite the sweat prickling in her armpits, and between her thighs, despite the oven-like heat in that hideaway under the pulpit, she would endure anything to prolong this moment.

'Peggy?'

'Yes?'

'You said they were looking for a murderer. So they are not looking for me?'

'No, no. Nobody knows anything about you. Nobody except Ernest. But of course if they catch you now . . .' The awful stillness of the looker's body came rushing back to Peggy. Her head rang with the howl of his dog. 'Oh, Henryk. I found him. His throat was cut. There was so much blood.' She wondered what they had done with the dog.

'Who, Peggy?' said Henryk very gently, stroking her arm with just one finger, or so it felt. What was she saying? Dear God, she was going to give herself away. She couldn't keep her mind on any track for ten seconds. 'Tell me who it was. Someone you know?'

'Not exactly. An old man. His name was Frank. He used to look after sheep on the Marsh. Before the war.'

'Poor Peggy.' His fingertips had found the tears on her face. She hadn't even known she was crying.

'Poor Frank. And his dog was just waiting there by him, making such an awful noise, as though he wanted to die too. As though he couldn't go on.'

'A dog? A black dog – black and white? I saw a dog this morning, through the window . . . far away . . . but it was alone.'

'Did you see anything else today? You would have told me if anyone had come here?'

'No, nobody has ever come here before, not once. Only you and Ernest.'

Thank God. A small hiccup escaped.

'Yesterday I thought . . .'

'Yes?' said Peggy.

'Yesterday, I saw a boy. I thought it was Ernest. But he was too big. He had a bicycle.'

'And?'

'He stopped. At the gap in the hedge, you know? I stood away from the window, watching. And he stared across at the church, for a long time. A very long time. I was ready to hide. And then he just went.'

'What did he look like?'

'Too far away. I can't say. He wore a cap, I think. He moved like someone young. That's all I know.'

'But that was yesterday . . . the looker died today.' Peggy dismissed this passing boy, whoever he was. She wondered if she would ever get the sight of the dead looker out of her head, if she could ever stop reliving that moment of realisation. 'Is it possible . . . can a man cut his own throat, Henryk? What do you think? People do, don't they?'

'Henryk?' she said, alarmed at his silence, suddenly twisting round. Her arm bashed against wood, and she cried out briefly. He soothed her, and she let him.

'You are right. It does happen. It can happen. For some. But I don't know what kind of man he was, this looker.'

'I don't either, not really.' She had the feeling that the looker could see things other people couldn't, that he had something like second sight. An inner eye. Maybe he knew the invasion was coming any moment. 'It was suicide. It must have been. Although . . .' At least she hadn't let herself see his eyes. She didn't think she could ever forget a dead man's eyes. 'No. I'm sure there's no murderer to find. Everything is so peculiar at the moment. Everyone rushing to conclusions – look, here we are, doing it ourselves! But why would anyone want to murder a harmless old man? It's ridiculous. It doesn't make any sense.'

Behind her, Henryk shifted the weight on his hips. Peggy felt his movements, and wished she knew what he was thinking.

'It will blow over. In a few days. It's sure to,' she said. Either it would blow over, or the Germans would be here. 'But they'll start looking for me soon too. They'll think something else has happened. I've got to get away from here. Don't worry. I'll make sure they're all out of sight and then you can come out too,' she said, her voice still low, but calmer and more decided. She listened carefully before pushing open the hatch, and felt the cooler air of the church on her cheek with a kind of relief. Blowing her hair out of her face, Peggy held down the skirt of her dress with one hand and wormed her way out of their hole. Her legs had to pass within inches of his lips.

Peggy checked the view from every window. The coast looked clear enough, but she knew how deceptive this landscape could be.

'Yes. Come out.'

Henryk emerged, creaky and stiff, and stood beside her, taller and lankier than ever. He wasn't getting enough to eat, Peggy worried. Look at the hollows in his cheeks. Look at the bones of his wrists, on those arms so much longer than the sleeves of her father's shirt. She was starving him. Raw vegetables and scraps simply weren't enough. Those beautiful hungry eyes, never still.

'I should go,' said Henryk.

Peggy tried not to let her voice rise. Her thoughts poured into the silence, and came out of her mouth too quickly. 'Where could you go? Where could be safer than here? You really can't, not yet, not just now.' She wanted to say something else. Lots of things. Like . . . Please don't leave me . . . I can't bear it if you go . . . I'll miss you forever . . . She tried again. 'Not now.'

'I cannot stay here forever.'

No. She could see how restless he was again. But still she could play for time. Peggy forced her voice to sound measured and thoughtful, kept it calm and steady.

'Of course not. Not forever.' She even made herself laugh out loud at the thought. 'But there couldn't be a worse time to go than now. When everyone is looking for a murderer. A stranger round here, goodness me! Y– you can't imagine. You won't stand a chance.' She could feel the distance growing between them. 'We've got to wait, sit it out,' she went on. 'And then . . . well, we can see. You can't do anything rash while there's such a fuss on. Nobody knows what's going to happen next, do they? Nobody at all. Tell me you won't do anything rash, Henryk.'

That would do. She mustn't plead. She was beginning to sound like her mother, pleading with her father. Pleading never worked. It made people go.

He shook his head. What kind of an answer was that?

Peggy reached up quickly and kissed Henryk on the cheek. There. Now she had to get out, as fast as she possibly could.

'Peggy?' She heard him call at her retreating back, but she was beyond speech now. 'Thank you, Peggy!'

And the door swung shut.

49

They followed the line of scrubby wind-beaten willows, Ernest making sure he kept ahead of the three men, to give himself time.

'How much further?' called Fred. 'You're sure you didn't see anyone?'

The men kept looking around. They were excited, Ernest realised. They were enjoying this. It was their moment, what they'd been waiting for at last. They were treating him like someone important, and he felt almost seduced by it. They trusted him because of the plane, he decided. He'd already proved himself reliable. That would help.

'No, nobody. Just . . . I was looking . . . I just noticed . . .' They couldn't expect him to say much when he was so out of breath. 'This way.' Be careful, he told himself. Careful not to say too much.

'I thought you were meant to be looking after Peggy,' said Fred.

'I am . . . I was . . . she went home . . . to lie down,' he lied.

The worry was finding it again. Was this the right part of the ditch? All the vegetation suddenly looked the same. Everything looked the same. There were lots of clumps of nettles. The reeds were the same everywhere.

'Hold on . . . look, over there.'

Ernest pointed. The farmhands who'd been working in the fields with them began to use their pitchforks. Ted and Harry, they were called. Prodding at the bank. Tossing the scummy old reeds aside to see what lay beneath.

'That's right.' He remembered now. He was sure. 'Look. Here . . .'

The earth was looser. He scrabbled at it, clawing with his hands, blindly. Yes.

'He's got it!' Fred was right behind him. 'Clever lad! Out the way, now.'

It really hadn't been very well hidden in the first place, even before Ernest's cover-up. The signs were obvious, once you knew what you were looking for. If it had rained hard, it could have been washed out. If this ditch had filled up, and the water had risen, it would have come up like a bloated corpse. Ernest stood back and watched as they pulled out the material, bundling it over several pairs of arms. There were yards and yards of filthy silk, unmanageable, damp and musty. The men poked around a little more, and discovered a deflated lifevest.

'But these have been here a while, I reckon,' said Ted.

Ernest felt sick. He looked from one man to the other, felt his eyes staring. He blinked. He mustn't give himself away. But maybe they'd have some way of telling – when it was buried, when it was covered up, who did it. Maybe that was the kind of thing you learned in the LDF, or whatever it was they called it now. The Home Guard.

'Do you think so?'

'Smell it.'

Fred made a face.

'Look at the stains.'

'Watch you don't tear it.'

Straps and cords began to emerge. Webbing, a buckle.

'Don't you think we should leave this to the authorities?' suggested Harry. He was beginning to look nervous. 'Tampering with evidence now, aren't we? What if someone's watching?'

Uncle Fred drew himself up. 'I *am* the authority round here right now,' he said proudly. 'But I will make it a priority to inform my superior officer of our findings at once. Harry, Ted: stay here and guard the parachute. Mr Carpenter should be on his way.'

50

By teatime, more discoveries had been made. A fisherman's waders stolen at Dungeness. A deflated rubber dinghy found washed up a few miles along the coast, towards Camber. An investigation was under way. And Peggy learned that in due course there would be an inquest, and she would have to speak.

For now she listened, but said as little as she could. She had acquired a victim-by-proxy kind of status. A hurt party, officially, the family tiptoed round her as if she were a sleeping patient. That was fine by Peggy.

'I don't want you two going anywhere without telling me where you've gone,' said Mum, standing up to clear the table.

'How far is anywhere?' asked Ernest. 'What if you're not here to tell? What if you're at the factory?'

'I've got the rest of this week off for the haymaking. I'll be here.'

'But do you mean . . .?'

'Ask no questions, young man . . .' interrupted their aunt, letting the words hang.

Peggy decided she actually hated her. Already that afternoon Myra had found an excuse to get to the post office herself, where she'd clearly been asking plenty of questions, and answering them too. And it wasn't true that Ernest would be told no lies, whether he asked questions or not. Peggy watched her aunt bustling about the kitchen in a triumphant, 'told-you-so' kind of way and couldn't understand what gave her the right. In all her doom-mongering, Myra had never predicted anything like this.

'Pass me the dishcloth, Ernest,' Peggy said. 'I'll wipe the table.'

Crumbs were weighing on her mind. And so was the difficulty of keeping Henryk fed, with all this extra alarm and suspicion abroad. He couldn't have many potatoes left. No more toast. They were getting through the carrots so fast Peggy was sure someone would notice. There was a helping or two left of that evening's stew but she couldn't think how to get it to him.

'Very kind of you, I'm sure,' said Myra. 'Put Fred's plate in the bottom oven, would you? He can have it when he's back from patrol. Lord knows he'll need it.'

'I'm going to check on Claudie again,' said June.

'She's fine, dear. I peeked in just before supper and she was sleeping like a lamb.' Peggy's mum put a cup of tea in front of June, and rested her hands on her shoulders to sit her gently down again. 'Here, have some sugar.'

'I hate to think of Dad out there tonight,' said June, making a whirlpool with her teaspoon, and staring down into it. 'Will he back before dark?'

'I very much doubt it, dear,' Myra replied. 'But don't you worry: your father can take care of himself.'

Peggy wiped her hands, and felt her eyebrows rise. Perhaps she had misread her aunt's stress on '*your* father', and the sideways glance, and everything else that implied, but it seemed unlikely.

'Let's go and do the blackout, Ernest. We might as well be ready.'

At the landing, they pressed their foreheads to the cool glass of the window and stared out across the Marsh, looking for movement. There'd be hours of light left. It was much too early, really.

'Do you think Fred will take the patrol back to the church?' whispered Ernest.

'I hope not. I don't see why he should. I think they're more interested in the coast now they've found that boat. They'll be looking in that direction, I expect.' Peggy had almost persuaded herself.

'I wish Dad was here. I wish we could have stayed in Lydd.'

'No point in thinking like that,' said Peggy. Not out loud, anyway. She gave his hand a little squeeze before pulling the dark curtains across. She thought about Jeannie and her family, safely in town, with houses all around, an air-raid shelter in the back garden and a whole camp full of soldiers just a shout away. But no Henryk. 'Don't worry, Ernest. The war won't last forever.'

He stomped into their bedroom without replying. The bedsprings winced as he threw himself onto the mattress, and Peggy knew Ernest's face would be buried in his pillow.

She didn't know why she'd said that. It wasn't helpful, and she realised now the war had barely begun. The thing that was getting to her was the waiting: this helpless waiting, humming around her, all the time. It had turned into something you wanted to reach out and grab hold of, to shake and throttle till it screamed. You felt you'd do anything to bring it to an end.

RULE SIX: ALL MANAGERS AND WORKMEN
SHOULD ORGANISE SOME SYSTEM NOW BY
WHICH A SUDDEN ATTACK CAN BE RESISTED.

51

The wind was up. You could hear it in the eaves. It made the church feel more like a boat than ever, miles out at sea. The light kept changing too, clouds scudding past the sun, pure white on top, dark grey underbellies, making Henryk feel as if he were moving himself, fairly speeding along.

One moment he was reminded how much he used to enjoy the challenge of flying in those gusty conditions. The next he felt trapped. It was like waiting at dispersal, sprawled on the grass in front of the readiness hut, listening out for the ringing, the order to scramble, eyes on the same page of his Teach-Yourself-English book, reading the same words over and over again. And all the time starting at the noise, the telephone's shrill tinkle, just to realise it was sounding only inside his head.

He hadn't spoken out loud in two days. He really would go crazy if they didn't come soon.

Then Peggy and Ernest burst into the church, talking over each other, faster and faster.

'Thank God you're still here. Did we frighten you?'

Peggy had seen how he sprang to his feet.

'The wind . . .' he said, carefully arranging himself on the seat, back to the harmonium. 'I didn't hear the door.'

'We thought we'd never get away,' said Ernest.

'They've hardly let us leave the house for days. It's been awful.'

'Take your sister,' Ernest mimicked.

'Take your brother,' said Peggy.

'Where are you going?'

'When will you be back?'

'Don't be long.'

'Don't go out of sight.'

'Stop!' said Henryk, picking up only the panic. 'Slow down . . . what has happened now?'

'Nothing more. Yet. That's the trouble.'

They told him about the search parties, the rumours, Fred's shaking head, Myra's hysterics. They produced food for him, which he ate while they watched, because he was too hungry by then not to. More eggs, hardboiled, which Ernest helped him peel. A prickly-skinned cucumber and cold tea, without milk, how he liked it.

When there was nothing left, and every scrap of shell had been tidied away, Ernest looked at him expectantly.

'Well?'

'Well, what?'

The boy nodded at the instrument.

'Can you play that thing? You're always sitting there as though you're just about to.'

Since that first, alarming note, Henryk had not dared press another key of the old harmonium. He shrugged. Ernest seemed on the brink of hysteria already; he didn't want to make the child worse.

'I used to play the piano,' he admitted. 'I don't know about this.'
Peggy's face lit up.

'Really? Oh do try! Nobody will hear today, not over this wind.'

'Go on,' said Ernest. 'Play. Play anything! We want music!'

Music would be a good distraction, thought Henryk. And it might make them stay a little longer.

'Please,' said Peggy, and that decided him. Henryk turned and slowly spread out his huge hands. He began to pump with his feet. Then down came his fingers in a thunderous chord that shimmered off the painted wood and brickwork. Peggy, who was in dungarees today, plucked at the loose trousers as if they were a skirt, and acted out a deep curtsey to her brother. Eventually he took the hint and bowed back, low and formal, and a little wobbly. Time he learned to click his heels, thought Henryk.

Then they were off, spinning up and down the narrow aisle, manic and uneven, and more over-excited than ever. Henryk only knew one piece by heart: a waltz which Klara had taught him long ago so that she could practise dancing with little Anna when Gizela was off with her own friends. *Ooom pah pah, ooom pah pah.* Fairground music, it sounded, on this unsubtle instrument: each note was as loud as the last, and you barely had the run of three octaves. Well, he wouldn't have known what to do with more. He was no musician. Not like his sisters. But he made more mistakes than he might, for he couldn't take his eyes off Peggy as she danced.

How would it be if she were dancing with him? One hand on the small of her back, guiding her, supporting her. He could show her how to waltz properly. If there was one thing you learned as a cadet at Dęblin – apart from how to fly, of course – it was how to dance. All those evenings whirling in the ballroom under glittering chandeliers. Silver and glass, ices and flowers, and a ceiling encrusted with stucco fruit and foliage too. Never a shortage of partners. Devil-may-care days, when evenings ended in duels and dares and shattered crystal. Everything at stake yet nothing mattered, nothing but the next flight: all this just an interlude before you could get back in the cockpit.

Peggy was leading, after a fashion, steering Ernest round as they danced. They both clowned around, deliberately exaggerating their clumsiness, elbows out and limbs loose, stepping higher than they needed to. Coltish. But all the while she kept looking across at Henryk, over her brother's head.

Up they went towards the altar, where there was a little more room, Peggy craning towards him as she turned, whipping her head round for the next chance for their eyes to meet. Henryk played a little faster, willing her back towards him, towards the font, where she might brush against him.

As they came back, their dancing got wilder. A slight step, and they tripped, and then all at once they were both falling, the stool screeching on the floor as Henryk pushed it back. Ernest crashed down against Peggy, something fluttered, and they all saw what it was. Lined yellow paper. In the silence left by the music's absence, everything changed. Peggy put up a hand to defend the bib of her overalls, and Ernest reached in, his face furious.

'You've got one too.'

'Leave it,' said Peggy, her voice a serrated knife.

'No, let me see.'

'It's not for you.'

Ernest was sitting on her now, holding down her hands, determined to get the paper out. Except Peggy was too strong for him, and soon she had his wrists instead. Intense and vicious, they wrestled while Henryk hovered, darting down just to rescue Ernest's spectacles. Then Peggy's head flopped back in resignation, and her flushed cheek fell against the stone floor.

Ernest pulled out the paper and scowled at it.

'It's not for you either. This is for Mum.'

'I know.' No expression in her voice.

'Will you give it to her?'

'No.'

'Why not?' said Ernest.

'I can't tell you.'

'I want to read it.'

She raised her eyebrows.

'You won't like it.'

Henryk had never seen Peggy's face so locked and hard. He felt invisible. This isn't my business, he thought, but there was no retreat.

Ernest put out his hand for his spectacles. His lips moved while he read.

Just a piece of paper. Just a piece of paper.

Peggy lay on the floor, with her head turned away from her brother, eyes glistening.

'I don't understand,' said Ernest. 'What does it mean, "behind bars"?'

Peggy lips broke apart, and then she swallowed and sat up,

but still she didn't answer. They both stared at Henryk, who felt almost cornered before he realised they weren't looking at him, but at his clothes, his collarless shirt, very worn, open at the neck. Their father's shirt. This was about their father.

'He's a prisoner-of-war?' said Ernest urgently, somewhere between a question and a statement. His fingertips were white and stiff as they gripped the paper. His wrist quivered. 'That's why he doesn't write. That's why Mum never talks about him. He's been captured. Already.' He looked from Peggy to Henryk and back again. 'Where is he, then? Tell me where he is.'

Peggy pushed him off her, and sat up.

52

'He's not a prisoner-of-war. Just a prisoner.'

'What?' Ernest said. 'Why? He hasn't done anything. Has he?'

Another gust of wind, and the church darkened, then brightened.

'What's he done? Tell me. Come on. Tell me.'

Henryk heard the collision of doubt and panic in Ernest's voice.

'He's been arrested.'

'But I thought . . . I thought he'd gone to . . .' Ernest couldn't quite say the word 'fight'. Or maybe he didn't want to say it in front of Henryk.

'Mum let you think that. She didn't want you to know. Other people went to fight. But Dad hadn't had his papers yet. He wasn't quite old enough.'

She held out her hand for the note, but Ernest shook his head, and held it to his chest.

'He must have.'

'No. He went in the night. Remember?'

Of course he remembered. At least he remembered the next morning. Henryk watched him remembering: the silence at breakfast, perhaps, and the unasked, unanswered questions.

'Did you ever see him in a uniform?' Peggy asked sharply.

'I saw . . .' He looked down at the yellow paper again.

'Other boys' fathers. Younger boys' fathers. And fathers who'd volunteered – the ones who went early, as soon as they could. That's who you saw.'

'I thought . . .' The shock of betrayal had taken the blood from Ernest's face.

'Exactly. You just assumed. We let everyone assume.'

'But why? Why did he go without telling me? Why did nobody tell me?'

Peggy's eyes darted about the church, as if the answer could be found lurking in a pew, or on one of the painted wooden ovals hung in the roofbeams . . . *let, I beseech thee, thine eyes be open.*

'They had an argument. A huge one. Worse than all the others.'

Ernest did not seem surprised.

'It woke you up?'

'Yes.'

'He said goodbye to *you* then?'

'Sort of. You were asleep.'

'He could have woken me up.'

'Yes. But then you would have asked.'

Ernest didn't deny it.

'And he didn't want to lie to you. You know what Dad's like.'

'But . . .'

'And he'd promised Mum.'

'But *you* lied to me too,' said Ernest.

'I know. I'm sorry.'

'And Mum did.'

'I think she thought she couldn't do anything else.'

'Oh, couldn't she? And this? What about this?' He scrunched up the paper and hurled it across the floor. 'Who wrote it? Why? How come they seem to know where he is and what he's doing?'

'I don't know how they know. I don't know who it is. I wish I did.'

Henryk wanted to hug her, and bring an end to this interrogation.

'How can we stop them?' asked Ernest.

'I don't know if we can. All we can do is keep hiding the notes and hope they stop in the end.'

'How many has Mum seen?'

'I don't know that either. I can't ask. Not many, I hope. Maybe even none. I've been looking out for them.'

'And Aunt Myra?'

'Oh.' Peggy realised what he meant at exactly the same time as Henryk. She shook her head firmly. 'No. I don't think it's her. Even she wouldn't . . .'

'No,' agreed Ernest, and Henryk had the feeling that if he ever set eyes on this Aunt Myra, he would know her right away. He hoped they were both right.

'So who do you think it could it be?' Henryk asked, and they both looked at him vaguely, as if they'd forgotten he could speak. 'Do you have an idea?'

'I suppose it could be anyone. There are lots of ways to find things out.'

Tentatively, Henryk picked up the ball of yellow and crouched down beside them.

'I can read it?' he asked. Eyes burning with hatred, they both just stared at the paper and eventually Peggy nodded. Henryk waited a moment, and then uncrumpled the note, and spread it flat.

REAL MEN FIGHT. THEY DON'T HIDE BEHIND BARS. HOW CAN YOU HOLD YOUR HEAD UP, MRS PANSY?

He frowned.

'Mrs Pansy? That is your mother's name?'

'No, no, of course not,' said Ernest. 'Pansy! Pansy? Pansy is a horrible word. Well, it's not really. It's a flower. But pansy means . . .' He couldn't finish. Henryk put a hand on Ernest's shoulder and nodded. The boy didn't need to explain. He'd heard the word in the Mess. Pansies and pacifists. Both words spat out, like something disgusting. No right to eat. That's what those men said. Why should pacifists eat food that reached them at other people's risk? They had no right to anything. Henryk supposed that applied to him now too.

Not everyone joined in. A few kept silent. But they didn't argue. As good as fascists, pacifists were, the squadron leader said. As bad as. After hearing talk like that, Henryk had never believed that pacifists lacked courage. He glanced at Ernest, at his skinny arms and flushed face, his trembling lip and broken spectacles and his serious gaze. Without asking, he knew that boys at school must have called Ernest pansy too.

'Peggy,' he said quietly. 'You are quite certain that your father is in prison?'

'It's not true,' Ernest muttered. 'It can't be true.'

Peggy lowered her eyes.

'Yes, I'm sure. Mum told me in the end, just before we came to the farm. When he went away, it was just to Eastbourne . . . just for a few days at first, to do his war work . . . that's what he called it. She could bear it, what he was doing, just as long as nobody round here knew about it. That's what she cared about. She said he had to go and do it somewhere else.'

'And what was he doing?' asked Henryk.

'Mostly helping the conchies get ready for their hearings. Conscientious objectors, that is. People who don't believe in war. You have to make a statement, you see, explain why you won't fight when you get called up. But then Dad was arrested, with his leaflets and newsletter, outside the conscription office. He didn't believe in military conscription. He said the state had no right to force people to take up arms.'

'He was arrested just for giving out leaflets?' Ernest asked, in disbelief.

'Yes. Arrested and charged and eventually convicted.' Peggy shut her eyes to get the words right. 'They said he was "spreading disaffection among the troops".'

'Disaffection?' Henryk was no clearer than Ernest.

'It means making the soldiers not want to fight. Or trying to. Spoiling the war effort. It means you're not a loyal subject.'

Henryk looked at Ernest, as if to encourage Peggy.

'And Mum wouldn't let him tell you, and she wouldn't let me either. Mum . . . Mum . . .' She could hardly say it. Her voice had dropped to a whisper. 'She didn't want anyone to know. Mum couldn't bear the shame of it. Of Dad being a pacifist. She thought . . . she said . . . if everybody knew, well, if everybody round here knew . . . if they knew what he believed . . . that she couldn't hold her head up. She said it was his choice. If he didn't believe in fighting Hitler, that was up to him. But she didn't see why the rest of us should suffer for it. Specially you.'

'But I just wish . . .' Ernest's face clouded, and Henryk knew tears were close.

'I'm sorry, Ernie. I really am. I didn't have much choice. It's not my fault.'

'Will your father get his call-up papers soon?' asked Henryk, trying to think of practical things.

'It can't be long now, though I don't know where they'll send them. The law's changed again, you see. They keep raising the age. Now it's thirty-six. And then he'll have to go through the whole thing himself, the tribunal and everything, when he comes out of prison. But I know he won't do anything to help the war. He says he won't be a cog in their war machine. He simply refuses.'

'I hate this war,' Ernest suddenly burst out. 'I hate him, and I hate Mum, and I hate you most of all, because you could have told me.'

He ran to the door, struggled with the latch, and vanished. Henryk was on the point of following, but Peggy pulled him back.

'Leave him. He's got to work it out on his own. He'll calm down. I just hope he doesn't do anything stupid, like talk to Mum.'

'Yes.'

She looked at him, and all the hardness that had frightened Henryk had gone. Her lower lip was quivering, and she could do nothing to stop it. Finally Henryk let himself put his arms around her. Immediately, she shuddered and gasped, her whole body wrestling with the effort not to cry. It was like a dam beginning to crumble, a huge weight of water pushing so hard at its structure that eventually it had to give way.

'He will be good and he will love you again. Do not be sad,' he whispered into her hair, and she nodded, shakily, and buried her hot face against him to block the flow.

Henryk began to hum. It was the waltz he had played earlier, but slower and more sedate now. They began to move, slowly circling, wrapped in each other, and she sank against him, all resistance gone. Round and round they went, her arms trapped before her chest, crossing and protective, until slowly they crept around his neck and he felt her tears burning his skin.

53

Ernest stumbled across the grass, running as fast as he could. He turned his face to the wind. He wanted to run out of his body and out of his mind. He wanted his heart to thump and his head to thunder, until it was so hard to draw breath that the effort would wipe out everything and leave him empty.

One knee jarred as his foot hit a dip. A few steps later his ankle turned, but he kept on going until he found himself trapped by water. He'd run so blindly he had forgotten he would have to cross it. By then his legs were shaky and weak and he felt heavy and earthbound. Breathless too. He slumped down by the reeds, curled up in a ball and let himself sob.

Why had nobody told him before? They called him a pansy at school because he wouldn't fight back. Dad always said he didn't have to. Nobody *had* to fight. Dad said it didn't matter. But of course it mattered. Dad was just as bad as him. They were two of a kind, both useless.

The grass under his legs was spiky and sharp. Funny how thinking about the big things made you notice the little things more. Like the sensation of burning in his throat as Ernest drew breath. Or the mosquito which had just landed on his arm. Its long proboscis was already drilling into his skin, just beside a freckle. Head down, utterly focused, with antennae waving, it swayed gently on legs beautifully banded, dark and light. Too absorbed to slap it away, Ernest watched its body fill, swelling with his blood, and he felt completely and utterly detached. Its head moved gently up and down as it fed, like a lamb sucking at the teat, dropping lower and lower as its capillary sank in further.

When at last he brushed it off, a bright splash of red appeared on his arm. Ernest wasn't certain if it had spurted from him or from the dead mosquito's body, which now sprawled, stuck to his skin, its legs feebly trying and failing to rise.

What did it matter? thought Ernest. Gradually his breathing slowed and his body uncurled. What difference did anything really make? The Nazis wouldn't come any faster or any slower just because of his dad. And why shouldn't making pots be war work? Why couldn't people choose?

There were a few swallows diving low over the dyke, following the clouds of insects gathered above the water surface. He watched the birds return again and again, swooping low but never colliding. Beaks open, gaping, scooping, the swallows continued to weave and wheel, mesmerising in their flight.

Ernest thought about all the letters he had written to his father and given to his mum. So many questions. He'd asked about the food, and the guns, and the training, and the other soldiers. He'd told Dad about his birthday, and the film, and the frogs and the rabbits. But what had Mum done with the letters? Probably never sent them. Surely he would have replied. Maybe prisoners weren't allowed to write letters. He had no idea what you did all day in prison. Ernest could only think of prisoners in *Robin Hood*, sitting in dungeons with rats and stale bread, and if you were lucky, a minstrel playing a song you knew outside your window, sending you a secret message that would help you escape.

He rolled onto his back. Something was going on, very high up, way away in the direction of Dover. There was always something over there. According to June, they called it Hellfire Corner. 'We should count ourselves lucky,' she'd told him with one of her slow winks. 'There's always some poor bugger worse off than yourself.' And then she'd looked over her shoulder, to make sure they hadn't been overheard, and said with a giggle, just like Uncle Fred: 'Pardon my French.' That was before the telegram, of course.

Even with the wind dying down you couldn't hear that much from here.

The tiny whirling forms overhead were only swifts, riding the thermals high above him. They'd be the first to leave next month. Actually – Ernest sat up hurriedly, and squinted at the sky, one hand shading his eyes – it wasn't just swifts up there. That was a hobby too, scanning the Marsh. Male or female? Not sure, without his binoculars. But it had set its sights on something. One particular swift. With height on its side, down it plunged. The swift spun out of the way, faster than you would have thought possible. But the hobby had power too, and determination. Up it soared again, turning, gliding, and then positioning itself for the kill, more deadly than ever. It happened so fast Ernest blinked. One moment they were apart. Then they were together, the swift struggling in the hobby's talons. Feathers drifting down, too small to see.

Ernest stood up, and shook his head, trying to empty it again. He would go to the Looker's Hut. Work things out there in peace and quiet. It was bound to be empty now.

54

Peggy kept her eyes tight shut, while the salty dampness spread stickily between their skins. There was no hiding the gulps that kept erupting from her chest. They were like waves slapping against a breakwater, refusing all her efforts to force them back.

She had never rated herself as a dancer. Two left feet, and all that. But Henryk made it easy. She didn't even have to think. Which was just as well, as she didn't want to think. The waltz he was humming seemed to sound right inside her, bypassing her ears and vibrating in her head and in her chest, until her sobs subsided and she found herself joining in. One-two-three, one-two-three. Her fingers, at first tightly locked behind his neck, began to relax. Her body swayed and turned.

Dancing was different when it wasn't with your brother or Jeannie. All at once Peggy understood why June's eyes went dreamy when certain tunes came on the wireless, and what she was thinking as her hips began to sway. It was a oneness like nothing else, perfection, legs working together, just gliding in and out, hipbone to hipbone, nothing between you.

Extraordinary, really, when you thought about it. That people did this in public and it was allowed. How on earth could it be possible to feel like this, like candlewax melting, this heat, this throbbing, with people watching and drinking and smoking and clapping and even brushing against you as you danced? Glorious.

She'd have to keep her eyes shut and pretend it was a dream. It didn't feel far off. Her head was airy and light, and strange images kept flashing by, one after another. Intense, random thoughts, that fed each other and disconnected her from the earth. Perhaps flying was like this.

Their movements slowed and their humming ceased. The wind had quietened and the church was completely still. Peggy felt the prickle of bristle against her cheek. Henryk's breath filled his lungs. Then came the touch of his lips on hers. Warm and moist against the salt-tracks along her nose and chin, tasting her. She couldn't open her eyes. If she opened her eyes the spell would be broken. It was like a wild animal, she thought. The moment it sees you looking, it's gone. She couldn't look at herself. But she let her lips loosen, and open.

He picked her up like a child and took her to the bench by the altar and there she sat – half-lying, really – across his lap. And his head was bent over hers and as he kissed her, she felt his tears on her eyelids and then he said her name. In the way people do when they want to check you are there. When they have just begun to worry.

'Yes. Henryk.'

'I want . . . I want you to know . . .'

Peggy felt she ought to be able to help him somehow, supply him with the words he couldn't reach. She nodded.

'Yes?'

He started again.

'I want you to know you are a bang-on job.'

She laughed out loud. Henryk never looked prouder than when he'd managed to remember one of these funny RAF words. He produced them so carefully. She put her arms round him again and gave him a tight hug, and maddeningly, a few more tears leaked out, but they were the happy kind this time.

'I think you're wizard too.'

For a while, they just looked at each other. Peggy found herself drinking him in, every inch. She had given up all hope, and now everything had changed, and if he could still like her after what he had heard and seen today, well, that was better than anything. He had seen her at her absolute worst. Fighting on the floor like a brat. Sullen. Dishonest, even. Crying. He knew she'd broken a promise she'd never wanted to make, let down her mother, upset her brother. She could hardly pretend to be a *nice* girl any more.

He obviously didn't care that she didn't have stockings and couldn't lay her hand on lipstick or that her legs were always scratched from walking through the fields to see him. Just as it didn't bother her that he trembled from time to time, and constantly looked behind, and around, and ceaselessly quartered the sky for danger.

He kissed her again, a strong simple kiss that pressed her lips against her teeth and broke the stillness. They looked at each other like conspirators, and then at the altar and up at the crucifix pattern worked into the lead of the window immediately above, and shrugged. It didn't feel wicked. It had happened now, and that meant it could happen again.

55

There was wool caught on the fence posts outside, on the splinters of the small pens where sheep used to mill. Droppings everywhere. Soon these fields would be ploughed too, grass turned to corn. But just at this moment, it was peaceful, and nobody could bother Ernest. Glancing at the sky, listening for planes, seeing a fading tangle of trails, his gloom lifted a little. Peggy should have thought of hiding Henryk here, instead of the church. It was a good place to escape – further away, but much safer, surely.

Ernest's thumb pushed down the iron latch. When it stuck, he nearly turned away. Still panting from his run, he leaned against the peeling wooden door instead. It shifted slightly with his weight, so he tried the latch again. With just a little more pressure, it gave, pinching the tender crescent of skin between his thumb and forefinger. A few particles of dust floated away from the groove worn down in the brickwork by the metal bar.

The window was small, so he left the door ajar, to let in more light. Ernest looked around. A wooden table, carved with dates and initials, and a drawer at one end of it. A single chair. A fireplace, with a pot-hook and a pan like a witch's cauldron in the corner. And yes, there was even a bed, with a lumpy ticking mattress, a bit damp-looking, and a couple of blankets with frayed stitching, folded neatly at the end. All you needed for a night of watching, and lambing, and warming milk, and waiting. Or just thinking, on your own. Ernest was tempted to settle down, to stay for the night, and if it made them fret, well, let them. It was all they deserved.

Should he look for a candle for later? No. His eyes would get used to the dimness. And there wasn't so much as a curtain at the window, let alone blackout.

Ernest inspected the stains on the bed and then sat down heavily, about to swing his legs up. The mattress sank and groaned. But it didn't go down like a hammock all the way, as he'd expected. There was something hard, just underneath the surface, tipping Ernest slightly to one side. You'd never notice unless you actually lay on the bed.

He knelt on the floor to inspect. Grit digging into his bare knees, he reached blindly into the darkness beneath, head turned as he thrust his arm out. It was odd. There was nothing there at all. Not so much as a mousetrap. Ernest returned his attention to the mattress, patting and pressing until he realised that the hard thing was right inside. When he pulled the bed away from the wall – revealing a scattering of mousedroppings – Ernest began to understand. The mattress had been hollowed out, very carefully, springs and flocking neatly removed to make space to slide in a small suitcase. Ernest dragged it out, then heaved it on top of the bed, which did indeed now sink, just as surprised as he was by the weight and solidity of the brown leather case. It was scratched and battered at the corners, but far from old. Perhaps it was full of tobacco, or maybe brandy, or whisky, he thought with a sudden thrill. Close-packed, with straw or something, so you wouldn't notice the sloshing. Contraband. Like the film.

Everyone knew there were smugglers on the Marsh, didn't they? There was that poem Dad used to chant years ago, like a lullaby, when Peggy couldn't get to sleep. Though as soon as Ernest heard Dad's voice, low, as he bent over the other bed, he'd find himself wider awake than ever, staring at the wallpaper so hard he thought he could see the shadows in the poem. Four-and-twenty ponies, trotting through the dark.

'"Watch the wall, my darling, while the Gentlemen go by",' Ernest muttered as he tried the sliding locks, one on each side of the leather handle. If it was brandy, he'd drink it, he decided, there and then. That would cheer him up, wouldn't it? You always saw men laughing outside pubs. There was something scary about the way they laughed, but maybe that was the point. They didn't care. And Ernest didn't care now.

Annoyingly, the locks wouldn't budge. Ernest growled at them.

He'd knock the spirits straight back – never mind a glass – and when the bottle was empty he'd throw it against the wall and let it smash, and then he'd light up a cigar (if there was one, and if he could find some matches) and smoke till dawn. If Victor could smoke, so could he.

You had to push the clasps back at exactly the same time. That was the trick. Ernest heard a click, and eased the lid up.

No brandy. No tobacco.

What was it exactly?

Grey metal. Two solid boxes, one square, one rectangular, nestling in compartments lined with maroon felt. Black knobs. White dials. The larger box had a grid of little holes, and a circular window with a needle. A row of small red sockets. Writing: *Off. On. Key. P.A. Tun.* Whatever that meant. *Volume. Phones.* He looked at the mess of black wires and plugs in the long thin compartment above the machines. Yes, there were headphones too. The whole thing was half the size of the wireless at the farmhouse. Ernest hadn't known it was possible to make one as small as this.

His scalp tightened. He took off his spectacles, and began to clean them on the corner of his shirt. He was breathing too hard and he needed to slow down. Then he put his glasses back on and picked up the headphones. Easing them onto his head, he adjusted the bar on top to make them fit, and the arms of his specs dug into his skull. The earpieces were big and black and hard, and he had to hold them on with one hand.

He licked his dry lips, and put the plug at the end of the lead into the socket marked 'phones'. Nothing. Just a beating sound inside his head. Nothing else at all. Of course there was nothing. How could there be, idiot? Ernest's finger and thumb lingered over the power switch. The white triangle on the black ridged knob was firmly pointing to the word 'Off'.

His eyes fell on the open door. It hadn't moved. He would have noticed. But he threw off the headphones anyway, and slammed the door shut. No, oh no, that was a mistake. Now he had only the window left from which to check. Nobody coming? Nobody watching? He could wedge something into the latch, jam in a stick to keep it locked. If he had a stick. But if somebody was out there already, if somebody knew *he* was there . . .

Ernest stood balanced between bed and door – no distance at all – weight on his back foot, like someone hesitating in boggy ground. You look for somewhere firm, a spot within jumping distance. And you feel yourself sinking as you steel yourself to leap. But you know that as you make that jump, you'll force your back leg in further.

He chose the door. He opened it again as slowly and quietly as he possibly could.

He was terrified that he'd suddenly see Henryk standing behind it, ready to clobber him. Revealing his true colours at last, just a fraction of a second before everything went dark. Then he would drag Ernest's limp body out of the way. Dump him somewhere, and get straight back to his real work. Tapping secrets to Germany with this transmitter. In code, of course.

He had made such a convincing coward. It was a brilliant disguise. Thanks to Ernest and Peggy, Henryk had stayed safely hidden, fed and warm all this time, and meanwhile he'd been sending back all the information his bosses could possibly need. Tap, tap, tap. Preparing the way. So when the Germans finally did arrive – all he had to do was hold on; no wonder he was in no hurry to go anywhere – why, he'd be laughing. And Ernest and Peggy would be collaborators.

Ernest emerged as quietly as he possibly could. But there was nobody outside. Just rabbits. More rabbits. Loping with an indecent lack of haste into the bottom of the hedge when they caught wind of him. Good. Ernest was used to watching. He could even be methodical, when he put his mind to it. He'd keep his head this time, and work out exactly what he should report to the authorities. He moved slowly round the outside of the hut, ducking through a few fences where he needed to, bending his body but not dropping his head. There wasn't a human being in sight.

If Henryk could hide a transmitter and a receiver so easily, never mind his true identity, he could surely hide a powerful pair of binoculars too. Not to mention a great many other things. Even now, further away than Ernest could possibly see, or worse, cunningly concealed somewhere closer, as only a successful spy knew how, Henryk could be watching him. Something else occurred to Ernest then. If Henryk was sneaking around out here, he could just as easily have gone to the farm too. It must have been Henryk who took Ernest's missing binoculars, and he was probably using them right now.

Was this how the birds felt, Ernest wondered, when he was watching them? Did their skin prickle under their feathers, and warn them when to fly? Ernest knew all about telepathy. ESP, they called it sometimes. That stood for Extra-Sensory Perception. They should have practised before, really. If he sent his thoughts across to Peggy, if he really, really concentrated, perhaps he could make her understand what awful danger she was in.

He wished he'd hidden the case inside the mattress again. When Henryk opened the door, he'd discover straight away that things had been tampered with.

To think he'd felt sorry for the man. He'd actually *liked* him.

And Ernest thought Henryk had liked him too. He remembered the way Henryk had looked at him. His sympathy. That strange little speech he'd made about courage. But he *knew* it was all a lie. All the time he knew. Now that Ernest knew too, his anger swelled and burned inside him. He'd make him sorry.

56

Peggy kept her eyes on the hands in her lap, interlocked with her own, gripping them more tightly with every word. She pushed back his sleeve, half-circling his forearm with finger and thumb. She wondered at the strength you must need to manoeuvre a Hurricane. These arms still had strength, despite everything. Her hand moved further up his arm, testing the muscles, marvelling at the subtle changes in texture in his skin, the smoothness of its underside.

Henryk said something, and Peggy realised she had missed his words completely. It was getting harder and harder to concentrate. Her arms were crossed awkwardly, high on her chest, so she wasn't sure if she was holding him, or he her. She was enveloped, giddy almost, and yet strangely in control. She could feel his breath on the parting of her hair. In and out. In and out. Cell-tickling and bewitching.

Peggy wondered how long she could wait before twisting round. To bring them face to face again, mouth to mouth. Melting wax again. That was exactly how it felt. Right through her body, right down her legs even. Minute and unfamiliar sensations.

His breathing became louder, and his arms held her more firmly. In the near silence, she caught the low futter of a distant plane, and tensed. These arms. Could they really be giving-up kind of arms?

She remembered the lifeboat leaving Dungeness for Dunkirk. The talk there had been. White faces everywhere. The shock of it all, and the time it took for the truth to dawn. There was giving up and giving up.

Without her own to contain them, Henryk's hands began to shake again. He steadied them against her thighs, and she felt their heat through the cloth of her overalls. And then she did turn round, quite suddenly, before she could scare herself with the idea of it, and she kissed him with a frightening urgency.

57

Aunt Myra was wheezing, a painful labour, repeated in cycles, over and over. Ernest would have been alarmed at the noise when he came into the hall had he not immediately heard the wireless crackle. Of course. It was Thursday. ITMA. More laughter spilled out of the front parlour, overlaid with Mum's, and even June's, which was more metallic, stretched and thin. *It's being so cheerful as keeps 'em going,* thought Ernest, in the charlady's graveyard voice. Well, they'd be even more cheerful soon. When they saw what he was really made of. When they knew how he'd saved them.

No Mrs Mopp just now. Funf the spy tonight, with a song about counter agents and a spypaper joke. A gigantic roll of yellow sticky paper unfurled in Ernest's mind's eye, dotted with tiny struggling figures in different uniforms. Then a horrible notion froze him in his tracks. How did counteragency work? Maybe that was why the wireless transmitter was labelled in English. It was quite possible to pretend to be a German spy and an English one at exactly the same time. Or perhaps he was getting confused between counter agents and double agents. There should have been a leaflet about that.

Spies are everywhere. It's that man again.

Another yellow envelope had arrived. He kicked it under the doormat. Welcome.

He wouldn't look. He wouldn't think about that. He just had to act now.

Then he retrieved it and read it. The writing was just the same. *PACIFISTS SHOULD KILL THEMSELVES, AND BE DONE WITH IT. THEY'VE NO RIGHT TO LIVE ON FOOD OTHER MEN HAVE SACRIFICED THEIR LIVES TO BRING HOME.*

He hid the note, climbed on the hall chair and stared at the two guns. Reaching for his own, Ernest wondered if the day would ever come when it didn't feel awkward. Uncle Fred's shotgun was like part of his own body. He handled it with ease and grace and it nestled against his shoulder as comfortably as Claudette asleep on June. Ernest shook his head, and replaced the air rifle that had never felt any part of him. With a choking, dry-throated swallow, he took down his uncle's shotgun. That was more like it.

The gun was heavy. With just one hand free, he couldn't lift the chair, so it scraped against the floor as he put it back in its place. The noise coincided with a pause in the programme. A pause for comic effect, demanding laughter.

Ernest waited for it. Then he eased open the drawer and quickly grabbed a couple of cartridges.

'Ernest?' His mother's voice had an uncertain ring. 'Is that you out there? Do come and join us. There's still another twenty minutes to go, and the programme's ever so good tonight. And get Peggy out of her room too, why don't you? Can't think why she hasn't come down yet. She seems to have been up there for hours.'

Ernest licked his lips again. Too loudly. He waited.

His aunt gave a kind of grunt.

'Oh,' said Mum. 'I was sure I'd heard Ernest. I simply don't know where he's got to tonight. I can't keep saying it over and over, and I don't want to frighten him, but I do wish he'd stay close by . . . Don't you think I should go and look for him?'

'Shhh,' hissed Aunt Myra. 'I can't hear the programme.'

Ernest set the gun on his shoulder. *Be like Dad*, the posters said. But he would be better than his dad. He caught sight of himself in the hall mirror, gave himself a brisk salute, and crept back out through the kitchen door.

58

Peggy pulled herself away. 'Oh God, what time is it?' Her eyes were bright, almost feverish. Henryk stared into them, imprinting her in his mind. 'I could stay forever, Henryk,' she said. 'Why don't I just stay forever?'

Stay, thought Henryk, imagining a night with her. He picked a wisp of hay from her hair. She still smelled of hay.

'You will come back soon,' he said. She didn't smile. Just nodded, no longer flushed, but pale and worried now.

'I wish it could be the present, all the time,' Peggy said quietly, unfastening his hands. Like a window held together by masking tape, waiting for the explosion, the world they had built between them seemed ready to fracture.

His head tilted in a question.

'Oh, that sounds so silly. I know it does. Of course it's always the present. It's now, and then now, and then now, always and forever.'

'So . . .?'

'If you could just keep each now separate and untainted, free of all the other nows that have been before and that will come after it. So that when we are together we're just together, pure and simple. And there isn't a then, in the past, to intrude on now, and there won't be another one, in the future, that we have to worry about.'

'That would be time standing still. You can do nothing if time stands still. We would be statues.'

'I know. I'm not explaining it at all well. That's not what I mean. That's not what I want.'

He stroked her hair and loved her with his eyes. She pushed against his hand with her head, like a cat.

'I wonder how late it is.'

'Will they miss you?' Henryk wasn't sure if this was quite the right word.

'Soon.'

He would miss her more. Every slow inch she moved away, he felt inside as a dull ache, more painful each time. In France a mechanic had taught him the word for magnets. *Amants*. It meant lovers too, he'd said with a wink. Now Henryk understood why. Now that he had felt that pull himself.

At the threshold, he tugged Peggy back one last time, and held her again.

'It's not dark yet.'

'It stays light forever now. Double summer time they call it. The government changed the clocks – to save fuel or something. Or make us work harder. There's no clock here, is there?'

'No. In Poland, our churches have clocks, on the tower.'

'Yes, here in England too, often. Haven't you seen?'

'I like there is no clock here. I can think always that you are about to come. That we are out of time. Like you say. Like you want to be.'

'That's right. That's what I mean. Instead of running out of time, which is how it always feels. Oh, Henryk, do you think we really are?'

'Running out of time?'

RULE SEVEN: THINK BEFORE YOU ACT. BUT ALWAYS THINK OF YOUR COUNTRY BEFORE YOU THINK OF YOURSELF.

59

Ernest imagined himself anywhere but here. Doing anything but what he was about to do. August should be a month of untroubled days, solitary evening ambles and freedom, not this grim and purposeful march. If he could only get past the barbed wire to the shore again, what would he see now? There'd be newcomers by now. Godwit. Whimbrel. Turnstone. Sanderling – wood and green. Oystercatchers, of course, always. And curlew. The other migrators. Sandpipers. Spotted redshank.

He went through the list in his head again. The names calmed him.

Godwit. Whimbrel. Turnstone. Sanderling. Sanderling. Sanderling. Wood and green.

He thought he heard the squeak of a bicycle pedal.

60

Despite the promise she had made to herself, Peggy turned at the end of the causeway. His face was a white blur at the window, unreadable. Her hand went up, very briefly – a quick, jerky wave. Too dangerous. If she went on taking stupid risks like this, there was no hope for them. Though when she saw a movement in return, she couldn't regret looking back.

There was still something he wasn't telling her, she felt. Peggy almost had the feeling she didn't want to know. He was protecting her, wasn't he? Just as she and Mum had thought they could protect Ernest. What you don't know can't hurt you. Except that wasn't quite true.

These long, light days were so deceptive. It was later than she'd thought. She'd have missed ITMA, which meant they'd have missed her. She began to hurry, turning this time into the little path with the overhanging trees, where she could walk unseen, yet keep the church just within sight through the branches. If she could see it, she knew Henryk was safe. The path was dead straight, but not empty. A figure was moving at the far end, coming towards her.

She squinted and realised it was only Ernest. She'd almost forgotten their fight. Now she waved, and smiled, and broke into a run. He'd forgiven her, then. He understood. Maybe he'd even managed to get hold of more food for Henryk – an extra loaf of bread, perhaps, or a hunk of cheese. Aunt Myra had been generous with the haymakers. The last few days had seen more opportunities than usual to squirrel away food, if not to take it to the church. It wasn't such a bad thing that Ernest had found out. It was good to have someone to share the worry with.

'Ernest?'

As she got closer, she could make out the fury on his face.

'Ernest?' she called again. 'I'm sorry. I said I was sorry. I meant it.'

Ernest was hurrying too. His lolloping walk turned into a run, and now she saw that he wasn't carrying food on his back, but a gun. When he reached her he didn't stop but brushed roughly past her, without a word.

'Hey! You nearly knocked me over! And where do you think you're going with Uncle Fred's gun?'

'Something I've got to do,' he muttered, not changing his pace.

'What?' said Peggy breathlessly, as she caught up with him. 'Tell me. Where are you going?'

'Why should I? You never tell me anything.'

'I – I – Well, I have now. I couldn't before.'

'And I can't now.'

He kept his eyes on the ground as he walked, just glancing up from time to time to look across towards the church.

'It's something to do with Henryk. Tell me,' she repeated. 'What's happened? Has someone found out? Why have you taken Uncle Fred's gun? Talk to me, Ernest. Just stop and talk to me.'

Peggy pulled at his shoulder, and he swung round. The gun knocked her chin, and she staggered a little.

'Go home, Peggy,' said Ernest savagely. 'You're not going to like this.'

She had never seen him look so grim before.

'I don't like it now. Stop messing around, Ernest.'

'I'm not messing around, I tell you. Just go home now. And forget about Henryk.'

61

He hadn't bargained on Peggy getting in the way like this. Why hadn't he thought of this? The awful look on her face made Ernest hesitate for a moment. Her eyes were so very bright and staring. Peggy loved Henryk. He hadn't known before. Ernest turned away from her. She was putting him off. He had a plan, you see. He had to stick to his plan.

'Look, he's not who you think he is.'

Insultingly, Peggy laughed out loud.

'Oh, Ernest, please stop! We've been through all this before.'

'I'll prove it to you.'

'Go on then.' She stopped and stood with arms folded across her chest, so of course he had to stop too. She was flushed, and trembling a little, but her look was still more mocking than fearful, which made Ernest angry again. 'I'm waiting.'

'Not here. You'll have to come with me.'

Ernest started walking again. He tried not to let his uncertainty show, but he realised he actually didn't want her to go at all. He needed to convince her, to confront her with the truth, so there could be no more betrayals. And he might need back up. There was every chance things could turn nasty.

'Where? Back to the church? I've only just left it.'

'And Henryk is still there?'

'Of course he is.'

'You're certain?'

'Yes, of course I am. Where else would he be?'

62

Henryk paced the aisle of the church, feeling more caged than ever. Perhaps because he also felt more alive. Anyone would think he'd just gulped down a whole handful of go-pills. Except this brightness, this energy, this weightlessness was something quite different. It made him want to soar again, to rise above the world and the mess it had made of itself. Dashing and brave and foolhardy in a way he hadn't felt for months, he longed to loop the loop once more, with Peggy by his side. To fly under a bridge or swerve out of a spin just for the joy of it, with nobody watching and nobody to watch out for.

But it was no good. They were both trapped, with the skies overhead busier by the day. Henryk sat down at the harmonium with a sigh and eased out a chord. He thought about Peggy and Ernest's father, and their mother's shame. He thought about his own.

What would happen if he turned up at the aerodrome tomorrow? It was surely far too late to pass himself off as lost, or confused, or forgetful. He was beyond AWOL. There would be a hearing of some kind. He would have to offer something like an explanation. There would be punishment.

But the punishment would only get worse the longer he left it. He couldn't put it off forever.

The echo of his next chord drowned out the sound of the outer door, as it opened and shut. Henryk did not hear the key turning in the lock, nor the muffled chink as it was removed.

63

Peggy saw him first, and nudged Ernest. 'Look,' she whispered. Victor Velvick was waiting in the shadow of the trees by the lane. He wasn't blocking their path exactly. But it was quite clear that he had no intention of letting them pass.

Peggy sensed Ernest shrinking beside her, so she took his elbow in her arm, and gave it a firm squeeze. Her brother straightened his back, and gripped the shotgun more tightly.

'It's all up now,' said Victor, looking them up and down as if he'd like to squash them under his foot. The gun seemed to amuse rather than alarm him. 'All over. I know what you've been up to. You and your Nazi-chum family. You're as bad as each other really, aren't you?'

The yellow notes. Peggy and Ernest looked at each other sideways. It was perfectly obvious really. Who was in a better position to know their family secrets than the postmistress? And who better to deliver them than the telegram boy?

'*Aren't* you?' Victor's voice was soft and controlled. He was rocking back and forth, from toe to heel, slowly and deliberately. He kept his hands clasped behind his back, and Peggy couldn't help wondering why. He raised his eyebrows. Peggy registered the fact that his jaw had become much stronger in the last few months, his chest much broader. His feet were huge. Even his voice sounded different. He was no longer a little boy Peggy could crush with a clever riposte. Victor Velvick was growing up fast.

Rigid and silent, Peggy tightened her hold on Ernest and willed him not to do anything stupid. Then Victor stopped rocking. Perfectly unhurried, he held out one pointing hand. The great iron key from the church swung tauntingly from his accusing finger.

Peggy didn't gasp, but her quick inhalation betrayed her. She knew this from the flicker in Victor's eyes, the brief flare of his nostrils. But if she was quick enough, Ernest could cover her, and perhaps – with a shotgun aimed at his head – might Victor leave them alone . . .? She darted forward and tried to grab the key, but Victor – always a tall boy, but taller than ever this summer – simply whisked it out of her reach. Shaking with rage, she retreated and turned in appeal to Ernest.

His face was white and tight and completely unforgiving. Ernest shook his head and began to edge away from her. He was lining up with Victor.

'Ernest. You've got to . . .' Her voice trailed away.

'No, Peggy. He's right.' Ernest's voice sounded clipped and strange. He wouldn't quite look at her. 'Now you need to see for yourself. I said I'd show you the proof. Otherwise you'll never believe it. Let's go.' He turned to Victor. 'You know what I'm talking about, don't you? You followed me to the Looker's Hut.'

'I know everything,' said Victor.

'Good. So we've just got to prove it to Peggy and then we'll get the Special Constable. Mr Carpenter will know what to do next. At least we can leave Henryk safely locked up.' Even Victor looked taken aback when Ernest continued: 'Well done. I hadn't thought of that. I was planning to try to bring him in myself, but it's much better like this. Yes, so much better.'

Peggy felt dizzy and cold.

'What are you talking about? What's wrong with you?' she said.

Ernest glanced in the direction of the church and back at Victor, who took over.

'He's lying to you, you little fool. No, I don't mean Ernest. That Hun in the church you can't leave alone. Oh, there's no need to look like that. I've seen you. I've watched your comings and goings. They ought to shave your head.'

Now she was burning all over, and sure it showed. She couldn't speak. She could barely stand. Victor looked her up and down disgustedly.

'He's properly pulled the wool over your eyes, you little . . .' He glanced at Ernest, and coughed theatrically. 'Right. Let's go to the Looker's Hut. But you really should have put the case away when you found it, Ernest. You'll get yourself in trouble like that.'

Ernest blushed, and nodded.

'Sorry. I – I didn't think.'

'For God's sake,' Peggy burst out. 'Just tell me what you're talking about.'

'Does she really have no idea?' Victor said incredulously.

'No, I don't, because whatever you think, you're wrong.' Peggy wanted to shake him. 'You don't understand.'

'Oh, drop it,' said Victor unhurriedly. 'Keep your breath

to talk your way out of the hole you'll be in when we call the Constable.'

He turned and started striding along the lane towards the Looker's Hut, jerking his head at Ernest to follow. The sight revolted Peggy: Ernest trotting after Victor Velvick, so eager, so conspiratorial, as if all the years she'd spend protecting him had never happened. She shook her head, and set off after them. For ten long minutes the three walked without a word, Victor leading the way. From time to time he whistled, but made little effort to hurry. *Run, rabbit, run, rabbit, run, run, run . . .* Drawing out the agony was clearly part of Peggy's punishment.

Peggy considered jumping onto Victor's back, wrestling him to the ground, fighting with him as she'd often wanted to fight with Ernest when they were younger, when he was driving her to distraction. She eyed Ernest's shotgun, wondering, her mind racing over every possibility, and getting nowhere. Victor was right. The game *was* up. Not just for Henryk, but for her too.

She wished she could know what that actually meant. She still had no real idea even of the nature of her crime. Words like 'treachery' and 'treason' and 'execution' rang through her head like axe blows. Harbouring a deserter. That would be the charge. But what would be the punishment?

'Get a move on!' Victor threw the words over his shoulder, and Ernest didn't even look round. Peggy glared at their backs, and returned to the dark gyre of her thoughts.

She reckoned she could bear anything if they didn't hurt Henryk.

They had reached the hut. Victor was as casual as anything now, now that he had everything under control. He released the latch, opened the door with a single kick and then stood aside to usher them in, waving a lordly hand. Peggy ducked into the shadows, and looked around.

'See. I was right all along. Henryk *is* a spy,' said Ernest, aiming a feeble kick at the leather suitcase on the floor. Its lid immediately fell shut, but not before Peggy had glimpsed the equipment inside. She dropped to her knees, and opened the case again. Dials. Switches. A headset. Everything inside her began to race again: her pulse, her heart, her thoughts. The blood seemed to drain from her head and rush straight back again. For a moment she could hardly see.

'No.'

She looked up at Ernest. Small as he was, just now he seemed to loom over her. Standing over the open suitcase, shotgun raised vertically above his head, he gripped the barrel with both hands and then smashed the heavy butt down onto the wireless equipment with all his force. There was a splintering sound as the dial cracked. One black knob hung at an angle, but he made little impression on the metal. He raised the gun again, spectacles askew, face twisted into a snarl.

'Yes. He's an enemy agent. Just like I always thought. He really is.'

Peggy covered her face with her hands and tried to think.

He couldn't have made everything up. He couldn't have. The Black Sea, and Constantinople, and Beirut and the boats. Flying over the refugees in France. His three sisters. Little Anna with her plaits and coloured ribbons and her grazed knees. The dancing. Was all that really a cover? The dancing.

And what about his fear? Nobody could act fear like that. She thought of the hours he had spent alone in the church. Could he really have been sneaking out to radio messages to Germany the moment her back was turned? It was impossible. Surely impossible. She remembered the warmth of his arms around her, and the disturbance of his breath in her hair, and the darkness under the pulpit they had shared.

And the looker . . . At that moment there was a loud slam as the door was pulled shut from the outside. The strangled cry that followed – it must have come from Victor – was quickly stifled. Peggy staggered to her feet, and grabbed Ernest, who was poised to smash the rifle butt down once more.

'Stop,' she whispered. 'Shhh! Stay here. Whatever you do, don't come out. He might not have seen you.'

Ernest looked as terror-stricken as she felt. Pushing him gently away, a finger on her lips, Peggy forced herself to take the few steps towards the door, where she stood and listened. There was the sound of struggle – grunts and blows – and then a dragging noise, and from further away, the crash of a gate slamming against a gatepost.

Cautiously, Peggy scraped back the door, just a few inches. Keeping her body hidden, she looked out.

64

Henryk began to pack. It went against every instinct in his body. There wasn't a great deal to take but the important thing was to remove every last bit of evidence from the church. Nobody must ever know he had been there. He crawled under the bench to retrieve his flying suit, which whispered as he pulled it from its hiding place.

He looked down at his borrowed clothes, still spattered with clay. He would have to keep the boots. He'd get nowhere without the boots. As for the trousers, the shirt . . . he'd dump them. And do a better job than he'd managed with the parachute and vest.

Now that he'd finally made his decision, Henryk wanted to hurry, to get on his way, and be done with it. If he kept walking all night, away from the sea, eventually he'd run into a checkpoint, an official of some kind. Then he would hand himself in, and avoid dragging Peggy down with him. He wouldn't breathe a word about Peggy.

It felt strange to be putting his uniform back on, all crumpled and smelling of damp stone and dust. He settled the revolver into the inside pocket, and remembered the feel of its barrel in his mouth. If he'd had the courage to see that through, he wouldn't have had Peggy. And without Peggy, he couldn't have begun to live.

She'd be back at the farmhouse soon, and getting ready for bed before long. The haymaking had worn her out, he could tell. And before she washed, she'd be slipping off her dungarees. Bending. Stretching. Yawning. That lovely mouth.

And then he checked himself. *You're making it more difficult for yourself*, he told himself. *Stop. You'll regret it.* Too much time. That was the trouble. He'd got used to having too much time to think, and to imagine, and to yearn for her.

The church was growing gradually darker. If only he could blow the dust around again and cover up his traces. It would soon settle back though. In a few weeks' time, his presence would be effaced. Just as the grass must be beginning to grow already over his lost Hurricane. He'd better open the door, let in the last of the light, and then he'd be able to see if there was anything he'd forgotten.

The door wouldn't move.

He rattled the handle, unable to believe it. But the key had clearly been turned. Should he check the windows? No point. It would be easy enough for his captor to keep out of sight. And it would hardly be a moment before Henryk found out if they were out there waiting for him or not. All he had on his side was speed.

Abandoning his bundle of clothes, his goggles and helmet, Henryk looked around for something strong and heavy. Hassocks. Books. A candlestick? Useless. He grabbed hold of the harmonium stool and threw it with all his strength at the nearest window. In an icy fountain of noise, twenty tiny panes of glass shattered at once. The lead between them buckled but did not break, and the stool crashed back to the ground. Again Henryk picked it up, and this time he didn't let go, but beat it repeatedly, over and over again. He heard himself roaring and grunting as he worked, while his boots crunched the shards of glass to powder on the hard floor. Once the metal had snapped, it became easier. He grabbed the altar cloth, sweeping a crucifix to the floor in his haste, and wrapped the white linen round his fist. Well, there'd be no hiding this mess, would there? But he wished he hadn't lost his gauntlets when he bailed out.

Pulling at the twisted leads, now oddly pliable, he bent back a space in the window, and as soon as it was large enough, he forced his way through it, ripping the back of his flying suit as he tumbled out onto the grass outside. He hardly noticed the blood seeping from his cut hand, colouring the cloth. Henryk staggered to his feet.

65

Ernest pushed Peggy out of the way, forcing them both out of the brick hut, and immediately fired. The shot went into the air. The recoil threw him back against the wall, against his sister.

'It's not Henryk,' she cried. 'I knew it couldn't be.'

Head dazed and ringing, he saw at once that she was right. Ernest had never seen this man before, this hollow-cheeked stranger in a fisherman's cap who was holding Victor like a shield in front of him as he backed away. He scuttled sideways towards the water's edge like a giant crab, moving faster than Ernest could believe possible. They were twenty or thirty feet away already, nearly at the sewer's bank.

Should he fire again? Ernest had just one cartridge left and then he'd have to reload. No spares. *A sudden attack can be resisted. A sudden attack can be resisted.* The words were jumbling in his head. *Remember. These instructions must be obeyed at once.* What instructions? He had no instructions for this.

He straightened his specs and put up the gun again, trying to focus on the unfamiliar sights, to work out where he might dare aim. He only knew about rabbits, and what Uncle Fred had said about killing them – go for the sweet spot, between eye and ear. It's got to be clean. His mind flashed back to the doe he had watched Peggy kill, remembering how the body had flown up in the air, like a toy thrown by a peevish child. Twisting, it landed, back legs thrashing. Kick, kick, kick. Head pulled in, rotating on the axis of its shoulders, in a deserted field. Kick, kick, kick. Until it lay still.

Victor was barely conscious. He flopped like a scarecrow, arms and legs and head hanging uselessly.

Peggy still stood by the wall, breathing heavily, her gaze moving jerkily from gun barrel to Victor to the stranger and back again.

He didn't look anything like a spy, of course, nothing like the Nazi officer Ernest had seen in the poster, sliced in half to reveal his disguise. More like a fisherman really, in waders and a nautical cap and oilskin dungarees up to his chest. That was how he had made it this far. Dark water rhythmically slopping against rubber up to his thighs, moving by night, hiding in reeds and under bridges, resting the case on his head to keep it dry. He had crept inland along the waterways, sluice by sluice, all the way from the shore, where the real fishermen still cast their nets among the mines, harvesting the odd shoal of dead and blasted fish. Had he known exactly where he was going? Was it chance or a map that brought him here, or had Henryk guided him?

Ernest ran a few paces forward and stopped.

'Halt!' shouted Ernest, hearing how thin and pathetic his voice sounded in all this space. He slung the gun on his back so he could cup his mouth with his hands and shout again: 'Handy Hock!'

The stranger just spat and swore. Victor's head was moving

again, slowly coming up, regaining consciousness. He began to struggle and scream, high-pitched with terror, half-choking as the man's hand tried to force his mouth shut.

'Peggy!' Ernest said, looking behind him. She was gone. Where? Where had she gone? 'Peggy!' She reappeared from the hut, the case in her hand.

'We've got to do something with this.'

She began to march towards the dyke. Towards the man. Ernest licked his teeth, urgently, as if his tongue might find a solution, hidden somewhere around his gums, in the space between his teeth right at the back. She must have a plan. Peggy always had a plan.

'Go, Ernest! Just run!'

He was so used to obeying her orders that, like a waiting batsman, he was already on his toes. He almost sped off. But he couldn't.

'No. I can't,' he said. 'I won't leave you.'

A rustling slither and a loud splash. The stranger and the boy were suddenly chest-deep in sludgy water, and Victor could shout out loud at last because now the man needed both his hands to force him down. They were pushing on Victor's broad shoulders with all their strength, and Victor's newly broken voice kept cracking between registers as he cried for help. Through the broken screen of reeds, Ernest watched them flail and flounder in all that mud and sediment and churned-up water. A tiny part of him thought, *This is how it feels, Victor Velvick. Like this.*

'Then we're three against one,' called Peggy, staggering, off-balanced by the heavy case. 'Come on.'

'Help! You . . .' Victor was silenced as his head went under water. But then he came up again, spluttering and choking and fighting for air.

Ernest looked at the gun in his hand. Useless, now that he risked hurting Peggy as well as Victor. And a new sound was building all around them, the low ominous throbbing Ernest always dreaded, dipping and rising and getting louder every moment: 'We're coming, we're coming, we're coming.'

66

You could feel it in your bones, even before your ears had worked out what the sound was. A slight vibration, building to a rhythmic moaning hum, and before long a vast wave of bombers was blackening the sky. Without looking, Henryk knew they were enemy aircraft.

But on their way home, or heading inland? He couldn't tell.

It was the first time he'd been completely out in the open for weeks, and he'd never felt more vulnerable, or disoriented, unsure of the direction of their flight and his own. He just knew they were getting closer all the time. How much worse to be below than above, he thought, surprising himself. From above at least you had a chance. You could emerge from the clouds without warning, dive down without a qualm.

He kept to the lane, wishing it wasn't so much higher than the land around. But he was ready to take to a ditch if he had to, and he didn't stop running.

Then he heard a new sound, much closer than the bombers: a confusion of voices that made him flinch. He had to stay away. He couldn't let himself be discovered yet, not here, not this close. Henryk ran beside the hedge to the nearest gateway and stopped, eyes narrowing as he tried to make out where the shouting was coming from. A little way away he saw a small, low building, brick, fenced off – a pumphouse, perhaps? No. Too far from the water running behind it, one of the larger channels that intersected the Marsh.

Height always helped. He would have to take one risk to avoid another. Henryk climbed onto the gate, and looked, and listened. The shot he heard was like a starting pistol. Henryk was over the gate in an instant, vaulting the next a few moments later. From the jumbled shouts that reached him, a few words detached themselves and rose above the rest. Peggy's voice.

'Let him go!'

No hiding now.

67

Peggy's yell caught the stranger's attention at last. He seemed to be looking straight at her, his face illuminated by the last bits of light reflected off the water. You wouldn't know he was German. How could you possibly know anything about him when you couldn't see his eyes for the peak of his cap, his mouth for the thick beard?

'Let him go! You're finished without this!' she yelled, as she swung her arm out over the dyke. At the far point of its arc, the momentum of the heavy case almost pulled her into the water; she just managed to keep her footing on the bank as it swung back to safety. Then she was dragged back herself, and this time was lucky to stay upright.

She stood panting, resting the case on the ground, vaguely aware of the noise of bombers in the sky, the distant sirens. She could see the man hesitate, calculating. His uncertainty lasted just long enough for Ernest to slither down the bank behind him, holding Fred's shotgun high above his head. For a moment it looked as if Victor had twisted himself out of the stranger's grip, and Peggy felt elated. But the distraction was only temporary. The man shouted again – violently, incomprehensibly – and his efforts to force Victor's head underwater resumed. She raised the case again.

From just a few fields away came the scream of falling bombs. 'Peggy!'

At the sound of Henryk's voice, Peggy turned, full of sudden hope.

'Henryk!'

Unstoppable, the transmitter case swung back out across the water at an angle, slipping from her grasp this time. Quite out of her control, it sailed towards the struggling pair, and hit Victor squarely in the stomach. All the breath knocked out of him, the boy crumpled and slid out of sight into darkness.

Then the stranger turned on Ernest.

'Quick, Henryk!' shouted Peggy. 'He's a spy. The murderer. He must be.'

Two great splashes. Peggy and Henryk entered the water at once, perhaps seven or eight feet apart along the bank. The mud felt like a living thing, sucking her in, dragging on Peggy's trouser legs, swirling and clouding the water.

'No!' she yelled, took a step forward and was lost. There was nothing firm around her. She was sinking. She lurched forward again, groping, half-fell against something. A log? No, a body. She had no choice. Peggy took a deep breath, clamped shut her mouth and squeezed tight her eyes, and then plunged both arms downwards towards Victor. The water closed over her head. Instantly, the beating engines in the sky were shut off, replaced by a bubbling rush in her ears and throbbing pulse in her head. She groped for something she could get a grip on – a limb, a belt, anything – grabbing blindly, and panicking as her hands closed only on water and weed. Her lungs could not bear this. She had to breathe. She needed air. A double thud pounded through the chaos. Two shots: there was no mistaking them, even so muted and deadened by water.

Ernie? Henryk? She had to find out. Most of all she had to breathe. But at last she had got hold of some cloth. She couldn't let go of Victor now.

His collar began to rip from her hands, and she felt him falling again, but she got her hand first under one armpit, and then the other. The water made it easier to support his weight. Finally some instinct for survival kicked in and he made a faint response to her tugging and heaving.

Peggy surfaced, gulping down air, with Victor coughing in her arms. She stumbled and caught sight of Ernest's horrified face.

'I'm sorry,' he shouted.

Barely perceptibly, the dyke was changing colour. Just where Henryk stood, the water was slowly darkening, reddening. The colour quickly began to disperse, the last ring of water on the surface expanded till it vanished, and the bubbles dissolved. The stranger – the spy – was nowhere to be seen.

Ernest was still staring at the shotgun he had just fired. Victor's eyes were fixed on the scorched hole in the arm of Henryk's flying suit, and the revolver in his hand. Peggy had never seen it before. She would hardly have believed Henryk capable of using it. He glanced down at the gun – as though he could barely believe it himself – then threw it across the water onto the bank, and looked straight at her.

It was like trying to hurry in a dream, when you never seem to get closer. They fought the mud and the water with hands like oars. Peggy didn't hear Victor's choking splutters as he finished clearing his lungs. She didn't care if Ernest was watching and she couldn't shake off the shivering. It seemed an age before Henryk's cold lips reached Peggy's chattering teeth. Her arms went round him. He felt bulky and unfamiliar.

'Are you hurt?' She didn't dare look.

'Not really.' Henryk didn't seem in any pain.

Still gripping the gun, Ernest turned to look the other way, towards the hayfields. Peggy and Henryk turned too. From down in the dyke you couldn't see the haystacks themselves as they burned. But you could see the smoke streaming into the sky, the false sunset made by the fires. It wasn't long before the smell began to reach them as well, and the first black embers were carried by the wind into their wet hair.

EPILOGUE

Victory Parade, London, 8th June 1946

The cheering came in waves, building in intensity as each vehicle passed, sweeping Peggy almost off her feet with its force. She stood on tiptoe, hoping for a better view, and with each new torrent of enthusiasm, she was caught up in the joy of the occasion. And then dropped down again. She wanted her heart to sing in tune with the others'. But with Henryk like a black dog at her shoulder, it was impossible.

'Come on, let's go,' she said at last.

They were too far back in the crowd to see much anyway. You couldn't possibly work out who anyone was through such a frenzy of flag-waving, and there wasn't enough room to open the programme she clutched in her hand. It was all very exciting – she couldn't deny that – but in a confusing, complicated way. She was no longer in the mood, and didn't think Henryk had ever been.

'I said, let's go,' she shouted into his ear. Perhaps he hadn't heard her. This drumming filled your head, and took over your mind.

He raised an eyebrow when she tugged at his arm, but he didn't object. As they moved away, the people who'd been squeezed against them fell into the space they left behind, like loose earth into a crater. Hopeless to try to talk. It was just a case of holding on to each other and battling through.

At last they made it to a quieter place, somewhere south of Oxford Street, Peggy guessed. She was beginning to find her way round London – it was nearly six months since she'd begun her work with the Red Cross, pursuing the intricate and too often hopeless task of trying to reunite refugees with lost relatives – but today everything looked different. Peggy wondered if she and Henryk would ever manage to find the others before the fireworks. Or if, by then, he would even want to. Five years and more, a few snatched meetings, and at times she felt she hardly knew him.

'Cup of tea?' she suggested. 'No milk?'

Henryk smiled as he bowed his assent and offered his arm properly. He had stopped clicking his heels a long time ago, but remained a stickler for courtesy. It still made Peggy glow. Hip to hip, they walked, aware only of each other. They ignored the gaps in the buildings they passed, the rhythm of holes left by uprooted railings, the windows still boarded. Their steps were in time, and whenever Peggy looked up at Henryk's face, she found his eyes already devouring hers.

Almost too soon they found a café that was open, and empty too, and the girl who served them very anxious to be gone. She kept looking out of the window, as if she might somehow be able to hear or see something of the action if she got a little bit closer to the glass.

Henryk was reading the programme again. Peggy studied the lion and unicorn design on the cover and knew he'd never find what he was looking for. But she noticed that he was wearing the cufflinks she had sent him at Christmas.

'Your own clothes at last,' said Peggy. 'I thought the day would never come.'

She regretted her words immediately. Today of all days Henryk should have been in uniform, preparing to fly. Henryk raised his eyes, and reached a hand across to hers. She kissed his fingers.

'But here it is,' he said.

She nodded, and coughed. The waitress tore herself away from the window and brought them their tea.

'Have you heard from your father?' asked Henryk.

That was easier ground.

'Oh, he's much, much better. The Research Institute closed a few months ago but he's stayed on in Sheffield, and Ernest is trying to help him set up a studio there, with another of the conchies from the Institute, an artist. It wasn't TB, it turned out. Just effects of Vitamin A deprivation, from the experiments. The "shipwreck diet", I think they called it . . . or maybe something else . . . I'm not quite sure. Anyway, Ernest said he hardly recognised him when he first arrived – he was like an old man. Awful. But his night vision has come back.'

'And no more itching?'

'Oh no . . . the scabies experiments only went on for about a year – human guinea pigs, the doctor called them. Urgghhh! How horrible to get yourself deliberately infected like that, for the sake of science. No wonder Mum didn't want to see him then. But she's planning to go up soon. I'm crossing my fingers. You never know.'

'I think I would rather have been a soldier, fighting, than do what he did.'

'Did I tell you about the first letter that came from the Institute, and how Mum put it in the bottom of the Rayburn to disinfect it and it went all yellow and crumbled when we read it?'

Henryk laughed.

'You did tell me.'

'Sorry. I can never remember what we've actually been able to say to each other and what I've just imagined.' Shyness unexpectedly attacking, Peggy lowered her head – but she had to make this confession. 'I talk to you all the time, you know. In my head. I can't help it.'

'Perhaps soon you won't have to. We must make plans.'

Peggy's heart seemed to do a double-beat. But Henryk didn't elaborate; he simply turned back to the Parade programme. He knew as well as she did that there would be no Polish pilots in the fly-past, but he couldn't seem to stop looking.

'Henryk,' she said, putting a hand out for the programme and gently pulling it away from him. 'Don't torture yourself. Please.'

'Sorry,' he said, but he wouldn't give it up until he had read every word. At last he looked up, his face transformed by an enormous smile. He jabbed at the paper with his forefinger.

'Look, Peggy! Look! The Central Band of the Royal Air Force. Poland has not been forgotten – not completely. Our musicians will play today!'

'We could go back, after this, if you like . . . if you think we'll be in time?'

His eyes alarmingly brighter, Henryk blinked a few times, and looked away, leaving Peggy wondering still. What kind of plans had he meant?

It had been so long now, with so many letters between them, and she had survived all that time, hadn't she? Whatever he was about to say now, whatever conclusion he had reached, surely, surely she could take it too. As June had said only the other weekend (tapping her toes impatiently while Claudette carefully tied her own shoe laces) if there was one thing you could say for a war, it makes a girl independent.

Peggy had managed to keep herself together when they took Henryk away for assessment, off to that horrible place – the NYDN centre, it was called: Not Yet Diagnosed Nervous. Where they stripped pilots of their badges, and made them parade on the seafront in their mutilated uniforms, and judged them fit to fly again, or not. Henryk couldn't have got through that ordeal without her. He had told her so.

And hadn't she spoken out without faltering at two inquests, telling the coroner exactly what she knew in an empty room at the George, shutting out the ominous sounds coming from the crowds gathered outside in the High Street? It had been far worse at her own trial, of course, in the juvenile court. Standing before the magistrate, ears singing and ringing, she barely understood the sentence. She had prepared herself for Borstal, imagined a cell of her own. If Dad could survive prison, so could she. It wouldn't last forever. So then, to be let off with a fine . . . she had cried with relief. And worked hard to pay it.

Peggy was twenty-one now, and her own woman, even if that did mean twelve girls to a bathroom in a bomb-damaged hostel in Marylebone. She had a job, and a life, and that was more than a start. In fact, she really ought to check her diary for the following week. Sort it all out in her head. She started to rummage in her handbag, and stopped almost as quickly. No – no more waiting.

'Henryk . . . tell me, what did you mean, before? What plans?'

Henryk turned back to face her.

'You know the choice we have to make? There is this new Resettlement Corps – it has an Air Force division – they'll look after us until . . . until we find something. Or we go back to Poland.'

She nodded, her mouth too dry to speak.

'I've decided,' he said. 'I can't. I can't go back. Not now. I've thought and thought about it and there's no point. There's nothing there for me.' He sounded almost matter-of-fact, accepting, which increased Peggy's bitterness on his behalf. He had told her in the end of his sisters' fate. A day didn't go by without her thinking about them. 'But there's work for good airmen all over the world – Holland . . . Argentina . . . Pakistan . . . They are all asking for us.'

So far away, thought Peggy.

'There's also a company near Bristol looking for test pilots. What do you think? Shall I put in for that? This is what I want most of all . . . so I can be with you.' He paused, and waited until he knew she had taken his words in. 'May I?'

HISTORICAL AFTERWORD

All the characters in *That Burning Summer* are entirely fictional, but the novel is very much inspired by historical events around the time of the Battle of Britain. I've taken just a few small liberties for the sake of the story, mainly with timing – sheep were actually evacuated before children, for example. Perhaps I've also taken a liberty in the creation of Henryk. I certainly don't know of any Polish pilots who either went into hiding or were charged with 'LMF'. But a German airman, Josef Markl, who bailed out of a bomber plane near Newbury in July 1940, survived for nine days uncaptured before giving himself up.

You'll find plenty of ideas for further reading and other resources on all the following subjects on my website, www.lydiasyson.com, where you can contact me with your own thoughts too.

LMF

Records of psychological casualties in the RAF during World War Two are far from clear. The peculiarly British term 'Lack of Moral Fibre' was introduced at speed in April 1940 to deter aircrew from refusing to fly without reason. Men with

LMF were branded as cowards, and received 'firm treatment'. In 1942 the Flying Personnel Research Committee (FPRC) admitted that there was a great deal of confusion about this among those in charge of psychological welfare. Thinking and terminology varied, but most medics agreed on one thing: men who broke down under the stress of flying in battle were 'constitutionally timid' and unfit to fly. Their characters were at fault, and their genes or family background were blamed. Yet the problem was seen as 'dangerously contagious', particularly in Bomber Command, where breakdown rates were highest. Some doctors recognised that flying stress built up over time and everybody had a 'breaking point'. But no official distinction was made between a crisis of confidence during a training flight and a collapse of nerve after an airman's twentieth sortie. By late 1945, 'LMF' had been abandoned. It is still a controversial and politically sensitive subject.

Peace protests and conscientious objection

The Peace Pledge Union was founded in 1934. Within a year, over 100,000 people had joined, promising to renounce war. In the first year of World War Two, over 50,000 men applied for exemption from military service because of their beliefs. Before the war ended, about 5,000 men and 500 women had been charged with offences relating to conscientious objection. Most were sent to prison. A number of PPU members were also arrested for holding open-air meetings and selling their newspaper, *Peace News*, in the streets.

Missing pilots

Many airmen on both sides could not escape when their planes went down, and are missing to this day. The excavation of crash sites on and around Romney Marsh was extremely difficult during the war. Sergeant Stanisław Duszyński was shot down near Lydd in September 1940, while attacking a Ju 88. Neither his body nor his Hurricane were recovered at the time. Decades later, despite several attempts – official and unofficial – his remains have never been found.

Spies

Spy fever was running high in the summer of 1940. Four rather incompetent spies landed on the Marsh coast in early September and were caught red-handed, although one had already managed to transmit several messages. Three of the four were found guilty at the Old Bailey and sentenced to death. In 1941, unknown German agents were suspected of the murder of a Lydd builder, found dead in an unoccupied rectory: his death remains mysterious. The only instance I know of an RAF airman 'faking his own death' was a Czech called Augustin Přeučil: his double-identity as a spy for Germany was revealed ten years ago.

Polish pilots in Britain

There's a myth that the Polish Air Force was destroyed on the ground within days of Hitler's invasion of Poland on 1st September 1939. But despite their outnumbered and out-of-date planes, Poland's highly trained pilots fought bravely for several weeks before accepting defeat. Most eventually managed to reach France to continue the fight for freedom.

By June 1940, France had fallen too. Over 8,000 Polish airmen were evacuated to Britain, arriving exhausted and battle-weary in yet another new country. They called it 'The Island of Last Hope'. On 18th June, Churchill declared: 'Hitler knows that he will have to break us in this island or lose the war. If we can stand up to him, all Europe may be freed and the life of the world may move forward into broad, sunlit uplands'.

Forty Polish pilots took to the skies at the beginning of the Battle of Britain, scattered among a number of RAF squadrons. In August 1940, two new Polish fighter squadrons were formed – No. 302, 'City of Poznań' and No. 303, 'Kościuszko'. By 1941 a fully fledged Polish Air Force was operating alongside the RAF. Polish pilots quickly acquired a reputation for unprecedented skill and bravery in action, winning 342 British gallantry awards.

Between 1939 and 1945 over 200,000 Poles fought under British High Command. But in the programme for the Allied Victory Celebrations in London a year later, you will only find a mention of Poland under one heading – the Central Band of the Royal Air Force. By this time it was Stalin, not Hitler, who seemed to require appeasement. The terrible fate of Poland, a subject far too vast for an afterword, had already been determined around conference tables at Tehran, Yalta and Potsdam.

ACKNOWLEDGEMENTS

Of all the books I read while writing this one, three stand out: Adam Zamoyski's *The Forgotten Few: The Polish Air Force in World War II*, Lynne Olson & Stanley Cloud's *For Your Freedom and Ours: The Kościuszko Squadron – Forgotten Heroes of World War II*, and Edward Carpenter's *Romney Marsh at War*.

Edward Carpenter was also extremely generous in sharing his vast knowledge of the history of Romney Marsh in person. Likewise, I had the great pleasure of discussing wartime memories with Doreen Allen, Esther Bourne and Marie Voller (also known as the Lyddite Chicks), who were kindly introduced to me by Alice Boxall (Friends of Lydd). Recorded recollections in the form of audio interviews and diaries formed a large part of my research, and those of Michal Leszkierwicz, John Anthony Kaye, Audrey Louise Hammon, and Miss M. Cooke made a particular impression on me. I'd like to thank all the museums, archives and libraries who supported my research in different ways: Brenzett Aeronautical Museum; the British Library; the Imperial War Museum (London and Duxford); Kent Battle of Britain Museum, Hawkinge; the London Library; Lydd Town Museum; Parham Airfield Museum, Suffolk; Sikorski Museum, London; Southwark Library Services. Thanks to Lydd Aero Club for making it possible for me to see the Marsh from above, to Barry Banson and Dorothy Beck for other Marsh information, Foppe and Lizzie d'Hane for vintage car expertise, Loraine Rutt for pottery know-how and Caroline Ridgwell for canine advice.

I am blessed in both my agent, Catherine Clarke, and my publishing team at Hot Key Books: special thanks to Sarah Odedina and Georgia Murray for editing with such sensitivity and insight, and Jan Bielecki for the vision and passion behind another superb cover.

Friends and family have been enormously supportive along the way, reading, listening, discussing and often re-reading with vast patience and good humour. I can't thank you all enough: my Finsbury Group (particularly Keren David, Becky Jones and Amanda Swift), Tig Thomas, Antonia Syson, Natasha Lehrer, Polly Radcliffe, Richard Taylor (special thanks for technical and military advice), and Bożena Burda (for whose unstinting help with all things Polish I am utterly indebted). As always, my daughter Phoebe has been invaluable in more ways than I can say, and she, Martin, Adam, Rufus and Solomon have lovingly endured my obsessions with a minimum of mockery. I thank them all with all my heart.

LYDIA SYSON

Lydia Syson is a fifth-generation Londoner who lives in Camberwell. She was once a World Service radio producer, and left the BBC after the birth of the first of her four children. Then she wrote a PhD about explorers, poets and Timbuktu and a biography of the eighteenth-century 'electric' doctor, James Graham, telling the full story of his extraordinary Celestial Bed. Lydia's debut novel, *A World Between Us*, was longlisted for the Guardian Children's Fiction Prize and shortlisted for the Branford Boase Award, with a special 'Highly Recommended' mention from the judges.

Find out more about Lydia at:

www.lydiasyson.com
twitter @LydiaSyson

Delve into the history behind the
story with the interactive edition of
Lydia Syson's A WORLD BETWEEN US,
available exclusively on the iBookstore.

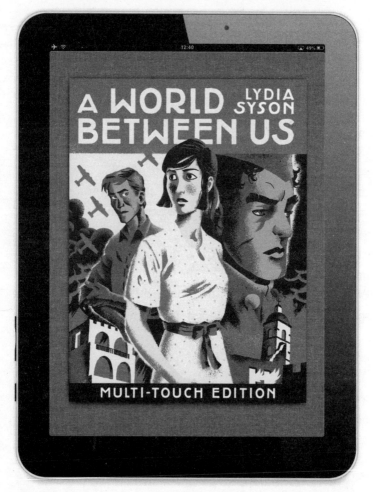

Explore the true stories of the Spanish Civil War
through primary source material including
photographs, letters, telegrams, audio and video.

www.lydiasyson.com